Gently Down

by

Michael Walterich

Copyright © 2013 Michael Walterich

All rights reserved.

"To be yourself in a world that is constantly trying to make you something else is the greatest accomplishment."

- Ralph Waldo Emerson

DIMMER

God may have said, "Let there be light," but human beings invented the dimmer switch. This didn't happen in anything like six days, of course. It took millennia of refining ideas. First, humans mastered fire. This gave them the power to have light and warmth whenever they wanted it, not just fifty percent of the time like their cheap-ass god provided.

Still, nature was harsh. Fire, like a human's unarmored, fairly hairless body, was vulnerable to the elements. So humans began to wall themselves in. Inside their unnaturally square boxes they were warm and safe and had plenty of free time for thinking. Eventually, they mastered electricity. Then it was light and heat whenever they wanted, at the flick of a switch, the turn of a knob, the press of a button.

With their basic survival needs taken care of, humans were free to tinker with the details. To discover what, exactly, is the ideal temperature of a room. And, exactly how much light would I like to have inside this room at this precise moment?

Thus, the dimmer switch was born.

Of course, the human mind had evolved to problem solve. Despite having accomplished precision control of their environment, some humans remained restless. They pressed on, finding all kinds of uses for electricity beyond merely allowing them to see in the dark. They created screens of light. Giant screens they gathered around with popcorn, and smaller screens to stare at in their own living room, and pocket-sized screens for personal communications. And on these screens, thanks to light shot between them over great distances, humans could view anything they wanted. Anything at all.

And for their next trick, humans invented the Stream. Finally, they could do away with all the screens and devices they had enslaved themselves to for communication and entertainment. Now light, which contained thoughts and pictures and information, could be beamed directly into their minds.

Yes, the Stream eliminated the need for gadgetry and brought about the interconnection of all human minds. One, all-knowing, Stream of light.

Humans have said, "Let there be God!"

But, can God control the dimmer?

SMILE

Killian Peterson's clients were not supposed to message him outside of business hours. Of course, if they could control when they freaked out they might not need a psychiatrist. Evan Hyatt had never broken protocol before, so when a message from him flashed [URGENT] in Killian's mind, just half an hour before he was due at the office, he figured he better not ignore it.

As soon as he acknowledged the message, Killian was looking through Evan Hyatt's eyes. He was hearing Evan's thoughts. Evan had sent him a live Stream feed.

[Too many voices] Evan thought. [Must silence them.] Killian watched his right hand pick up a flathead screwdriver.

[Stop!] Killian yelled with his mind. Evan didn't stop. He couldn't hear Killian. He had muted all incoming messages. Killian winced as the screwdriver thrust toward his forehead. He tightened his abdominal muscles in anticipation of an overwhelming burst of pain. But no amount of preparation could ease the horrible sensation of the tip of the screwdriver tearing through flesh and cracking skull. The metal shaft squished through the meat of the brain and the pain decimated Evan's awareness.

In the darkness, Killian notified the police. There

was no way they'd arrive in time.

Sight returned. Evan was in the bathroom. Thought returned. [I'm in the bathroom,] he thought. [I have a screwdriver stuck in my forehead.] He pulled the instrument out. Hot blood followed. An image of Evan's parents, standing in an audience looking up at him on stage, surfaced from the mist of his mind. They were clapping, smiling. He warmed inside. The scene dissolved into wet sand near a lapping ocean. His ex-girlfriend jogging playfully away. His warmth turned to hot anger.

He lifted the screwdriver again.

"No!" Killian yelled aloud. But he was miles away and powerless to intervene. Condemned to watch. Over and over he'd watch this scene. Later, he'd have to study the moments leading up to this and try to explain why this Streamer chose to end his life. This was part of his job. A big part lately.

He could smell the rusty blood, which flowed from the first puncture hole, along the side of his nose, then dangled from the precipice of his nostril. Evan steadied his hand and aimed above his left eyebrow once more. He believed there was a chip there. He believed that destroying it would sever his link to the Stream. Evan believed this because his psychiatrist told him so. Killian told him. Killian told this lie to all of his clients.

[Must stop the voices, the swirling thoughts and pictures,] Evan thought. [Can't breathe.] Killian felt the wind stir the hairs on his forearm as it thrust toward his head again. The pain was less severe this time, but the darkness was deeper. No thoughts surfaced for several seconds. Only the cold of the intruding metal shaft among the warm bundles of neurons pervaded. Evan dropped to his knees.

Killian was on his.

Vision cleared. The bathroom sink was at eye level,

just a few inches away. He grabbed for the shaft that protruded from his forehead. He missed. Twice. Wobbly on his knees, he sat back on his calves. Another swing of the arm and Killian felt the hard plastic handle in his fingers. He pulled the screwdriver out and immediately thrust it toward his forehead for a third time. [Take that God!] Evan thought. He felt the sharp stab tear through his thoughts. Pain smothered existence. Pain became existence. Then pain too, faded. "Take that," Killian mumbled as the image dissolved. He was lying on the floor of his own bathroom. He felt frantically at his forehead, but there were no holes. There was no blood.

"Why, Evan?"

This was Killian's third suicide in a month. Progner was not going to be happy.

Killian grabbed the sink with his left hand and pulled himself to his feet. In his right hand, he still held his toothbrush. When he looked down at it, his right arm jerked and he poked himself in the forehead, just above his left eyebrow.

He put the toothbrush back in its charger. [1:45] flashed in red in his mind. He hadn't reached the minimum recommended brushing time. Now he wouldn't see her smile. He'd have to start over and brush for the full two minutes.

Killian loved his Streamlink 3.0 ImageCaster Tooth Management System. It was so much better than the 2.0, which merely allowed him to see a smiley face in his mind if he brushed long enough. The 3.0 allowed him to insert his own images. While Killian brushed, the dark-haired goddess he had a crush on in high school stared sternly at him. But, if he brushed for at least two minutes, she would allow just the slightest smirk to lift one corner of her lips. The subtlest of approving smiles from her could start his day off just right.

Killian thought a hot shower might comfort him, but found himself hesitant to undress. The screwdriver haunted him. He knew the image would sneak attack him over the next several days. The sound of Evan's screams would interrupt his thoughts. Tinges of the pain would stab his mind without warning. But he would watch his own experience of it all from a distance. Commenting on his experience of the experience. Like the narrator of his own consciousness; detached and unmoved.

Professional numbness. It didn't come naturally. He had to work at it. Avoidance, denial, repression. The coping mechanisms he was trained to recognize and help alleviate in others had become the tools of his own survival.

He stepped into the hot water and let it blast him in the face first. It seemed not to touch him. He turned and let it massage the base of his neck and run down his back. But he didn't feel it there either. He could feel the trail of blood running alongside his nose and pausing to linger on the edge. Each panicked breath threatened to inhale the drop that dangled there. It was not his blood. Yet, it seemed more real than the water that cleansed him.

Killian turned off the shower and stepped out to towel off.

The screwdriver returned. He relapsed into the sensory maelstrom that had swallowed Evan's mind. Sights, sounds, smells, all mixed together and competing for his attention. Was he experiencing Evan's insanity or his own?

Insanity. Who could tell what insanity was any more? Many claimed the Stream itself defined the word. The damn Jadonist priests disagreed. They claimed that insanity had nothing to do with being in or out of the Stream. That for both Streamers and non-swimmers alike, a lack of faith made one insane. They claimed the 'psychiatry elite' needed to examine their definitions and help start healing the Stream. Killian did not want to admit he was a Jadonist at that moment any more than he wanted to admit he wasn't sure if he was sane. But there was no way he'd be able to focus his mind that morning without Jadonist meditation.

He sat cross-legged on his damp towel and straightened his back. He lowered his eyes and tried to imagine his consciousness existing just below his navel. His hands rested softly in his lap. He counted his breaths and felt his energy flow in and out of him with each one.

Killian called up his calendar and looked over his day. Something was bothering him. The background of the calendar was that drab purple he switched to yesterday, even though he knew he'd end up hating it. He stood and began to dress while cycling through calendar colors. It had to be a solid color, pictures distracted him.

Last week Killian spent thirty-seven minutes of his life changing background colors. He spent another six minutes thinking about how much of his life he'd wasted thinking about background colors. Screw it – white for the calendar.

His schedule for the day was full. Wait a minute! He was supposed to see Evan at eight this morning but there was another name there. A new name that he didn't recognize. Damn it, he already had a noob scheduled after lunch. Killian called up Progner's face and thought a message at him. [Two noobs in one day, are you kidding me?] He stopped himself. It was never a good idea to send emotional reactions to the boss.

Damn noobs. Helping the nutjobs was one thing; he did what he could for the lost causes. But Killian found it increasingly difficult to help convert non-swimmers these days. After all, why would anyone want to Stream up now? Don't they know that one third of all Streamers are insane? Of course not. How could they access that information? Or any information? Ignorant fools.

He looked down to the left and his clock appeared in his mind in glowing green digital numbers, just the way he liked it. Though, maybe it would be better… No! He was running late. He should go. Right now. But he picked up his toothbrush instead, thought the command to have it fill itself with paste, and began polishing.

How did his world get this fucked up? Killian avoided that question by scrubbing too hard at his teeth. Raking the gums until they bled; until his questions drained into the porcelain with the ruddy spit and toothpaste and swirling water.

He focused on the woman who ogled him critically. The dark-haired beauty of his dreams. He would please her this time. He could do it. He would see her smile. A message from the office reminded him that he was going to be late. He pushed it away, shielded himself against all extraneous noise. He focused on finishing the job this time, scouring the inside of his bottom teeth relentlessly, waiting for the timer to flash green, for that beautiful mouth to smirk slyly at him. But he suddenly pulled the toothbrush from his mouth and poked himself in the forehead with it and felt the screwdriver penetrate his mind for the third and final time.

He opened his eyes and looked in the mirror. No holes. No blood. But his own lips were curled slightly upward.

S.O.S.

Killian was ten minutes late to work. He was fairly certain his new client would already be waiting in his office, but he cracked the door and peeked to make sure. Unlike another Streamer, whose presence would be sensed when close enough, a non-swimmer, could sneak right up on Killian without him realizing it. He found the thought unnerving.

From the moment he saw him, Killian wanted to grab this new client by his skinny little neck. Such anger issues. Maybe he should see a shrink. Oh, wait; he is a shrink. But not a real one. A Short Order Shrink. A band-aid tossed into the gaping wound of society.

The first few months after the Stream came online were a nightmare. Wellspring Inc., anxious to launch its product before the competition, decided to go ahead and iron out the bugs after release. Sort of beta test it on the public. Life for early Streamers was riddled with glitches. Wellspring responded by releasing an endless array of patches and software updates. These smoothed out some of the wrinkles, sure, but they didn't even attempt to address what was clearly the biggest problem with the Stream. The biggest problem was that the Stream was moody.

At its most melancholy, the Stream faded to the faintest whisper and data retrieval became frustratingly slow. At its most excited, it overwhelmed people with the speed and volume of information they received. Such events were called Streamquakes, and the worst of them forced people to sit down and breathe deep and call to their mommies until the quake subsided. Some people passed right out. This was a big problem, as people could be doing anything when a Streamquake hit.

Eventually, Wellspring realized that it wasn't an equipment problem at all, causing all this vociferous behavior in the Stream. It was simply user error. Human brains, it turned out, were not as cookie-cutter identical as factory-made computer chips. You couldn't just plug a bunch of them into a server and expect them all to perform the same. Chalk it up to design flaw or individuality or free will; whatever. It amounted to big trouble for Wellspring.

Killian entered his office and circled around the noob who sat in the chair across from his desk. This guy finished high school out in non-swimmer land, knew it sucked out there and was going to get worse, so sign me up, sign me up for the Stream. Hurry up! I'm seventeen years behind already. Go, go, go! These kids didn't need a Stream connection for Killian to read their minds. They were all the same.

This one was pale and wiry. His body was wiry. His hair was wiry. His industrial strength glasses were not wiry, and looked to be a terrible burden.

"Good morning, I'm Doctor Peterson," Killian said. He didn't catch the mumbled reply.

Taking a seat behind his desk, he waited for the noob to say something. Usually they were anxious and it was best to let them blurt out questions right away. But not always. Sometimes they sat real quiet at first. Like this blank slate. His giant eyes merely blinked away the moments behind those thick lenses. Probably nervous. Eventually he'd settle in and the stupid questions would flow out all over the damn place. And it would be Killian's responsibility to mop up as best as he could.

"Let's start with what you know," Killian said.

"Well, I know that you're called an S.O.S. because so many of you were trained in such a hurry when the Stream came online and everybody went crazy."

Maybe he wasn't nervous. That was pretty bold. It was also correct. Once Wellspring realized that the people themselves were the problem, a network of psychiatrists were quickly trained to begin the arduous work of diagnosing and adjusting all the minds that were contributing to the disruption of the Stream. The Short Order Shrinks, as they became known to the public, had minimal psychiatric training. And due to their overwhelming, and growing, number of clients, they probably wouldn't be squeezing in advanced courses any time soon. No real need though. They mostly just filled orders.

A client couldn't stop hearing two songs at the same time? Killian adjusted his audio filter. Another couldn't sleep at night? Killian adjusted his bio-rhythm filter. That was the job; listening to the complaints, consulting the manual, adjusting their filters. He took their orders; he shrunk their heads.

A screwdriver appeared threateningly in front of Killian. He clenched his eyes.

"Doctor Peterson?"

"Hmm?" He looked around his office for the voice.

"You alright?"

"What's that?"

"Are you okay?"

"Yes, of course," Killian said, "Why?"

"Well, my name is Patrick Fitzgerald, but you wrote Jerry Futzpot. And I told you I'll be staying with my cousin, but you wrote uncle. And under 'Career Intentions' you seem to just be scribbling."

Of course, the Stream eliminated the need for pens. And paper. And therefore, paperclips, file folders, staples, scissors, copy machines, and pretty much anything categorized as office supplies. Killian's office was bare. Aside from his desk there were three chairs. One on his side of the desk, and two on the other. His desk drawers were all empty except for one. The top drawer contained three identical pens, a clipboard, and a stack of New Applicant Forms. The pens said "Wellspring, Inc." on them. The clipboard said "Wellspring, Inc." on it. The noob forms each said "Wellspring, Inc." on them. Killian's *degree;* the only framed object decorating the walls of his office, said "Wellspring, Inc." on it.

Killian might as well have had a tattoo on his forehead that read: "Wellspring, Inc." That way noobs could identify whose property he was as easily as Streamers.

Killian looked down at the pen. The law insisted that he write down notes from his sessions with new applicants, so the applicant would have a record if he or she chose not to dive in. As if anyone ever chose not to dive in. As if, faced with the dazzling technology of the future, any of these hicks ever said, "No thanks. I'll just go on back to the countryside, where they'll hopefully have TV and phone service for another five years. Ideally, we'll still get electricity for a decade or more. So, no thanks. I'm gonna pass."

The fact was that anyone with any kind of technological savvy at all had flocked to the cities, the bright source of the Stream, like moths to light bulbs. There was almost no one left out in non-swimmer country with the skills needed to keep the Internet, the cell towers, or even the outmoded computers running any more.

Killian grabbed a new form from his drawer. He removed the picture of this noob and the paperclip from the old form and transferred it to the new one. He started over.

"Name?" When he got down to career intentions the noob got into some involved story about when he fixed his uncle's TV as a kid and he knew right then he'd be good with technology.

"...and I have this old video game system that I keep running, and no one can beat me, at any of the games. So, I figure, I can probably design Stream games, right? Anyway, I just feel like life has been holding me back. I know I was born to Stream. Once I get immersed in the technology, and up to speed, I'll be able to do anything I want."

Killian tapped his pen on the clipboard. Tap, tap, tap. Quick little taps. He tried longer ones next. Dash, Dash, Dash. Morse Code. Quick again. Dot, dot, dot. He paused, then repeated the pattern. Three quick taps, three long taps, three quick taps. S.O.S. Save our society. Save our souls. To whom was he calling? Who could possibly help him?

MUSTACHIO

"How about the Stream then?" Killian asked. "What do you know about that?"

"Well," the noob twisted uncomfortably in his seat, "I know the Steam is like, beamed into your head, right?"

"Don't think of it that way. The Stream is everywhere. It's broadcast into the air, like television or radio waves. The implant simply allows you to receive the waves and interpret them with your brain, instead of needing an external device."

"So, can I really read other people's minds?"

"Well, sort of. But only with their permission. And only what they send you. We'll get into filters and transmission levels much later, but it will be possible to communicate with anyone who answers. Just like a phone call. Without the actual phone. In fact, once you adjust to the Stream, life will be little different than it is for you now. You'll simply be removing all the little devices and gadgets you rely on and living without them. Music, movies, phone calls; everything will be internal."

"So, when can I try it out?"

"Well…."

Standard operation for noobs required two full

sessions before they could be connected to the Stream. The first session was for dispelling myths. What they heard out there in non-swimmer land could be shockingly stupid. Can Streamers really move things with their minds? Can I fly? Will other people be able to control my body? Ridiculous. Yet, unoriginal. Killian had heard it all. This noob had nothing remotely novel to say. As he sat there stroking his greasy, fuzz-lined upper lip, Killian writhed.

"Doctor Peterson?"

"Right. Um... not today. I can't just throw you in. On the third session I'll begin slowly introducing you..."

"How come it doesn't cost anything?"

Oh it costs, Killian thought. It costs time. Maybe a little piece of the soul. The Stream worked like television originally did. People got so much Stream, seemingly for free, and then a commercial interrupted. Back to the Stream, then another commercial. Of course commercials were no longer something one could walk away from. People couldn't just get off the couch and leave the room for a snack or a quick tinkle. StreamAds bombarded them with sound and intense visualizations. Some even used the illusions of smell and touch and taste. Meanwhile, they whispered all kinds of suggestions to the mind. People couldn't hear the suggestions, due to the sensory overload, but they got in there and did their naughty little magic. They created cravings, suggested fixes for those cravings, and then revealed the best place to buy such fixes. People couldn't help but listen. And it was hard to complain, since they didn't really know they were listening. They thought they just happened to want that Beta Bar, and, lucky for them, they just happened to have bought a whole case this week.

"Well, of course you'll have to get a job," Killian explained. "Then you'll be able to pay for longer uninterrupted Streaming. It's no different than society has always been. The more you work, the more free time you get."

Killian recognized the paradox, but this kid across from him was just bursting with questions, and didn't seem overly concerned with the answers.

"Is it true I won't need glasses?" he said, adjusting his heavy frames on his nose.

Killian looked into the noob's oversized, rapidly blinking eyes. "No. Well, not when you close your eyes. Not to see things in Stream. But you'll still need them to see the real world." Whatever that was.

"But I'll be able to think about thousands of things at once, right?"

"No, look, that's a big misconception. As far as we know, the human mind can only concentrate on one thing at a time. What most people refer to as multi-tasking could more accurately be called rapid focus shifting. All the Stream will do is give you a billion more foci."

The noob crunched his forehead.

"Focuses," Killian sighed. "A billion more focuses. That's what's so dangerous. That's what makes people go crazy." Killian stopped himself. He wasn't ever supposed to mention craziness to noobs. It was in bold in the Wellspring handbook.

Also in bold in the handbook: "Euphemize! Words like: Streammadness can be scary. Instead, try: Temporary Stream Regulation Concerns."

Bullshit. His entire job was peddling bullshit. He wondered if he could convince this noob not to Stream. Now there was a challenge to alleviate numbness.

"You see, my job is not just introducing people to the Stream. Most of my day is actually spent trying to cure Streammadness. Essentially, what happens is that people lose control of their consciousness. It skips around all over the Stream on them and they can't seem to choose what to focus on any more. You can imagine how maddening that could be."

Bad, bad shrink.

Killian grinned. He needed a name for this noob. He had to give a nickname to each of his clients. It helped him adopt the elitist attitude he believed was essential to doing his job well.

Killian looked down at the photograph clipped to the upper left corner of the Stream Applicant Form. He placed the tip of his pen on the spot just below the man's nose. He drew a dark line out to one side and curled the end of it. Returning to center, he drew a line the other way, curling the end just like before. A mustache.

"Where are the vandals of old?" Killian wondered. Where are the merry pranksters who once would deface a poster with an ink mustache? As if to say, "You think you're important enough to have a poster of your face blown up and advertised publicly? Well, I'll show you." A mustache – a slash right through the ego. Sorry, sir, but you are not that important. In fact, you are ridiculous. And I will dismiss you with a simple swipe of my pen. Where are the graffiti artists and bathroom stall poets? No longer anonymous in a world where all thoughts are recorded. Maybe a little mysterious fun would do this brave new society some good.

Killian looked up to the man sitting across from him. He was not as baby-faced as the previously un-defaced photo suggested. He had dark, wispy hairs on his upper lip. Mustachio! Yes, he'd call him Mustachio. Mustachio, because it was a silly child's mustache he wore. One that should be shaved out of shame, not flaunted as a symbol of manhood. Killian looked down his nose at Mustachio.

But what he saw was Evan Hyatt's reflection in the

mirror. He saw a hand raise a screwdriver toward his forehead. He saw Evan's memories and felt his frustration and confusion and pain.

"But it will make me smarter, right?" Mustachio asked.

Killian exhaled through his chapped lips.

"No, the Stream cannot make you smarter. All it does is give you access. Access to all the information that human beings have ever collected. Access to all the opinions that any Streamed individual has ever formed. But it doesn't help you understand this information."

Mustachio tilted his head. Killian was supposed to gently encourage here. He was supposed to explain that the Stream provided the potential for one to grow intellectually and spiritually, and certainly this meant becoming smarter. Bah!

"Look, Mus… man. Say they open up a massive library next door to your apartment. Thousands of books. Millions. And they give you a free library card. And it's open twenty-four hours a day. Would that make you smarter?"

Mustachio looked to the ceiling for advice.

"The Stream is just a big library inside your head. It'll even read the books to you. But it can't make you pay attention to them or comprehend them or learn from them. It isn't the answer to all your dreams, it won't give you super powers and it can't help you get laid."

[Peterson!]

Killian looked up to where Progner stood in his doorway, his suit coat casually held over one shoulder.

"Dr. Peterson, why don't you introduce me to this interested young applicant?"

"Um, yes. Of course." Killian jumped up and clumsily circumnavigated his desk. "Dr. Progner, this is Mustachio."

Oops.

VENTING

"Fitzgerald. Patrick Fitzgerald," Mustachio said, rising and offering his hand for shaking.

"Nice to meet you Mr. Fitzgerald. I'm Dr. Progner, head of the Department of Stream Psychiatry. I was wondering, Mr. Fitzgerald – I hope you'll excuse any indiscretions on the part of my associate Mr. Peterson, you see, he experienced an emotional trauma early this morning. I was wondering if you would allow me the honor of finishing up your introductory session. I don't often have the opportunity to meet many new applicants, what with all the administrative tasks that occupy my day, and I like to stay in practice. You understand."

Progner led Mustachio out of Killian's office with one hand on his shoulder. He continued to chat him up all the way across the lobby. Killian dragged along behind them, staying back a few feet as they entered the elevator and turned to face him. Mustachio wiped a filthy finger across the thin greasy hairs under his nose. He looked to Progner.

"Is it true that the Stream is like ninety-five percent porn?"

"Jadon help me," Killian sighed.

[You're on thin ice Peterson. My office, 4:05.]

The elevator doors closed and Killian waited patiently until it was out of range of his voice. Then he screamed a string of obscenities at it until his breath failed him.

Sucking for air, his brain throbbed. Pain localized in his forehead. The left side of his forehead. He saw the screwdriver again, coming toward him. He closed his eyes and felt the metal slide into his mind and erase his thoughts; replace his thoughts with pain.

In his office Killian killed the fifteen minutes until his next client arrived playing quiZblitZ. Addictive gaming was an amazing alternative to thinking.

Super Sweats, donning his usual matching primary colored sweatpants and sweatshirt, found Killian in his office with his eyes rolled to the ceiling and waited patiently for him to finish up his game. An hour with Super Sweats. An hour with Goat. Then an hour with Filter Whipped. Three hours of listening to the mundane problems of typical Streamers. Seemingly minuscule problems when compared to Killian's own life. Were they responsible for the deaths of three people this month alone?

As their psychiatrist, it was Killian's job to prescribe fine-tuning of their filter. To adjust for their complaints. Complaints that piled up inside his own head, smothering his mind until it cried out for air holes.

The moment his fourth client of the day left his office he saw it again. The sharp end of a flathead screwdriver. He jumped up and walked briskly to the elevator, forcing his eyes to stare at his feet. Still, the vision commanded his attention.

Stab. Stab.

Killian reached out to stop the phantom screwdriver but it pulled away from him for another thrust. He ran straight into the closed doors of the elevator. The screwdriver stabbed again while he slid slowly to the floor.

Once Killian sat down and focused on his breathing he gained control of his memories. Jadon be praised. He attempted to dial down the background noises that drove Evan crazy. He isolated thoughts, visuals, and sounds. This is exactly what he needed to do for his report. He would analyze every moment leading up to Evan's suicide and attempt to determine what went wrong with Evan's filtering programs.

The filtering programs Killian was responsible for tuning.

Evan was overwhelmed by too much incoming data. Killian heard, saw and felt that barrage of sensory data last night. He felt Evan stab at the center of the noise. The source. The imagined chip above his left eyebrow. Three times he stabbed at it.

There wasn't really a chip. That is, there wasn't a little square of plastic or silicon that existed in a very specific location in Evan's forehead. Evan believed this because his psychiatrist told him it was true. Killian told all of his clients this. The Wellspring manual insisted on it. It read: "Tell them the only thing different about them will be the tiniest little chip just under the skin of the left side of their forehead."

So that's what Killian did.

It wasn't like that at all though. There was no incision or insertion. Not a single slice. To dive into the Stream, all Evan had to do is lie on his back and receive a quick injection. It was as easy as getting pregnant.

The injection went up one of his nostrils. He could have even picked which one, if he had a preference. The spray contained nanobots. Nanobots are microscopic robots designed to do very specific jobs. These nanobots assembled in certain areas of Evan's brain. Areas that controlled vision and hearing and memory. When they got to these locations they reproduced. When there were enough of them, they set up tiny transceivers. This allowed all of the information shooting around Evan's brain to be shared across the network of the Stream. It also allowed all of the information crossing the network of the Stream to shoot around inside his mind. When the information shooting around inside Evan's mind was not properly restricted by his filtering program, the result was Streammadness. Just like Evan Hyatt. And Elena Gratz. And Hector Horowitz.

No more nicknames. Not for the dead.

"People don't want to know that miniature robots are setting up transceivers in their mind," the Wellspring manual continued. "This will scare them. They would much rather believe that there is only a small chip in their forehead. It sounds less invasive. It sounds like it can be easily removed."

The Stream connection could not be easily removed. It could not be removed at all, in fact. It *was* a scary notion.

So Killian told his clients that the nasal spray they received culminated in a small chip in their forehead, somewhere above their left eyebrow. He then felt incredibly guilty when one of them tried to destroy that chip with a kitchen knife, or a power drill, or a screwdriver.

Getting to his feet, Killian wiped tears from his eyes with the end of his sleeve. He called for the elevator. He didn't need a button for this. Inside the elevator he told it what floor to go to. He didn't need a button to do this. There were buttons. They were there for noobs.

He dropped all the way down to ground level. There he followed the aisle past unused storage rooms to a door at the end. As he approached it, a voice in his mind said,

[Warning: the door ahead leads outside. Air temperature is ten degrees Celsius.] He opened the door and allowed the icy wind to blast him in the chest. His eyes and nostrils widened. His forehead was washed clean of imagined holes by the numbing cold. He tensed every muscle and became rigid before the purifying oxygen that rushed through the gap in the door.

He imagined the heat circulators in this section of the tower whirring up in response to this crack in their perfect world, this venting of reality, which interrupted the meticulous regulation of ideal settings. He closed his eyes. He closed the door.

GOD?

Human beings sure like religion. Just because they evolved brains capable of complex, imaginative thought, doesn't mean they have to use them. Why bother contemplating the world around them, and their place in it? That's exhausting. Simply follow the prescribed road map for a good life, and let God take care of everything. Free up that mind for important decisions, like whether or not you should just have both of those last two pieces of cake now, that way you can wash the plate.

Religion is supposed to explain the world in a way that makes sense and promotes healthy living. But how can it do that when it refuses to keep up with the times? Science and technology have made it very difficult for those whose faith hinges on literal interpretations of ancient texts. The Stream makes it nearly impossible Being constantly connected to, and therefore influenced by the minds of all those sinners makes purity hard to even imagine.

And yet, Stream society has seen the most successful rebirth of religion in modern times. Jadonism has made converts of ministers and fakirs and lamas alike. In a few short months it became the dominant religion in Stream. Within a year it became the only one.

Why? Well, like any religious prophet, Jadon was good at describing what was wrong with people's lives. He was good at telling them how their lives could be better. But Jadon had one thing traditional prophets did not. He had proof. Instead of relying entirely on the faith of his followers, Jadon offered proof of the changes he promised. And he delivered on that promise.

Jadon claimed that the moodiness of the Stream was a reflection of the chaos of the minds connected to it. He claimed that if people learned to focus their minds, the Stream too would settle down. To prove this he suggested that during the next Streamquake as many people as possible should sit down and focus on counting their breaths. Just that: sit and breathe. Nothing more.

And it worked. The next Streamquake was short-lived and dissipated with unusual swiftness. People were convinced. Jadon began promoting forms borrowed from tai chi and yoga and Zen meditation to help people focus their minds. As more and more people adopted the ways of Jadonism, the Stream seemed to lose its reputation for being grumpy and unreasonable.

But humans quickly lose sight of a good thing once they have it in their pocket, and as with most fads, Jadonism began to wane as swiftly as it had waxed. Now, while a good swift waxing is highly preferable to the excruciating tearing of a slow waxing, a swift waning of a new religion is never really desirable. Jadon realized that his people needed more than a fix for today's problems. They needed hope for the future as well. So, in his now famous Sermon That Should Count, Jadon promised his people God.

"It is obvious that the creator of the universe does not micromanage humanity," Jadon began. "You cannot speak to God directly whenever you want and hear a reply. Yet this has been the desire of human beings for thousands of years. It is why we have built the Stream. The Stream knows everything that we collectively know. It hears our voices constantly. But can it answer our prayers? I believe it can. If we continue to focus our minds together, we can bring harmony to the Stream. Then we can help the Stream evolve a consciousness of its own. A voice. An all-knowing voice that can guide us toward our greater destiny."

So humans could create God in their own image. The ultimate democracy. Every person contributing to the Stream; the consciousness of the Stream able to speak for humanity. Nirvana. Heaven. Right here on Earth.

Naturally, disciples were needed to constantly refill attention deficits with rosy visions of this future. To remind people of their role in helping to create it. A priesthood began to grow. It was made up, mostly, of clergy from other religions. People who were already good at crowd control. People who realized the old holey ship they were steering was sinking fast, and they better jump on that there passing ship with the shiny new name right quick.

Of course, when the Jadonist priests surmised that the more in-tune, the more similar the minds of its flock grew, the calmer and more manageable the Stream would become, they began to suggest filter adjustments to their followers. They began to prescribe a set of parameters for a 'Faith Filter' that all who really wanted to hear the voice of God should adopt.

So, even though the S.O.S. were the only ones with the technical know-how to tune the filters, they could no longer hold back the waves of clients that began to wash into their offices demanding very specific tune-ups. Jadon faded into the background and the priests began competing with each other over the best ways to purify the Stream. When one priest demanded, "God should not have child pornography in his mind," for example, it sent loads of clients in to their shrinks demanding their filters on nudity be clenched down a touch harder. When another priest suggested, "The day God comes online, do we really want him to think his people are so violent?" psychiatrists' offices overflowed with requests for sterner anti-violence filters.

Killian hated the clergy. He loathed the fact that he'd probably be working with them much more in the near future. Their power continued to grow as the psychiatrists' diminished. As he stood in line in the cafeteria, waiting to pay for a slice of pizza, pushing out the image of the floating screwdriver, he missed Evan Hyatt. Evan was a fellow devout atheist. He and Killian would talk during Evan's sessions about the idea that maybe bringing about some sort of God whose digital teat we could suckle, instead of thinking for ourselves, wasn't really a sound evolution to promote. In the interest of survival of the species anyway.

WISH

Killian grabbed a seat by himself in the cafeteria. He usually ate alone. He spent his whole day listening to people whine at him. Lunch was a welcome relief.

That day, however, Killian would have preferred not to be alone with his thoughts.

Actually, he would have preferred not to be alone with Evan Hyatt's thoughts.

Killian didn't want to think about anything more complex than chewing at the day-old cheese on his pizza. He needed to have a preliminary report ready for his meeting with Progner though, and lunch was the only chance he'd have to work on it. He desperately needed to find some connection between Evan and the others. Something to give Progner so that he didn't conclude the only link between the three cases was their incompetent psychiatrist.

What Killian would really like was someone to listen to *him* for a change. Face to face. In the same room. Where he could see their eyes looking at him. Where he could be certain they were real and paying attention. Being connected to millions of minds through the Stream had only deepened Killian's loneliness.

He suspected this was all that was wrong with many

of his clients.

Not all of them though. Some of them had much more severe problems. Like Evan. Some of them really needed a good psychiatrist. Like Evan. Some of them were beyond Killian's ability to help. Like Evan. And Elena. And Hector.

But why? What did these three suicides have in common?

Evan and Elena were both big gamers. Elena spent most of her time in a world called Edenite, where she was a level seventy-two Necromancer. Killian first tried prescribing her a duration alarm that sounded every three hours. She was supposed to come out of Edenite for at least ten minutes when the alarm sounded. A week later, Killian received a call at two in the morning. He had set the biometer in her filter to inform him of any health concerns. It informed him she had fainted. She hadn't eaten, slept or used the bathroom in twenty straight hours. She was dehydrated. After that Killian had to prescribe timed shutdowns. If she remained in Edenite for longer than six hours her filter would kick her out for thirty minutes. That worked. For a while.

But then Elena had started talking aloud while she was outside the world of Edenite. Only, she wasn't talking to anyone. There were no responses to her questions, in Stream or in her own mind. She was having one-sided conversations out loud. It worried Killian a great deal. He was convinced it was some kind of echo effect of overexposure to a virtual reality. But his attempts to further restrict her access to Edenite were met with hostility at first, and a cease harassment notice from her lawyer eventually. Killian could do nothing but wait, and then watch as a kitchen knife penetrated the mind he couldn't.

But Evan never obsessed on a single world. He liked

military mission games and galaxy roaming games and fantasy sports and porn. It was tough to keep up with his shifting interests. Evan was a pretty damn good hacker too. He found ways around any restriction Killian could prescribe within a few hours. His problem was the opposite of Elena's. Instead of being too long in one world, he jumped too frequently from one to another.

Hector's problem was think tanks. Or chatterboxes. These were Stream "rooms" with a simple topic as their only label. The idea was that he would enter and focus on the topic. And thousands of other minds would do the same. There wasn't any type of organization programming or filtering of the conversation at all. Everyone's mind spoke simultaneously. Killian couldn't understand the appeal. He spent a good deal of his time wishing he could escape all the noise. Hoping to tune out the voices.

But Hector didn't really game at all. So where was the connection? Killian wished he could see it.

Wait. Hector was being booted from chatterboxes. More frequently in his last few days. Yes, he would be removed from a room and would receive a message saying he violated rule seventeen section eight. Every time, the same message. Killian searched, discovering that rule seventeen involved intentionally straying from the topic of the room. Section eight had to do with speaking aloud and clarified the disruptive potential of continuous unrelated speaking, and how it embodied the very antithesis of the purpose of the room.

Killian listened to some of the dialogue Hector got booted for. Once, in a room labeled "Stream Society Gender Roles," Hector began asking someone to please leave him alone. Over and over. He answered yes three separate times for no reason and received a warning from the room monitor. Then he screamed, "Stay the hell out of my head, you bastard!" and was booted from the room.

Killian chastised himself for not reviewing Hector's time in the chatterboxes previously. He just couldn't do it. All those random thoughts. It made him want to... He saw the power-drill that Hector used. He heard it's high-pitched whine.

He shook it away. Had Evan also been speaking to no one? Killian chomped a mouthful of pizza. Was that the connection? One that wasn't his fault? It was a possibility.

It meant he needed to go back to Evan's apartment. He needed to stab himself in the head again.

He'd rather do just about anything else. He wished for a distraction, for someone to talk to.

[Praise be to Jadon.] It was Paul's voice in Killian's mind. He spied the priest across the room, finishing up at the cash register. He was heading toward Killian's table, holding his lunch tray high across his chest. Killian reminded himself he had to be careful what he wished for. Now he wished that memory of the screwdriver would shatter the teeth in Paul's approaching grin.

"May I join you?"

"No fucking way," Killian thought. "As you wish," he said aloud.

SCREWED

"I thought I'd catch up with you informally..." Paul said. He sat and reorganized his sandwich, chips and coffee on his tray. He put a paper napkin in his lap. He looked up. "Before our next official meeting."

[Great, because the time I'm forced to spend with you just isn't enough for me. In fact, I was wondering if I could get me a personal priest. You know, one to follow me around *all* day.] Killian's mind was exhausted. It wasn't easy to keep what he was thinking to himself. Had he broadcast all of that?

Paul took a bite of his sandwich and managed to chew without relaxing his smile. That damn priestly smile constantly curled his lips. It caused his beady eyes to sink deep into the surrounding wrinkles. Empty approval. It was a magnificent mask.

Paul used to be Father Paul, a Catholic priest. Killian couldn't wrap his head around how so many priests and ministers became Jadonist clergy shortly after diving into the Stream. For the masses, sure, new religion, new god, why not? But someone who devoted his life to the one true God? How could he have been drawn so easily into another explanation of the universe?

Paul's vacuous gaze revealed no answers. Killian

picked at the crust of his pizza. Neither man thought directly. They allowed their minds to drift through the random questions of the uncommitted consciousness. To daydream. To wonder. It became a familiar contest. Who could stare the longest. Who could stand the other's mind and fail to react the longest.

[I wonder if his hair is naturally that uniformly white, or if he just prefers that distinguished wise man look?]

[I wonder if that's his original eye color] Paul thought [that radiant pale blue that almost forces you to look away?]

[Why do priests always adopt that patronizing paternal tone?]

[Why can't some people accept the inevitability of a shift toward Jadonism?]

[Does he think I care that the priests are growing more powerful than the psychiatrists?]

[What purpose does it serve a shrink to help clients, ultimately, become more insane?]

[Why would someone spend so much time smiling?]

[Why would someone sabotage his own job?]

[Why does he take his so seriously, does Jadon give bonus points to clergy?]

[Is he really incapable of seeing that his little jokes are defense mechanisms, with his psychiatry background? – But then, it wasn't really very authentic training, was it?]

[No.]

Killian lowered his eyes after thinking it. He had lost the battle of wills. He responded. Paul didn't yell, "statement" or "response", or "I win" like when kids played. It was obvious that his will was stronger than Killian's indifference, and that this would set the tone for their conversation.

Paul could afford patience now; could wait for

Killian to begin.

"What do you want from me?" Killian shoved the last of his pizza crust in his mouth.

"Only what I want for everyone. Peace. Progress."

"Don't start with that shit. What, specifically, do you want from me? Now. At this lunch. Why did you sit with me?"

"I can help you."

[Doubt it.] The image of the screwdriver flashed into Killian's mind again. He drove it out, focused on chewing and swallowing. He took a sip from his drink.

"Have you figured out yet what connects your three clients?"

"That's none of your business. It's confidential. How dare you...." Killian saw it. The connection. He winced to hold the thought in but he couldn't. [None of them were Jadonists.]

Paul's smile neither expanded nor contracted. It didn't judge in increments. It provided blanket approval. He opened his bag of chips, selected one, and inserted it between his rows of teeth.

[That's your help, huh? Rubbing your religion in my face. And that's why you're here. These suicides are leverage, aren't they?]

Paul did not respond. He chewed. He dug for another chip.

[Three dead because they refused to follow Jadon. Admit it, it's just what you wanted.]

"Killian, you yourself employ Jadonist techniques when you feel overwhelmed. Why do you refuse to share that knowledge with your clients? Don't you want to help them?"

"I don't want to deliver them to your cult. Who knows what brainwashing Jadonism will employ when enough Streamers buy in completely?"

"Because Wellspring's goals are much purer, right? They have no ulterior motives whatsoever. Killian, call up a picture of Evan Hyatt's apartment. Look into the details."

Killian did. He saw the body. He saw the screwdriver handle. He rewound until Evan walked backwards out of the bathroom and into his kitchen. His thoughts had been unlocked by the police and Killian had unlimited access now. He stopped while Evan was slugging soda from a large plastic bottle. He threw the empty across the room. The apartment was a mess. There were six bottles of Wave Blast soda scattered across the floor. Two torn open packages of Health-Es littered the table. There were Beta Bar wrappers on the counter, the couch, and the floor. The whole apartment was littered with snack containers.

[Do you see?] Paul asked.

Killian squinted into the beady eyes across from him.

[Who owns Wave Blast?]

"Wellspring," Killian said.

[And Beta Bar, and all the products you see there?]

[Wellspring, Inc.] Killian thought.

[And you're afraid of brainwashing by the clergy?] Paul swallowed and then resumed his smile. "Killian, at least if we work together we'll have some checks and balances."

"Yeah, well I don't know how to counsel someone if his basic life premise is out of whack. I mean, some of the clients I have that are real hardcore Jadonists; the ones who believe they're actually helping to create God, they're impossible to reason with. How can you fine tune a mind that thinks its purpose in life is divine, and therefore needs no logical explanation?"

"Well, we can work on that together."

"I'm afraid not."

"Killian, the Faith Bill is going to pass. And that means…"

"I know what it means." Killian stood abruptly and grabbed his tray. He stomped to the trash and tossed out what was left of his lunch. Paul remained in his seat, chewing.

The Faith Bill required that all noobs be introduced to Jadonism before being hooked up to the Stream. Specifically, it added a third mandatory preStream session to the new applicant agenda. This joint session was to be run by both a psychiatrist and a priest. Killian and Paul, working side by side. Good times.

As unappealing as this was, it wasn't the worst detail of the new Faith Bill. The worst part of the bill was the crazy catch. The crazy catch said that anyone who was determined to be psychologically unsound must regularly meet with both a psychiatrist and a priest. The catch came when the priests began declaring any Streamer who wasn't a Jadonist to be crazy. So, if you're a Jadonist, you see a priest; and if you're not a Jadonist, you're crazy, and therefore you need to see a priest.

[The only step left is for you priests to become the shrinks,] Killian thought. [You already 'counsel' your believers. You already suggest Stream filter settings for many of the *faithful*. If you could actually prescribe settings, you'd have total power over your flocks. Baa, baa bah!]

Paul waited for Killian's ranting mind to slow.

"Dr. Progner informed me you have a particularly difficult new applicant that you are scheduled to hook up tomorrow."

"So." Killian had nicknamed her Lightning. She was dull. She was slow. She was fat and predictable. She was safe and in no way dazzling or mysterious. Exactly like lightning.

"He would like us to work together with her today. A trial run of the new meeting format. I for one am honored by the opportunity."

[Oh, please. If he thinks for a moment....]

Killian sensed Progner approaching. "Hello Paul," Progner said. Paul moved to allow Progner to sit.

"I was just telling Dr. Peterson of our plan for this afternoon," Paul said.

"Excellent. I'm sure Dr. Peterson approves."

Killian ran through protests and excuses in his mind but Progner stopped him with a single image. He sent a picture of a screwdriver to Killian's mind. Paul had already made the connection. Evan was Killian's third recent suicide, and none of them were Jadonists. Progner had no choice. He had to work with the clergy if he didn't want them to focus media attention on these nonbeliever suicides.

"I'm glad you agree," Progner said. "Paul will be joining you for your eleven o'clock tomorrow."

quiZblitZ

Killian walked the deserted streets alone. Everyone else was crammed onto the metro at this hour, where they could sit and tweak their backgrounds, or send messages, or watch images. But the metro was too fast for Killian. He needed to slow his thoughts, to align them rhythmically with his footsteps. The air between the giant towers, where the sun struck for but minutes a day, was frigid. Huddled into the inadequate warmth of his light jacket, he kept reminding himself to slow down.

The walking woke his body some, but not his thoughts. He arrived at his apartment door, surprised, wondering how he got there. Of course, he could have rewound and watched himself drift backward toward his office. Then he could replay the entire walk and every thought he had on the way. But if he blocked out his own thoughts the first time through, they couldn't have been very interesting, could they?

Few of the moments that made up his days were. Did he even need to go into work ever again? Couldn't he just rewind and fast forward the index of identical days that had been stored up as the bulk of his life for years now? Did he really need to create any more duplicate memories to add to the stack?

Killian's door unlocked for him and closed behind him. He dropped onto his couch. He surfed some news feeds. Audio wasn't enough to keep his mind from wandering, so he called up a generic newscaster. Then he rotated through the options, shifting the newscaster's gender, hairstyle, outfit and voice. Who was the ideal reporter? Could looks be so average as to neither attract nor repulse? Could a voice sufficiently grab your attention without strangling it? Could a set of clothes be invisible without being appealingly naked?

Details. That was the key to distraction. If he could manipulate all the details, fine-tune the minutia; he would't even have to think about the big picture. Keep the mind busy, bombard it with trivia and meaningless tasks.

He checked his messages. His filter was set to let him know if Progner called. He hadn't. No one else would. He checked again. He played with the background color of his mail program.

Maybe he could give his whole filter a drastic makeover. He liked the new voice he'd chosen for it though. Same voice as his toothbrush. Sultry yet calming. He was a little bit in love with that voice. No, he couldn't give it a body. Too weird. He'd be chatting her up all day. Too distracting. Look at how obsessed he'd become with oral hygiene since he added her image to his toothbrush.

Perhaps the other direction? Did he need a less appealing filter? A man's voice? No, that seemed weirder. A clone of himself? Now that's insane, mister.

No. He'd spent, let's see, a total of seven hundred eighty-three hours of his life adjusting his filter. Wow! Imagine what he could have done with seven hundred eighty-three hours. Of course, he had four hours until he could go to bed that he had no idea how to fill, so, careful what you wish for and all. Besides, that worked out to less than fifteen minutes a day adjusting his filter. That was nothing. He spent more time moving his bowels.

He checked in on his favorite game shows. The latest episode of *Million Dollar Hunt* was released last night. Killian watched as the randomly selected Streamer's name was called by the host. A skinny woman appeared next to the host in striped pajamas. She blushed, then changed her clothes to camouflage fatigues with the bat of an eye. The host gave her the standard rifle with one bullet and a hunting knife. The current hunter had won seven matches. If he won ten he'd get the million dollars. If he lost once, he'd be off the show. Out of the Streamland fantasy world and back to his couch.

This woman was shaky and indecisive. She circled around the same patch of jungle for the first twenty minutes. Killian began by watching through her eyes, but it was nauseating because she wouldn't stand still. He panned out to the objective view. The other hunter was in a tree, sighting her through his scope. It was only halfway into the show though. Of course he stalled. He waited to see if she'd come closer. Reality programming, sure. Killian predicted correctly that the guy would somehow miss her when he did fire, then have to jump out of the tree and wrestle her gun away. This happened five minutes before the show ended. Suddenly Killian was bombarded by a soap commercial. It was so loud and flashy that it was over before he recovered his wits enough to block it.

Never mind. He skipped over to some entertainment news to see that the hunter did win a record eighth hunt. Killian would bet everything that next week's *random* pick was just home from the front lines of whatever war we're supposed to be fighting this year. Some expert soldier, recruited to ensure the safety of the elusive million dollar prize money.

Paul's smile appeared in Killian's mind, floating, Cheshire style. Progner's voice told him to cooperate, for his own good. The image of a screwdriver invaded. Crystal clear, preserved, forever unchanged by the flawless memory of the Stream. Killian needed a better distraction. He needed something more interactive to suck his mind in. He decides he'd game for a bit.

Not a shooter game though. No more blood today.

He pretended to search for games for a while, but he knew what he wanted. quiZblitZ. He lay back on the arm of the couch while the game booted.

quiZblitZ worked in fifty question batches. Killian sat at a virtual table and every seven seconds another player appeared on the other side of it. Simultaneously, a question appeared in the air. It was in white lettering, and a bit transparent, so it was hard to read, especially with some random person's face behind it. People would yell or adopt ridiculous expressions or wave their hands to further distract him from reading. The first one to shout out the correct answer to the question got the point.

Of course, everyone knew the answer. Or at least, every Streamer had access to it. It was a game of processing speed. It measured how fast a person could identify what was being asked, search the answer, and spit it through his mouth. The answer had to be spoken to count. Since it usually took more time to draw the answer from the memory center of the brain than to Stream search it, to be good at quiZblitZ one had to either know very little, or be really good at tuning out any thinking his brain might try.

Killian was pretty good, averaging thirty-two points per game. This evening he was a little sluggish though, and lost five out of the first six points.

He held his breath waiting for the seventh question. For weeks now he'd held his breath on the seventh question. As if there was any more chance of her appearing on the seventh question just because she had appeared on the seventh question that one time.

That one time over a month ago now.

Still, despite having recently survived several second-hand suicides, her appearance across the quiZblitZ table had been the single most emotional moment he'd experienced in years.

The seventh question had in no way obscured her beauty, which had immediately seemed familiar to him. He'd felt alive, looking into her dark eyes. Yet, the excitement she spurred was something he knew he'd felt before, in some distant memory he could no longer force to surface.

He would have done anything to recapture it.

[Who are you?] he'd asked her, that day, over a month ago.

Her eyes had tightened, but then loosened in recognition. Her full bottom lip cupped her thinner upper lip as it curled into a seductive grin. Then her lips had parted. She spoke.

"Minerva."

And then she was gone. Minerva? He'd never known anyone by that name.

A bulbous man eating a sandwich had appeared behind the next question. He answered correctly. Another figure appeared and shouted the next answer. Killian wasn't even trying to read the questions. He withdrew from the game. He rewound to the instant she had appeared. When had he known her? The straight, honey-brown hair had seemed all wrong. So had the heavy eye makeup.

He paused the moment in time, the very instant she smiled. He held the image in his mind. He had dreamt of kissing those lips before, he was sure of it. Who was she?

He backed up the view some more, but the question obscured her. It said, "Who was the Roman counterpart of the Greek goddess Athena?"

Ah. Minerva! She had been answering the question.

Still, she had seemed to recognize him.

The game was anonymous, so there was no way to get her information from it. Killian zoomed back in and stared into her bottomless eyes throughout that evening. He didn't want to forget her. Not again. So he adopted that smirk for his ImageCaster 3.0 toothbrush. Every morning and every night he puzzled over that subtle grin. It finally hit him just a few days ago. Her real name. It just sort of floated up out of the monotonous fog that was his daily existence. Ophelia Redenbacher. The girl he lusted after in high school.

How could she be in Stream? After all the protesting…

How could he have forgotten her?

Killian had searched exhaustively, but her name appeared nowhere in Stream. She must be using an alias. There was no way he could think of to track her down. So, for now, he watched as that smirk mocked him and his sparkly clean teeth morning and night. He spent hours at a time playing quiZblitZ, hoping she too was playing, and that he might just bump into her again. Then he berated himself late into the evening for being so pathetic.

But not tonight. Tonight, exhaustion helped him escape self-flagellation.

RECOLLECTION

If you could look in on other people's dreams, would you? Would you waltz within the cave of Echo to watch how daily observations are melted into memories, then refracted into shredded scripts of new fantasy? Would you spy out the secret desires, hopes and fears of the vulnerably unconscious? No, you are too noble for that.

Liar! Of course you would. How could anyone resist such power?

And while you were in there, checking out the wonderlands of any Alice you chose, could you prevent yourself from suggesting? The sleeping mind is so very vulnerable. Could you help but play hypnotist?

Would you be able to resist, for example, offering promotion ideas to the boss that never notices your hard work? Or dating suggestions to unrequited love? How about advising a wealthy stranger to invest in the new business you're trying to get off the ground? Easier still, why not try (just to see if it would work) asking directly for his bank account passwords. Tempting, huh?

It did not take Streamers long to submit to temptation.

One of the first patches Wellspring released was the

sleep boot. Less than a week after the Stream went online, an emergency update was downloaded to every Streamer. The sleep boot literally booted a mind out of the Stream when the biometric programming sensed it was asleep. Disconnected. No chance anyone could speak to you, look in on your thoughts, or suggest you transfer all of your money into their account.

So when Killian Peterson lay down and closed his eyes, no one could see his madness purge itself. First, the images that haunted him; the screwdrivers and power-drills and kitchen knives came. They stabbed and stabbed until the blood and pent up frustrations and fears and anger flowed steadily from the holes in his forehead. Images of Paul and Progner and every single one of his needy clients begged for his attention as they dripped from the stabbed holes, and ran down across his face. Until his entire mind had run out. Until he stopped panting and returned to rhythmic breathing. Until he was completely drained.

And then Killian's mind, freed from the gift of the Stream, would return to his past. The past, which during waking hours, he could no longer find. He had become so accustomed to rewinding life when necessary, that inquiries about his childhood sent his mind back ten years, to the moment he entered the Stream, where it would stop, befuddled about how to continue.

But at night, with the shutdown of the amalgamation of Stream and consciousness, his mind could go further. Freed from the current, Killian drifted back, ladling images from this past. He collected his most memorable childhood moments. His favorite action figure. That train ride his uncle once took him on through the mountains. And the year he got to know Ophelia Redenbacher, his first love. He spent a good portion of his nights back in the summer of his fifteenth year. When she had smiled at him, and kissed him gently on his lips.

Each night Killian set sail across his true mind, collecting these memories anew.

Sometimes, he woke with the vague feeling of these dreams still on the edge of his mind. The details, the names, faces, events and places were gone. He knew his dreams were of the past, however. He was sure of this because, although the details had dissipated, they left a faint aftertaste. What was left behind, he realized, was a tinge of joy.

He woke now. Memory dissolved into mist as awareness was immediately caught up in the flow of the Stream. He wanted to hold on to his feeling, but the current was strong and he would drown if he fought it. Row, Killian, row your mind, gently down the Stream. Merrily? Why not try merrily? Life's replaced your dream.

NIGHTMARE

Dona. How long had it been? Ten years? Maybe more. She hadn't changed so much. Gained a few pounds, maybe. She didn't ever look directly at Killian, so he found it wasn't awkward to stare continuously at her while she spoke. Her deep eyes peered out at a spot on the floor just past the tip of her left shoe. She scrunched her unplucked brow, as if trying to focus on something that wouldn't hold still for her. But there was nothing there.

He was examining her features, somehow, without really seeing her. He never really saw her. Now, as when they were kids, he was looking only at what she was not.

For example, her nose did not curl ever so slightly upward, then come to a cute little tip. It was wide and flat and yet, hid unnoticed in the rest of her face. She also did not look out through pupils that reflected the potential energy of the world around her while floating in warm, coffee brown irises. They were cold little lumps of coal, set deep into their sockets, and fixated on the floor just in front of her left shoe.

Her hair was not a collection of lightly bouncing, dark curls that drew his attention away from her face just long enough to be pleasantly surprised upon rediscovery. No, her hair lay in thick layers. The bottom layers were frizzy, but contained by matted, greasy top layers.

She was not animated. She did not radiate. She didn't exude an indescribable energy. Her bottom lip was not full and her top lip did not curl slyly, invitingly. Nothing about her mouth made Killian imagine kissing it obsessively.

She was not Ophelia.

Poor Dona. How many boys and men had done this to you? How many, beside Killian, had formed the question in their minds? How could they be sisters? There was absolutely no resemblance. None. Not one similar feature. And in every comparison, Ophelia was superior.

Dona's breasts were larger, and some might think she'd have that going for her. But they were overly large and dragged the eye down, toward her slightly chubby belly, where they rested insecurely, forever in danger of submitting to gravity's pull and rolling off to the side.

Killian tried to look away. All the while she was talking in a low, grumbly monotone he was unable to find any link to the voice that, with a single word, had revivified his ambition.

"Minerva," she had said, and he had never heard such beauty in a voice. But that's not true, exactly. He just hadn't heard it in such a long time. "Minerva." He replayed it again and again.

It didn't sufficiently distract him from Dona's ranting. She was droning on about something to do with the moon and Killian couldn't seem to tune her out.

Dona. Her full name was Jacinda Donatella Redenbacher. And as Killian forced himself to study her plain face, he could only conclude, as he must have many times in high school, that their mother's propensity for ridiculous names was the only proof at all that they were sisters.

Ophelia Cassandra Redenbacher. Three years older,

a hundred times more beautiful. Where was she now?

Killian remembered the elation that overtook him this morning when Progner mentioned there was a Miss Redenbacher waiting in his office. He hadn't cared that it was an hour and a half before his scheduled workday. It didn't bother him that Progner had said she was suicidal. He never stopped to consider that it couldn't possibly be Ophelia because she wasn't using her real name. He'd checked. The only sign of her anywhere in the Stream was whenever she was mentioned as the daughter of Steve Bates, inventor of the Stream. Nor did it ever occur to him to remember that Ophelia had a sister, one who had no reason not to use her real last name. No, he had somehow managed to completely overlook the possibility of Dona. After all, he'd forgotten Ophelia, and Dona was so much more forgettable.

While she was standing in his office door, Killian had only recognized who she was not. She had to speak before he began to see the truth of her.

"Hello, Killian, it's me, Dona. Dona Redenbacher."

She hadn't spoke the words so much as allowed them to dribble from between her lips. Killian had shaken his head for effect and said of course it was her and how good it was to see her. But his heart had sunk, and he had trouble holding up his head as he took his chair behind his desk.

She had started right in on this theory about the moon affecting evolution or something and had been droning on for a good ten minutes before it occurred to him that her not being Ophelia wasn't all that bad. After all, she was her sister. She must know how to contact her, right? All he had to do is figure out how to bring it up.

[Our moon is fairly unique, you realize. It is unusually large. I mean, most other known planets have relatively small moons. There are one thousand four hundred seventy-eight planets. Known planets. Of course there are infinite planets, but we've only catalogued one thousand four hundred and seventy-eight. Then we stopped looking. Shortly after the Stream was born. It halted curiosity in outward directions. That's another theory of mine. But ours is big. Our moon. Real big. It's like one-quarter the size of Earth. A moon of anywhere near this size is unheard of in our catalogue of known planets. And, it has a great effect on the oceans, right? The gravity of the moon controls the tides. So, anyway, the human body is like ninety percent water, did you know that? So, obviously the moon's gravity has some effect on us as well. Studies have shown that moods become intensified during a full moon. So, what I'm suggesting is that maybe it was the pull of the moon that created human intelligence, and therefore, a moon of such extraordinary size being pretty rare in the cosmos, maybe we are a fluke. Maybe we are all alone out there.]

    She paused, sucking in the starting of a canker sore on her lower lip and picking at it with one of her upper teeth. She continued to stare at the floor, just working at that little sore with that tooth until Killian pictured her biting it right off and swallowing it and had to muffle his own gag reflex.

    "So, tell me where your sister is," Killian thought. But aloud, he said, "So, tell me what's bothering you Dona."

    "Same thing as Hamlet, Doc." She let out her lower lip and flashed her coal eyes at him for an instant. He waited for her to continue, but she only rocked gently back and forth in the chair, staring at the floor.

    "Your uncle killed your father?" Killian tried.

    "Bound in a nutshell," she said, knocking on the side of her head with a fist. "I could be queen of infinite Stream. But I have bad dreams."

"You remember your dreams?"

"Remember them? I wake up in the middle of the night screaming." She was rocking a little faster. Forward and back, at an angle, toward whatever her left foot pointed at. She wrung her hands. She waited for him.

"I didn't think it was possible to remember dreams. I seem to have trouble remembering anything outside the Stream."

"Oh, you don't think that Wellspring actually lets you out when you're sleeping do you?" Dona said. "I mean, right, Wellspring discovers that people can be manipulated even more effectively during sleep, and out of their general concern for humanity, they close up that little loophole entirely? Really? Isn't it much more likely that they narrowed that little loophole, and encoded it so they're the only ones with access?"

"That sounds a little too paranoid." He saw the segue he'd been seeking. "If you remember your dreams, do you remember your childhood?"

"Well, you have to work at it, don't you," she said, rolling her eyes and sighing. "You have to work at anything you can't just rewind. You have to spend a lot of time exercising your mind to do the things it used to do naturally." She pulled in that canker again and gnawed. Killian looked away.

"Do you want to hear about the dreams or not?"

"Yeah. Yes. Proceed, please."

Dona curled her disproportionately thin legs up onto the chair beneath her lumpy torso. "Well, it's really just one dream. I'm sitting in a car, in the middle of a forest. Sometimes it's day, and the sun warms my chest, and sometimes it's night and the moon... Did I ever tell you my theory about the moon?"

"You just did." How could he slip Ophelia's name in now? She was back on the moon.

[Right. Well, so you see, that if we're just a cosmic accident, then we're unique, and we kinda realize that and so we're egocentric and that's why we think we're entitled to some kind of afterlife.]

In session, Killian's clients could speak aloud to him or through the Stream, whichever made them more comfortable. Most clients preferred one or the other. Dona seemed to be a flopper. She switched from voice to thoughts and back again without warning.

Taking a large breath, she exhaled while speaking. "But don't you see that eternal life is unfathomable, ridiculous, and above all else undesirable? Nothing lasts forever. What would be the point?" She found that sore again and pulled her lip in and transmitted her thoughts. Even in her thoughts her voice was dreary and slow and hard to pay attention to.

[If the universe really was created in a few days, created as is, and was to remain as is forever, what purpose would that serve? Seven days, seven million years, infinity. If there's no change, then infinity is the same as a week and therefore a week is sufficient. God, no God, random chance or some intelligent design, it doesn't matter. It's obvious that the universe is interested in only one thing: evolution. Change, by experimentation. It doesn't stay the same for a moment. All possibilities must be explored. So why would there be eternal life? Why preserve the soul of a little insignificant creature on a single tiny world within an infinitely large experiment like the universe? It's like you owning an ant farm, and saving every single ant turd, preserving it forever, because it's special to you as it is. But the soil needs that excrement, doesn't it? It's all part of the circle of life and makes plants grow that the ants eat and turn into excrement, right? It's a mere human ego problem to want to survive past death. How long would be enough?

Imagine living for a thousand years as a ghost, or soul or a heavenly spirit. Imagine another thousand. How long would it take, being an unchanged you, just your personality afloat, disconnected from everything that made you alive, until you begged for an end?]

Killian didn't realize he had been asked a question. He couldn't stop examining every facet of her crazy rant for something he could relate to Ophelia.

Dona cleared her throat. "So you into Jadonism, Doc?"

"Well, no. Not the… just the breathing, I guess, when I need to center myself…" Wait a minute! Killian was not supposed to answer such questions. Dona got his head spinning, reversed things. *She* had a nickname for him it seemed. She kept calling him Doc. She was supposed to call him Dr. Peterson. And she was asking the questions. Those stupid theories of hers were so dizzying. That was it! Stupid Theory Girl. That's what he'd call Dona.

Killian sat up. Armed with a nickname, he could take control of this session. Then casually, masterfully, he'd work in a question about Ophelia.

"Dona, maybe you better tell me why you're here." Yes. If he could get her to give him a reason to adjust her filters, he might just accidentally uncover an address, or … well, he'd need her alias.

"Told ya, Doc, bad dreams."

"Well, are you going to tell me about them?"

"I guess we'll have to get into that next time," she forced a weak smile. Adjusting her sweater, she rose with a puff of air.

"Why is that?"

"Because our hour is up. I'm sure you have other clients to see."

He did, of course. His eight o'clock would be in any

moment. Just how many stupid theories had Stupid Theory Girl spun? It was too long, that nickname, wasn't it? Dona's tiny black eyes searched the room quickly until they discovered Killian, startled and then darted away again.

"Dona, why did you threaten suicide if you didn't get to see me today? I mean, you didn't reveal very much, and now you're content to go home and wait until our next appointment?"

"I guess just talking to someone familiar eased a lot of my tension."

"Maybe, I should just take a look at your filters. Perhaps some slight adjustment to your sleep sensors will help with these dreams."

"Doc, I don't want to forget the dreams. They're obviously important. I want you to help me figure them out."

"So you're not going to kill yourself?"

"No. That was just a tactic to get what I wanted."

"Which was?"

"To get an appointment with you."

"But why me? I haven't seen you in ten years. Why did you need to see *me*?"

Dona stood up and stretched her arms above her head. "Because in my dreams I'm sitting in the passenger seat of a car. I'm screaming. Always screaming. It's the most torturous scream you can possibly imagine. It hurts me physically to produce it," she said, finding that spot on the floor again, just ahead of where she might, at any moment, put her foot down and begin a new journey. A journey out of his office. Without telling him what he wanted to know. No, that would be a nightmare, Killian realized. He opened his mouth, but she spoke first.

"Someone else is screaming," she said. "Sitting in the driver's seat. I'm screaming, and this other person is screaming; two distinct screams. It's always the same."

"Maybe…" Killian started.

"It's you Doc. In the car. In the dreams. Every time. Screaming. That's why I knew I had to see you. You must be the key to figuring it out." She chewed at her lower lip a second. "Well, let me know when you can schedule me again."

She put her foot down, onto the spot she'd stared at for almost the entire hour. She put her foot down and she walked out of his office.

PERIOD

It used to be that only the rich were crazy. Not drooling and twitching, uncontrollably insane, of course. That's always been reserved for the poor. If the rich dwell that far into insanity they soon become poor. Or else their friends and relatives use their exorbitant wealth to bury their afflictions deep from the public eye, which amounts to the same as curing it.

No, only the rich used to be crazy, as in: just neurotic enough to be alleviated by two hours a week of talking it out with an emotionally neutral, bearded and sweatered, older gentleman. This was not because the working class wouldn't benefit from bitching about their problems twice a week to someone who wasn't their friend. Someone who could say honest things a friend couldn't. Things like: "Hey, the solution is easy: just stop being a jackass so much." No, it wasn't that the poor wouldn't benefit from seeing shrinks. It was merely that they couldn't afford them.

But a Short Order Shrink?

Once it was determined that the Stream was broken and it was Wellspring's fault and that psychiatrists would be able to help the situation, then it was inevitable that psychiatry would be made affordable. Reasonably priced complaint departments. All of a sudden everybody was crazy.

And so, overloaded with clients, Killian spent his hours being handed off like a relay baton from one needy, infantile mind to the next. Sure, there were those who were actually being driven mad by the Stream, who actually needed him. But they had to wait in line. Or else find their own solution.

The screwdriver appeared in his mind.

Killian wasn't yet sure if Dona really needed him. She didn't seem to be crazy, crazy. Either way, he didn't want to spend too much time considering this. He wanted to catch her before she reached the elevator, and somehow bring up her sister. But the baton had been passed.

"Dr. Peterson," PMS said as Killian came out through his office doorway. "Dr. Peterson," he said again as Killian walked past, oblivious to his presence. Killian turned back toward PMS, then looked back to Dona, who was now being swallowed by the vertical mouth of the elevator doors. He sighed and headed back into his office, PMS lapping at his heals.

"Well Dr. Peterson, I'm getting my period again." This was his favorite opening line, and had earned PMS his nickname. What he meant was that he intended to come in and bitch for an hour, while Killian nodded his head and listened, like a good husband. PMS was kind of a chauvinist jerk.

"The Stream was to be the technology that revolutionized education," he said, taking off his coat. "And not like the computer revolutionized education. Nor how the Internet revolutionized education either. No, and it wouldn't just be something that sounded good to say at a faculty meeting, like when every single new piece of software that helped organized this, or add pictures to that came along. No, the Stream would actually revolutionize education. School would never be the same again. How *could* it be?"

PMS often started out this way. A big dramatic intro. A hook. He clearly rehearsed. He was good too. Came from being a teacher, perhaps. He put the right emphasis on just the right words, allowed his voice to get soft for a moment, then boom, he hit the desk while making a significant point. He had decades of experience trying to keep kids' attention. It made it very difficult for Killian's mind to wander. Killian's mind would have liked very much to wander.

PMS finally sat down. He leaned far in over Killian's desk. He waited until Killian's eyes locked with his. "No more pencils, no more books, no more over-paid, too much-vacation, know-it-all teachers' dirty looks. What would you need them for?"

And here he paused the perfect amount of time. Just long enough that Killian wondered if he was supposed to answer that seemingly rhetorical question. His lips fumbled nervously to form words, but that's when PMS jumped right back in.

"After a decade of trial and error, however, it turns out teachers are needed for the same reason they always have been. Most kids just aren't going to sit at a desk and learn on their own all day. Even if they have every tool available in their mind to do so. No, teachers are needed to guide children toward good information, and to help interpret literature, and to relate history to the students' own lives, and blah, blah, blah. But when it comes right down to it, somebody has got to keep an eye on these kids all day so their parents can go to work. It might as well be teachers. Right?"

Again the pause. Killian wouldn't bite this time. He sat waiting, staring back into PMS's icy eyes. They pierced deep, drawing out his comfort. He grew nervous, wondering if he missed something in the conversation. He turned away and spit out; "Right, I…"

"The Stream ended up revolutionizing education in much the same way every other technological advancement has." PMS was on his feet again, circling his chair. "It served as an excuse to put more students in each classroom, despite endless research which clearly demonstrates that nothing so negatively impacts learning as too many students in one room."

Killian wanted to scream. He needed time to process. He needed to think about Evan and his possible connection to Elena and Hector. He needed to consider Dona. But PMS was back again, throwing his palms flat on Killian's desk.

"I mean, try getting a kid to write an essay these days. They fire it off like it's a message to their friends. They're so used to instant communication that they can't, literally can't, stop and think before they form a sentence. Never mind trying to convince them to go back and reread it. It's been said. It's been sent. There's no editing for them. No refining. And then it's my job to take this stream of consciousness mound and segment it. Divide it. To chisel in breaks and say, hey, you need a period there. To bracket ideas for them. This is a complete thought, and this is a different thought and you need to separate them with a period.

"But that's how my whole day is laid out. Periods. This hour is devoted to these thirty-seven kids and their inability to form a coherent thought, and then a bell rings and a new period starts. The bell marks the shift from one group to the next. At 10:41 the bell marks lunch. Ring a bell and I salivate."

Killian realized his life was laid out like this too. This hour he listened to PMS complain. Last hour he listened to Dona. Who was next? His life was a schedule that measured other people's misery. A schedule packed full. There was no room for his own problems.

Ophelia's smirk came into his mind. She wasn't miserable. Her face, unlike the faces of his clients, did not blacken his soul. That subtle grin warmed Killian and filled him with life and hope. But why was she even in the Stream? She had tried to prevent it from coming online. And Killian had betrayed her, hadn't he? The minute he thought it he realized it was true. He couldn't recall the details, but the feelings were beginning to surface. A nausea in his intestines. He had definitely betrayed her.

Wait a minute? What had caused him to think of her just now? Killian rewound PMS's banter and listened to the last few moments again.

[She's always saying that teachers have enormous power that goes unrealized. I eat lunch with her twice a week, and man, it is difficult not to fall in love with this woman. I mean, I'm aware of the fact that I'm an old fool and even if I was young and single I'd have no chance, but I can't help it. She's just so damn delectable. Anyway, she's always saying how we have the tools available to influence the minds of the entire youth culture. If you're not willing to use all available resources, you can't win a war.]

That was it! He'd heard that dozens of times. He couldn't call up a single example, yet he was sure he'd heard it. In her voice.

"Can I see this woman you work with, I think I might know her."

PMS sneered his lip and held Killian's gaze a moment. "I guess."

Killian bit his lip as PMS called up an image of her. Yes! He tried to contain his excitement. She had the same hair and eye color as when he saw her in quiZblitZ, which still seemed wrong on her, but it was definitely the same girl he knew in high school. Ophelia!

"So?" PMS said.

"What?"

"You know her?"

"Oh, yeah, I guess. We went to high school together."

"Lucky. I'd have fallen deeply in love with her and followed her around every day if I went to high school with her."

"Yeah," Killian thought. "That sounds about right." But he couldn't remember.

He'd go to her. At the school. When could he find the time? He couldn't. Every hour of his life, every minute, was scheduled. He certainly didn't have a free moment during the school day. Maybe he could convince PMS that he needed to visit him in his classroom next session. Yes, tell Progner it was a field observation. That would work, wouldn't it? No. PMS wasn't scheduled until next week. He needed to go see her right now. He needed to run to that smirk, that one symbol of hope that sparkled between the cracks of his bleak schedule. Without it he would wither. Besides, if he didn't help himself, he wouldn't be able to help others. Right?

He had a right to happiness. Period.

DRONE

It was dark still. Killian forgot about that. The unnatural darkness at that hour. The sun had risen, somewhere. But not above the towers. The slit of true sky above him was pale blue, but the light did not penetrate down into the gray atmosphere he inhaled. The current his cheeks created by parting the stagnant air was chilly. What season was it? Did that matter? Did the passage of time matter here, where every moment was recorded forever? Where every moment was rewindable and pauseable and impossible to lose.

He walked quickly. The school where PMS worked was a good two miles away. He'd definitely have to take the metro back. He should have taken it both ways, but he needed to wake himself, to think of something to say to her. He believed fresh air and exercise would inspire him. Why did he believe this? It had been so long since that simple formula was enough.

Whatever thoughts his walk did inspire escaped him completely by the time he reached Wellspring Middle School 42. The sun was just peeking over the buildings as he entered the huge lawn at the front of the school, and the sheer amount of bright space overhead wiped out the entirety of his mind.

This had been happening frequently. Large amounts of time where he didn't remember going from here to there, let alone what he thought along the way. Of course, it was all there, in Stream, if he wanted to retrieve it. For some reason this bothered him more. It was as if he wasn't thinking for himself at all. His thoughts served the single purpose of filling up the Stream. If Jadon was right, and God was some day to come online, Killian's thoughts were helping to complete God's memory. It wasn't important what *he* got out of them. Yeah, disturbing.

Inside a hive of sand-colored bricks, where the school day droned on, Killian found a woman sitting behind a window. She was labeled, [Please check-in!] Killian approached, but before he could speak she held up a finger. She stood, then turned, lifting her chin a touch and rigidifying her body. A booming voice in Stream recited:

> [I pledge allegiance,
> To the Stream,
> Of the United People of Earth.
> And to the God,
> For which it formed,
> One mind,
> Indivisible,
> With morality and justice for all.]

Killian retrieved his jaw. How long had this been going on? These kids were being brainwashed. The United People of Earth! Bullshit. [What portion of the world is Streamed?] Killian asked, yet received no answer. Curious. He knew the translation programs were worked out quite a few years ago, and that the Stream had reached most industrialized countries. But it still only existed within the borders of major cities, which was less than half the population in those countries. The people of Earth. Right. And now, God was the reason the Stream formed? Jadonism was already rewriting history. If history meant a decade ago. These kids would grow up believing it though. All of it. They knew no other world.

The woman behind the window continued to telegraph her disapproval by scrunching her eyebrows and lips to maximum strain. He smiled. No effect.

"I'm here to see Lorelei Anders," he said, rolling his eyes to confirm this was the name PMS gave him.

"Do you have an appointment?"

Killian shook his head.

"Well, of course, *sir*, she is with students right now, and unless this is some kind of emergency…"

What the hell was he thinking; that he would just pop in and start chatting her up? If he thought about this for a moment he would have realized how absurd he was behaving. But he didn't want to think about it. He didn't want to admit that the obvious route, now that he knew her name, would be to message her and ask her to meet him. He sensed Ophelia did not want to see him, but he couldn't recall why. He couldn't remember anything about her. In fact, his entire childhood was blank.

[Killian,] Progner's voice invaded. [You've got fifteen minutes to be back in your office or you're fired!]

"Shit."

"Excuse me?" the woman behind the window gasped.

"Shit, shit, shit," he said and turned around and walked out of the school building. The building *she* was inside, somewhere. So close. He crossed the street and took an elevator up to the metro stop, just like the map in his mind directed.

Killian believed he spent the three minutes on the

metro reviewing Evan Hyatt's last few weeks of life, trying to determine if he was talking aloud like Elena and Hector. But he couldn't be sure. By the time he was in the elevator, rising toward his floor, he was already beginning to doubt that he'd actually just taken a field trip to a middle school.

"Ah, Dr. Peterson. Come in." Progner was sitting behind Killian's desk.

Killian entered to find Mustachio lounging in one of the patient's chairs.

"Mr. Fitzgerald and I have been getting along so well. I've explained to him that the note you left was not intended for him, and that it was an inside joke between you and a colleague, though certainly still unprofessional of you to leave out. In any case he is a little nervous around you. Says you seem edgy. I explained this is only due to the excessive stress you've been subjected to of late, and that normally you are quite skilled in your work. Still, we've decided that he will be seeing me from now on."

Killian nodded a bit lamely. Mustachio turned away from him, running a finger along his upper lip.

"Anyway, Mr. Fitzgerald, if you don't mind terribly, giving me and Dr. Peterson some privacy for a few moments, I will change your scheduled hour to an hour and a half tomorrow. That'll be in my office. Seventeenth floor."

"Sounds good," Mustachio said, standing to shake hands with Progner. Killian took a few steps back to clear the doorway and Mustachio left his office, hopefully for the last time.

"Sit Killian," Progner demanded, showing no sign of abandoning Killian's own chair. Killian sat. He glanced around the room from a client's perspective. There was his degree in the small gold frame. There was nothing else to look at but Progner's disappointment.

Killian dodged a phantom screwdriver. Justifications raced through his thoughts, but Progner erased them all with a single sentence.

"She doesn't want to see you Killian."

"Who?"

"Are we going to play that game, old friend?"

Here it came. The usual speech.

"Killian, I got you this position, not because we were casual acquaintances that lived on the same block, but because I believed that the boy I knew back on Springer Street had potential. I thought you'd go far, given half a chance. So I gave you that chance. And yet, you continue to flounder."

Yes, he'd heard this all before. And the guilt trip usually worked. Partly because Killian didn't really remember his past relationship with Progner, and so he wasn't sure if he owed him for something or not. He squirmed down further into the leather chair.

"Ophelia. She never wants to see you again. She tried to use you, remember? And she hates you for refusing to be used in the end. But you made the right choice. That's why *you* have a job and didn't spend several years rotting away in jail."

Killian swallowed hard and opened his mouth to protest, but no words formed. For all he knew, what Progner said was true. Why would he betray her? He couldn't remember. But he felt that he had. He closed his mouth.

"I need to rely on you, Killian, but you're cracking up on me. I can't believe you would leave, what did it say: 'Sorry Mustachio, no head shrinky today!' I mean, are you fucking kidding me? You didn't inform anyone you were leaving, Killian, I could have had your shift covered if you needed an hour. I'm not unaware of the difficulty of your situation. That's why I've overlooked all this somber droning of yours lately. But then, you just run out during the workday to go visit a dangerous terrorist, on a whim. Unforgivable. Frankly, I should fire you for even considering talking to her. What she's doing here, in the Stream, is certainly suspicious. Stay clear of her. Do you understand?"

Progner leaned forward and waited for Killian's eyes to return to him. "As for her sister Dona, that's another story. As far as I can tell she's never done anything nefarious and hasn't had contact with her sister in many years."

So much for that route back into Ophelia's heart. Killian wilted.

"But the fact that she's an avid anti-Jadonist, and came in here threatening suicide could be very useful to us. Couldn't it?"

Killian wasn't so sure. Then he saw it. "You mean, if I can help her heal, without Jadonism…"

"It'd go a long way to taking the edge off this case Paul is trying to build. I reviewed your session with Dona from this morning though and I must say, you really let that hour slip away from you. It's almost as if *she* were running the show. I'm going to try to get her to come in again tomorrow morning, in place of Fitzgerald. I'll take him off your plate. I understand that you've been overwhelmed with these… unfortunate cases, Killian. But I need you here, right now. I can't allow the clergy to just snatch all of this out from under us. You understand that, right?"

"Of course."

"Because, some of our fellow psychiatrists are already climbing into bed with the priests. But I've always liked your feelings about Jadonism, Killian. You don't love it, nor do you outright detest it. You separate what's useful from what's nonsensical."

Progner got up and headed toward the office door.

"Your client and Paul should be here in ten minutes. Get yourself together. This has to go smoothly. I'm not saying to let him have his way with her, not at all, mind you. But I won't be able to defend you if you fuck up any more. So just be a good little worker bee. Got it?"

LIGHTNING

Lightning looked from Killian to Paul. As her skull slowly shifted, it pulled with it the mound of dough that coated the area her neck should be. This mound continued past when her skull stopped, stretching to its limit; then rebounded in a series of diminishing ripples, until finally, it waggled to a nervous halt. All of this happened in slow motion, reminding Killian of that viral video of the fat kid dancing with no shirt on that got messaged to everyone a few weeks ago. First it was raw at half normal speed. Just rolls of fat jiggling hypnotically. Then it was sent out again with a sound track. Then a better soundtrack. Then an ideal soundtrack. Fat Kid Dancing Seven added close-ups of the bellybutton. There was a string of messages with faces added so the bellybutton looked like a mouth. New music was added. A contest developed around which song looked most like Fat Kid Dancing's belly button was singing it. It was officially decided that 0.73 of the original speed was funniest. There was a vote and everything.

Of course, this sort of communication disease was a big part of why Killian didn't have any friends. A friend to him was someone that did not deliberately add to the pile of ridiculous signals he must eternally sift through.

Still, he got the gist of the awesome fun he was missing out on from his clients. They loved wasting their sessions filling him in on the latest crazes. The week before last it was the superimposed machine gunning squirrel. Next week it would no doubt be Machine Gun Squirrel versus Fat Kid Dancing. With so many possibilities, *that* face off might have a full two week run.

The power to create anything and share it with the world, and this is what people did with it. They tweaked Machine Gun Squirrel versus Fat Kid Dancing versus Monkey Drinking Own Pee until it got just the right backdrop and music and play speed. Until it was edited to maximum hilarity. Until everyone had had a hand on it and could claim contribution. Until it was a globally filtered product representing the finest in human creation. "If only God would come online now," Killian thought. "Damn proud, God would be. Damn proud."

Lightning's entire form drooped so heavily it pulled Killian's eyelids down with it. He yawned. He looked away. There was Paul. He tried to cut the yawn off early. Paul rolled his eyes. With a quick thought Killian boosted his stim level, just slightly. He'd pay for the privilege of self-prescription later, when he crashed on his couch after work.

"Well, *Doctor* Peterson, why don't you fill me in on what the two of you have covered already."

"Of course." Lightning looked back to Killian when he spoke, causing her mesmerizing waves of chins to dance. Killian looked away. "Last session we left off reading multi-genre viewpoints, trying to give her a better overall view of just what it is we call the Stream."

"I still don't get it," Lightning admitted gleefully.

"That's fine," Killian soothed. "We can pick up with that. I want you to listen to a few more descriptions. Let the words wash just over you. Then we'll go back and try to piece together an understanding of the whole for you, okay?"

Lightning waggled her chins in reply.

Killian quoted positive descriptions of the Stream, mostly from advertisements, mostly ridiculously idealistic drivel. None of these ads specified that the process was irreversible. None of the scientists who spoke on Wellspring's behalf predicted the instability that would result from hooking up so many minds in such a short period of time. None of the Wellspring commercials admitted that their main interest in the Stream was a massive captive audience for flooding with advertisements.

Many writers and artists did predict the sharp division that would form in society between the Streamers and the group of abstainers who would come to be known as non-swimmers. For when everything could be communicated with the mind, when the need for devices was eliminated entirely, when no one had a telephone, how could they possibly keep in touch with the fossils who stayed behind? But nobody listens to artists. Paint cannot stop progress, only color it.

"You see, the Stream is not everything it was supposed to be," Killian lied. "It fluctuates. Sometimes more wildly than others. No one has ever really been able to explain why. At it's weakest it's startlingly silent. The voices whisper, the pictures fade. At it's strongest, it's overwhelming. The sheer volume, not to mention the influx of incalculable sounds and visuals forces one to freeze up.

"Of course, Wellspring continues to put out better filtering programs. Good filters are the key to Streaming. Without them, everyone would be venting their foreheads with screwdrivers."

[Careful Killian.]

Killian squirmed. He didn't like having someone else in the room with a client. He had to think about everything he said before he said it. And he had to be careful not to transmit his every thought for Paul to hear.

Killian quoted from the Wellspring manual. "Your filter program is a virtual interface with the Stream. It can take on many forms, but for most people it looks like an organized page in their mind. A home page. Streamers evolved from Internet users after all. Your filter decides what news feeds you pick up. It organizes your music and movies and friends. It recommends information and entertainment based on previous preferences. Many people give it a friendly voice. Some give it a virtual body.'"

Killian had spent hours listening to clients who were fighting with their filters. It was a lot like marriage counseling. "She doesn't listen to me, Doctor Peterson. She just decides what's best for me, without even asking. Can't you reprogram her just a little?"

Paul watched skeptically as Killian's eyes drifted off. He cleared his throat. Killian refocused on Lightning. "This is the brilliance of Wellspring's S.O.S. program, of course."

[Yes, *brilliance*,] Paul thought.

"Having a personal psychiatrist to fine-tune your filter helps minimize possible interruptions to smooth..."

[And if Wellspring owns the filters and the shrinks who adjust them, it maintains control over everyone in the Stream,] Paul's thoughts interrupted.

Killian paused, unable to remember what he was saying. Paul, sitting next to Lightning on her side of the desk, turned and looked straight into her eyes.

"Kathryn, let me try to help explain," he said, taking hold of her floppy paw. "When it first came online, the choppiness of the Stream upset a lot of people. You could be right in the middle of an important business meeting and half of your audience would disappear. Or you might be chatting with a friend and suddenly get bombarded by hundreds of other people's communications."

[Or crash your car into a tree!] Killian thought. [But we don't want to scare her with reality.]

Paul continued without acknowledging Killian. "The improved filters and the psychiatrists helped decrease these problems, sure. And life was fine again for most people. But not for one man. No, for one man among us it was not okay to live in a world of chaos when peace was possible. One man fought for, still fights for, the dream of an ideal society."

[Is he faster than a speeding bullet?] Killian chided.

"His name is Jadon. Jadon insists that the Stream can be everything it claims. It doesn't have to remain a disappointment. Instead of a bookstore in the wake of an earthquake, the Stream can be organized into the greatest library of knowledge in human history."

Killian blew air through his lips.

"Excuse me, Dr. Peterson, but don't you frequently use Jadonist breathing techniques to calm and focus your mind?"

[Bastard.] "I wouldn't say frequently."

Lightning waggled from one man to the other and back again.

"But you do admit that you employ the benefits of Jadon's techniques?"

Killian blew air again. "Yes. Now let's get back to…"

"I want to hear more about this Jadon," Lightning whimpered.

Paul geared up for his sales pitch. Killian tuned out and drifted through news portals, half listening to updates on crime and celebrities and sports. He had heard this spiel of Paul's so many times he could recite it, even if the Stream didn't allow him to rewind any one of the times he'd heard it and play it back verbatim.

"We can help the Stream evolve a consciousness, a voice," Paul was spouting when Killian returned. "An all knowing voice that can steer us toward our greater destiny."

[We can make God!] Killian thought in the mocking tone of an excited child.

Paul didn't take his eyes off Lightning.

"There aren't many Streamquakes now because most Streamers are Jadonists. As Jadonists, they practice their breathing techniques and meditation regularly. They help calm the Stream by calming their own minds."

"Yes, well…" Killian blurted, rising from his chair, "Wellspring has significantly improved its software. And the devotion of the psychiatrists, who individually tailor filter tuning to each client, has made the biggest difference in the overall calming of the Stream."

Paul leaned further in to capture her slowly wandering gaze. "Well, Miss Kathryn. Let me ask you this: would you rather visit occasionally with a spiritual advisor to discuss the future of humanity's faith, or with a head shrinker because you can't maintain control of your thoughts on your own?"

[So believing an agreed upon set of delusions makes one sane?] Killian thought.

Paul rolled his eyes toward Killian. [According to you, having faith makes you insane. Evan Hyatt didn't have faith. Is suicide the act of a sane mind?]

"Oh, please!" Killian stomped around his desk and took Lightning's other hand. He took it a bit roughly. She jumped. It took half a minute for her upper arms to stop rippling. "Once all the kinks are worked out in the

Stream's programming, people won't need shrinks. And they sure as hell won't need ridiculous religious rituals. For Jadon's sake, we've been trying to escape them for centuries! Why should society go backward?"

Lightning pulled her paw from Killian's grip and leaned her head as far back from him as she could.

[You're scaring her! Idiot.]

Killian growled and returned to his seat. He turned away from the two of them and tried not to listen to Paul describe the new Faith Filter.

"Wellspring and the Jadonist clergy have invested a lot of time working together on it. It will prevent any nasty thoughts from getting in. It will help determine a righteous and healthy mind."

[It'll censor the shit out of you!]

Unable to feign interest in this woman long enough to compete, Killian let Paul take over the rest of the session. By the time Lightning's hour was up, he'd cooled down a bit and offered her a very polite farewell. She was scheduled to be hooked her up to the Stream at the end of next week. She asked that Paul join them for all future sessions. Killian could not refuse. By law. He looked away as she hoisted herself out of the chair and wobbled out through the door.

"Killian," Paul said when her panting faded completely out of hearing range. "Your behavior in front of a client was noticeably odd. The way you were always staring off, like you were listening to someone else. It's rude. And a little creepy. Next thing you know you'll be talking to no one."

Killian's eyes clenched against the phantom screwdriver.

"I'm going to have to report your behavior to Dr. Progner," Paul said.

"You're not my superior," Killian snapped. His fists

clenched. "I'm sure he'll be plenty interested in what you had to say. I'm on my way to meet with him now."

[You mean.... Perhaps he didn't tell you. Curious.] "The meeting will include all three of us."

Smile, smile. Killian did not contain his wish to smash that wall of teeth.

"Look, Killian, you like this new Faith Bill as much as I do."

"Oh, really?" Killian drifted toward his door.

"Don't you want to know why?" Paul said.

"Okay. Why do *I* like the new Faith Bill as much as you?" He walked to the elevator and commanded its presence.

"Because you know damn well that noobs need a priest. You've seen what happens when they charge in unfiltered. They become mumbling idiots in weeks. Or worse.... You know they need Jadonism, but you don't want to admit it, because of your whole anti-establishment obsession. The Stream is a big world. You could get lost in it. But as long as you're against the system, you maintain some individualism, some sense of identity among the rest of the school of fish. So, this way, with it being a law that you set noobs up with a priest, you can make sure they get what they need and still have the satisfaction of complaining about it."

Paul stepped into the elevator. "Not coming?" He tilted his head.

"I'll take the stairs."

"You see, anti-establishment. You know, there's one other reason you like the bill."

"Enlighten me *father*," Killian said through the narrowing slit between the doors.

[You get to see me regularly. You need that. Who else would set you straight?]

He was gone. Hot anger erupted within Killian. He

swallowed, holding it down until the violent acid soup percolated an idea. Yes! An idea struck him. A flash of inspiration. A solution to all his problems. He bolted toward the stairwell and burst through the door.

VOICE

"Human memory is not very reliable at all," Progner was saying as Killian approached his open office door. "Say you remember playing catch with your Dad one time. You remember this particular time because Dad was about to leave for a trip, but he had promised to play catch and you started to cry and so Dad called and moved his flight and played catch with you until your arm hurt. You can see it, right? The sun in your eyes and everything? But the truth is, most of that memory probably didn't happen."

Paul sat on the arm of one of the chairs, his back to the door. Progner sat on the edge of his desk, his eyes locked on Paul. Neither man acknowledged Killian's presence.

"It was a sunny day right?" Progner went on. "The sun set golden orange behind you as you caught and returned Dad's tosses? Mom sat smiling on the porch sipping iced tea. You felt warm inside. You felt loved. Maybe.

"Or it was drizzling rain and you and Dad had an argument. He screamed, you cried, until, pissed off, he whipped line drives at you until your palm ached and you ran in the house to wail away the afternoon into your pillow.

"Which is the truth? Hard to say. The memory is colored by time. It is viewed now by an adult, as old as the father in the scene. It is viewed now from a perspective of experience the child couldn't imagine. It is viewed now through a lens of complex emotions the child was only beginning to glimpse.

"It is also viewed for a reason. Why did you remember this scene? Did you see a father and son playing ball, and wish for a similar memory? Did you see a father and son playing ball and need to remember your father wasn't like that?

"Did you ever hear a story about yourself as a kid, perhaps even as a baby, so many times that a visual memory forms? You remember it. But you *remember* it as a conscious being, not from the limited perspective of a baby or small child, so it can't be true.

"Maybe your father never did make that call. Maybe he never once played catch with you. Yet you can see it. You can feel the excitement well up as he hangs up the phone, or the pain in the heel of your palm. You can hear the ball move through the air. How can this not be real?"

"Memories are the lies people tell themselves so the present makes sense," Paul added. Killian could see that arrogant grin even through the back of his head.

"But Stream memories can't lie," Progner said. "Isn't that right Dr. Peterson?"

Paul turned his grin to Killian and said something welcoming.

"Stream memory is a recording," Killian said.

"That isn't to say the world of Streamers is some idealistic land of truth and reality," Progner said. "Quite the opposite. The Stream is made up of human minds, and therefore, it is full of lies. It is full of fiction. It is full of artificial realities and make believe personas. Filled, but growing. Bulging the sides of a container of eternal depth.

"But Stream memories are as accurate as the day they happened. The dream of a fair and speedy trial has come to fruition in Stream society. Once someone is accused, all the police have to do is recall the alleged criminal's memory of the time of the crime. Now, you not only have to hide the crime, you have to hide the memory of the crime.

"Still, even if no one suspects you, and therefore no one looks at your memories, they're still there, for you. This alone has begun to deter major criminal activity. Without the ability to work with your own memory over time, you have to face the exact scene of every evil deed for the rest of your life."

The image of the screwdriver stabbed at Killian. He resisted swatting it away.

"For example," Progner continued, "say you killed your wife and her lover Pre-Stream. Your guilt would go to work on that memory immediately – softening her screams, lessening the look of terror on her face, heightening your feeling of justified anger. Over time, this would help you live with what you had done. The human mind is adaptable. It's programmed to survive. To live with great tragedy. But, robbed of this ability by accurate Stream memory, criminals are left with only one way to rid themselves of guilt: confession."

Killian shifted his weight on his feet. Paul was taking up both chairs, sitting on the arm like that. Progner stood suddenly and turned to the wall behind his desk, peering out at the gray sky beyond the rows of black skyscrapers.

"I'm not trying to justify inappropriate behavior, mind you, I am merely trying to explain to you why it is so disturbing for us. Once we experience a client's memory, it remains that way forever. Stream memory cannot be manipulated. The cold hard facts of the event are etched in stone. The psyche can't soften the scene of a suicide. It comes back to the mind as fresh as the first time. Every time."

Killian felt the screwdriver pierce his skull and slide into his brain.

Progner turned to face them. The transparent wall behind him faded to black, obscuring the outside world beyond. It could display any scene Progner chose. The windowscreen was antiquated just months after it hit the market. After all, in Stream, Killian could close his eyes and become completely immersed in any scene he chose. He didn't need to stare at a wall. For that matter, he could have closed his eyes and tapped into the security cameras on the exterior of the building if he wanted to see outside. That was the excuse they gave him for not having put a window in his office anyway. Progner liked to show off his windowscreen to noobs though. He probably dazzled Mustachio with it.

"So, we're agreed then," Progner said.

"I believe so." Paul met his glare.

Killian had lost the thread of the conversation.

"Killian," Progner said, extending his hand toward the seat next to Paul, "please, sit. We've been discussing your day of course, and I've been trying to explain to Paul just how difficult experiencing other people's suicides can be. Still, we've decided that you probably need a little time off."

Paul moved from the arm of the chair to the seat, leaving room for Killian to sit. Killian unfolded his arms but stood his ground. The last thing he wanted was time off. Sure he hated his job, but what the hell would he do with himself for an extra eight hours a day? He looked at Paul, who made a genuine effort to dampen his smile.

"They all talked to God!" Killian blurted.

Paul's face froze. For the first time since Killian had entered the room, Progner locked his eyes on him.

Killian hesitated, his mouth half open. He closed his eyes and forced the words out. "Hector, Elena and Evan. They were each talking to someone, starting about two weeks before they did themselves in. They spoke aloud. They reacted as if they heard replies. But there was no one there in the Stream."

"This is preposterous," Paul said.

"Schizophrenia," Progner whispered, dismissing the entire idea with a brush of his hand. "Let's not assume that just because they're in Stream, they can't contract good old-fashioned psychoses."

"But three of my clients? All so close together? The odds are astounding. Besides, wouldn't they hear the voices in their heads? And then I would be able to hear them when I rewound their memories. But there were no voices. Nothing originating from them, nothing from elsewhere in Stream. They were having conversations with nothing."

Paul uncrossed his legs, momentarily relaxing his plastic grin. "Aha," he said, crossing his legs the other way and retightening his mask, "so now you're going to believe in God, now that you can point an accusatory finger at Him."

"No," Killian said. "Shut up."

Progner lowered his eyebrows.

"Sorry," Killian fumbled. "Listen, though, I'm trying to explain. Evan did not believe in God. He didn't want a God. Not a creator of the universe and certainly not a man-made techno-god. He believed it would negate our motivations and strengths. It would ruin us as a species. But just before he stabbed himself for the last time, his final words were, "take that God!"

"And is this all you have to go on?" Progner asked.

"Sounds like a desperate attempt to save face," Paul added.

"It makes perfect sense," Killian went on. "God is great as an obscure, unreachable, future figure in people's lives. It helps them behave, allows them to have goals. And that's why people are so taken with Jadonism. But do people really want to ever reach the goal of creating God? Think about it. Many religions describe how you couldn't survive the presence of God. That hearing His true voice would drive you mad. Maybe that's what happened?"

"So you believe the Stream has actually developed a consciousness of its own?"

"Possibly. It could very well be more of a glitch than a God really. A program that believes it's supposed to help guide us. Wouldn't it start with those who needed the most help? Those who don't believe?"

Killian had been pacing the room wildly. He stopped. Paul and Progner were looking at each other and squinting in that way that signified they were communicating through the Stream. Privately. Killian steeled himself.

"Dr. Peterson..." Progner said. "Killian. We appreciate your enthusiasm and your devotion to helping your clients, even beyond their deaths. However, we feel this has been too much stress on you. You're not yourself, and now you're stabbing in the dark for a scapegoat. It is not a healthy time for you to be seeing clients. I want you to take a few days off and recuperate."

"While the priests slip in here and begin sinking their teeth into our clients?"

"Dr. Peterson I'll have to ask you not to sling about inappropriate accusations," Progner said. "Today is Wednesday. I will contact you on Sunday and hopefully you will be back in your office, with a refreshed attitude, by Monday. Now please, there is nothing else you can say.

You need to take care of yourself and trust that the rest of us can take care of this transition period. I only hope you will come to understand we have your best interest in mind."

Killian opened his mouth then closed it. His head dropped. He wanted to say something, anything not to have to turn around and drag himself out so defeated before their judging eyes. He opened his mouth again, but no voice would come.

SCREAM

When he closed his eyes he heard screaming.

Sometimes it was Elena Gratz's closing remark. It started when she shut her eyes, and pulled back the kitchen knife. It was a nervous, terrified shriek, which anticipated incredible pain. It continued, unwavering, for a few seconds, helping to build her nerve. It rose an octave in response to actual pain, then ceased almost immediately.

He felt the scream burst from his lungs, burning up his windpipe as it erupted not only from his throat, but through his ears and nose and eyes.

It was the scream of absolute terror. One should not experience such a scream for more than the few seconds Elena did. Her last few seconds. But Killian would live with it forever. It was sewn into his spine.

Other times, when he closed his eyes, it was Hector Horowitz yelling at the power-drill he had plugged into his bedroom outlet. He told it to "come on", and to "bring it." He pulled the trigger and the drill screamed it's high pitched whine, but Hector yelled louder, a deep warrior's scream, from the scratchy depths of his voice box.

Hector's throaty howling compressed Killian's chest

until he gasped for his life.

Evan never screamed out loud. Not with his mouth. Not with his throat, nor his lungs, which were limited in their capacity to produce actual noise. But his mind screamed out with each of the three stabs from the screwdriver. Screamed with an intensity his dying body couldn't possibly match. It screamed with pain. Yet, simultaneously, it screamed with satisfaction. It wailed both in shock and relief. This scream, hailing from the intimate mind of a friend, took Killian the longest to recover from.

It was Evan's scream that kept Killian from falling asleep.

But it was not Evan's scream that woke him.

It was dark and he was sitting in a padded seat of some kind. These facts floated in the hazy peripheral of his consciousness. The screaming, which came from his own throat, occupied his entire being. His lungs provided it with life. His throat tightened to channel its energy. Every muscle of his face strained to widen his mouth and allow its escape. The rest of his muscles, right down to his feet, tensed up to help absorb the impact. His mind could not wander from the shriek. But it was not a scream of physical pain. It was not the scream of the anticipation of death. It was not the paradoxical satisfaction of Evan's final scream. This was a new scream.

It was a yelping of confusion and loss and complete helplessness. It was the wail of an infant slapped into awareness by the cold rubber glove of a delivery room nurse.

His lungs emptied of all air and the scream faded to nothing. He gasped for breath. There was panting beside him. Another person breathing. Gasping as he gasped. He opened his eyes and saw a steering wheel. He saw a shattered windshield. Through it he saw a large tree trunk which had inserted itself into the center of the car's hood. He turned to his right, spying the legs of the passenger.

The scream began again. He screamed again. But *he* hadn't started it. He had screamed in response. He screamed to keep out the screaming. From the center of his being he spewed as much noise as he could, emptying all that he was. But it was not enough. It was still there. Someone else's scream. But whose?

He opened his eyes and both screams stopped. He was sitting up in his bed in the darkness. There was no one beside him.

CATALYST

Turning on every light in his kitchen, Killian poured some orange juice and tried to puzzle out what had happened. "Okay, so Dona shows up," he said to his juice glass, "and tells me about her dream." He grabbed a bowl from the counter. "Her dream is about the two of us sitting in a car together, screaming, right?" The bowl did not answer. He poured in some cereal and tried to involve the jug of milk in his musings. "Then I come home and have a similar dream. Can't be coincidence, can it?" The milk jug snubbed him too, so he knocked it's top off and tipped it over his bowl.

Returning the jug to the refrigerator, Killian grabbed a spoon from the drawer. "Obviously my subconscious grabbed the idea she planted there and ran with it. No biggie." The spoon was ambivalent. "But why did I remember it? I haven't remembered a dream in nearly ten years. So why now?"

Killian shrugged, scooped some cereal on his spoon and lifted it to his mouth. He paused midway. Dropping the spoon, he rushed around the couch and stared down at a dark green sketchbook that was lying on his coffee table.

"How the hell did that get there?"

He quickly checked the Stream, but there was no trace of an intruder having entered his apartment.

It was definitely the sketchbook he had in high school. He recognized that stain on the lower left of the cover. The small blob of slightly darker green. But it couldn't be his old sketchbook, could it? He opened the cover cautiously and was drawn into memory...

"Mr. Progner? I'm the, uh..." Killian stumbled, having remembered he'd decided fifteen was too old to be a paper*boy*. "I deliver your papers."

"Good timing kid," Progner said, moving to the sink and filling a glass with water. Killian could see through the kitchen now into what resembled a slightly handgrenaded living room.

"Should I come back?" He didn't want to come back. He wanted what this guy owed him.

"No, what is it?"

"Well, I realize you usually pay by mail. But you see, well most people don't. They pay me. That is, I usually come around collecting, Monday nights. Mostly. But, well, the newspaper called me and told me you haven't paid for a while. They wanted me to, you know...."

"How much?" He reached in his back pocket for his wallet, but it wasn't there. The wallet, the pocket. He was wearing plaid pajama pants.

"Three months."

"Really? Three months. That's what, like ninety newspapers? I could guarantee you kid, I haven't read a single paper in the last three months. Not a headline."

"Well. You should have canceled it then."

"You're right," Progner said, "I should have canceled it." He turned to look out the window at the row of houses across the street, his water glass held at an awkward level of indecision.

After a minute Killian cleared his throat. "You are still going to pay for them though, right?"

"Hmm? Oh yes. That's not what I meant. Come on in, I'll get my wallet."

Progner tiptoed through the wreckage in the living room. Two bookshelves, a computer desk and an entertainment center had all been overturned. They had each vomited their contents into a pile in the middle of the rug. Progner began moving some of the bigger items off the pile. "How'd you know I was home?"

"I saw you ripping down the curtains."

"Right. Sorry about the mess."

"No problem," Killian said, setting his sights on his sneakers.

"Come in, come in and sit. I might be a minute. I think my wallet was in the computer desk, but the drawers seemed to have fallen out and…."

Killian allowed the uncluttered corner of the black leather couch to suck him in. Progner bent down to rummage through the scattered papers and electronics. He moved from item to item in a squatted position, peeking under an overturned drawer, then a pile of papers.

Killian froze the scene in his mind. Progner was paused in the center of the mess, peering under an upside down keyboard. There was something important about seeing him there; squatting, head tilted sideways as he lifted and peered under that keyboard. Poised like an ape rummaging curiously through a heap of abandoned technology. Like he'd been reduced. A man in possession of everything modern, reduced to foraging through wreckage. There was great symbolism here. He couldn't quite wrap his head around it, but he could feel the power of it.

Killian sensed that he could save this scene and

examine it later. He closed his eyes and could still see every minute detail of the room. Not only could he see it, but he could rotate the entire scene and view it from different angles. Tip the lights and shadows across the multitude of three dimensional surfaces. He could see each line, each degree of shading he would use to reproduce this image on paper.

He opened his eyes.

Progner had moved near the window and was checking behind the pile of curtains.

"So you cheat on your wife?"

"What?" Progner said, looking up. "What kind of a question is that?"

"I'm sorry, I just thought with the mess and all." Killian put his feet on the coffee table, just to see if he'd be asked not to. It went unnoticed.

"Well it's kind of forward don't you think? No, I'm not married."

"Mid-life crisis?"

"I'm only twenty-nine."

"Lose your job?"

"No. Sort of. You just jump right in there don't you? Here it is." Progner pulled out his wallet and held it up.

"So you quit?"

"Not exactly."

"I don't understand."

Progner was standing now, surveying the various piles of drawer contents on the carpet. He took off his glasses and cleaned them on his shirt. His glasses defined him. He was, you know, that guy with the glasses. And without them he was nothing.

"Well, let's say I won't be going to work for quite a while. I kind of erased myself from existence. How much is it anyway?"

"What do you mean, you erased yourself?"

Progner explained to Killian how his job involved compiling television listings and selling them to newspapers and web sites and cable stations. He wrote a program that would take all of the incoming data and redistribute it for him. He replaced himself with software.

"Not too smart," Killian said.

"Well, I was paid for the program. A year's salary. But no, not too smart. I hated that job anyway. God, I'm glad to be out of that office."

"So why'd you trash *your* place?"

"Well, I'm tired of screens. For the past seven years my existence has served a single purpose: provide accurate television schedules. Can you imagine anything more menial?"

Killian could not. He didn't understand what menial meant. But he didn't interrupt.

"Then after work I'd come home, surf the net, watch TV, and wonder why I had trouble sleeping. I'd been asleep all day. I want to feel alive! So, I've paid all my bills in advance, canceled my cable and Internet services, pulled out my phone. TV, DVD, CPU, MP3 – I want nothing abbreviated to remain." He squinted further out the window, trying to bring something vague into focus.

"Disconnected. Reconnected to the breath of reality. You know what that office smells like? Electronic dust. It makes the lungs itch to breathe, infects the bloodstream with static." Progner sighed. "It breeds dreams of imprisonment."

Killian slid off the couch and moved toward the front door. "Well, thanks," he said. Progner continued staring out the window.

Killian leapt out the door and ran down the driveway toward the next house on his route. He had to get home. Something was very right here and he needed to work it out. What was so appealing about this man and his act of rebellion?

He burst into his bedroom and began sketching. He spent hours filling in details from Progner's living room, taking a break the third time Mom called him to dinner, then returning to draw late into the night.

When he woke the next morning he stared at his creation. The skill of the drawing surprised him. He'd never before rendered something so lifelike. But it was more than the technical skill that astonished him. The scene itself had meaning. It was as if he had captured a man, an entire man and all that he was, in this one scene. Man as idea. Man destroying his own creation, then, reluctantly sifting through the remains out of necessity. Rebellion followed by reconstruction. It was the beginning of... something.

Killian closed the sketchbook and fell back into his couch. Memory. Real memory. He felt the excitement of youth and the thrill of the creative process, as if he were there again. But how was this possible? Recent attempts to remember how he knew Progner before the Stream had produced only frustration.

Maybe he just needed a catalyst. That drawing. Had he really forgotten his sketchbook, his boyhood dreams of wanting to be an artist? How could he have?

"Thank you," he said aloud. But whom was he thanking?

He checked the security features attached to his apartment door again. He even checked the windows. No one else had entered today, yesterday. In fact, it had been a long time since anyone else had entered his apartment. So how could this physical object have gotten here?

He picked up the sketchbook again and rubbed the outside, feeling the hard green cover. It was worn fuzzy and smooth to the touch. It was real. Right?

He saw a screwdriver floating, poised to stab his forehead. That was not real. But he could touch it. He could feel it in his hand. It stabbed and he could feel that too. But that was not real. Right?

And Ophelia's smirk? He could see that, by rewinding the Stream if necessary. He could see it and it inspired real emotion. But was that real?

Was he no longer able to determine? He felt the hard cover of the book again. Logically it couldn't be here, yet he could feel it. *Was* it real?

Did it matter? He had been forced to take several days off of work and needed something to occupy his mind. Unlike many Streamers, Killian's job demanded eight to ten hours a day of face to face time with real live people. Despite the weight of this burden, it grounded him in a way he was afraid to drift too far from. He'd seen, heard, felt through the minds of others what groundless Stream drifting could do. He looked to his clock and calculated the hours remaining until Monday and moaned aloud. He wouldn't make it. Not without distraction.

So, he could spend the next several days ducking phantom, forehead-seeking objects and the responsibility of recuperating, while drifting further and further from anything that still made sense in his world, or he could open this book and recapture a time in his life when hope still existed.

Killian opened the sketchbook.

PROJECT

Killian stared into the etched likeness of a younger Progner. Progner exposed. Progner unraveled. One day he was simply 1575 Oakenfield Lane, paid by mail, lived alone, and the next day he was a man in search of his soul. Killian remembered wondering if all of the addresses on his route hid real people? How many had he drawn?

He turned to the second sketch. Yasanori Haroki. So life-like; the wine glass in his hand seemed to jut out of the page. Time hadn't faded the drawing. It was crisp and clear and made Killian doubt he was once capable of such skill. But there it was.

It was a Monday evening, his usual collection night, but Killian seemed to have caught Mr. Haroki off guard. He sputtered a nervous invitation to come in while he looked for change. Yasanori Haroki. He said his friends called him Harry. He seemed desperate to convince Killian of this.

"Just minute. I get cash," he said, disappearing down the hall. The living room was simple: a modest TV, minimal furniture. It occurred to Killian that perhaps people weren't all interesting. He stepped further into the house. The dining room was in complete contrast to the living room. The antique hand-carved dining table sat in front of a brick fireplace with a carved wooden mantel. Over the fireplace was an expansive, silver-framed mirror. No photos, just the mirror. The table was set with what was probably formal china. Set for two with china and an open bottle of wine tilted in an ice bucket. Killian had never seen anyone but Mr. Haroki come or go. Perhaps he was expecting a big date. It would explain his nervousness.

"Ah, here we go. Four dollars, twenty-five. Yes?"

Killian nodded. He took note of the starched pinstriped shirt Mr. Haroki wore; his carefully gelled hair.

"Thanks Mr. Haroki, see ya next week."

"Yes, ah, nex' week."

Killian glanced back at the house as he made his way down, and then back up the street. He checked again when he emerged from each of the three perpendicular roads that made up his route. No other car ever arrived. At home he snatched up his sketchbook and got to work. He had to transpose his memory of Mr. Haroki over his memory of the dining room, but the result was a unified portrait. He was able to remember Mr. Haroki in detail. In fact, even his reflection looked real in the drawing of the mirror over the mantel. Killian drew him raising a wine glass to toast someone off the edge of the paper, but the mirror revealed that no one sat at the other end of the table. It worked. It captured the mood Killian felt there. Mr. Haroki toasting his own loneliness.

Killian compared this work to the sketch of Progner. Both figures were captured in time, alone, lonely, dealing with something important. Important, but not present. Again he felt that excitement build in his gut. He was on to something.

This was a mature art project. A character study, of

sorts. The faces behind closed doors and drawn blinds. A rendering of the brief glimpse he had into the homes that he collected his salary from.

Killian flipped the page again…

Mr. Halloway had his trophy case and that lumpy dog in front of it that never moved. A pure-bred mastiff. A trophy itself. His shelves were lined with ships; models in glass bottles. The room defined him. Mr. Halloway, Timothy P. Halloway, had to get up to answer the door, but Killian knew he probably rarely moved from the hardback leather chair. When he drew Mr. Halloway, Killian added a pipe in his mouth, as the stale scent of tobacco always greeted him at the door.

He flipped the page…

Mrs. Appleton had a life-size, framed photo of Marilyn Monroe in her hall. She had a genuine beauty mark above her lip, but the resemblance, which the photo forced one to consider, ended there.

Flipped page… Mr. Jordance had the biggest collection of movies Killian had ever seen. Three bookcases, filled with neatly stacked movie cases. And who would have guessed – flipped page… that grumpy Mr. Heindlich, curser of neighborhood dogs and their obsession with marking his azaleas, had four fish tanks in his living room. One on each wall.

The objects in their rooms defined them. This was after all, their den, their roost, the room they worked to pay for, to pass their lives away in.

Flipped page…

They were all there. An artist's first collection of his prospective talent. Seven portraits.

And the blank pages beyond.

The countless blank pages behind the first blank page.

The first blank page was hers. He remembered. He swore he wouldn't go past it until it was filled. But he never could capture her.

Killian closed the book and set it on his coffee table. He summoned the image of Ophelia smirking across the quiZblitZ table from him. He tried to see it as a drawing, to translate the scene into lines and shading. But he could not see her the way he needed to. He ran his tongue over the fur on his front teeth. He should brush them.

No. No distractions.

He needed to remember more. He needed to remember her.

The drawings brought back the memories of the others. Maybe it would be enough. He grabbed the book and flipped to the eighth page. He stared into the empty whiteness, zooming in on the divots and flecks that made up the surface of the paper. He went deeper, blurring the details out of focus.

He saw the faded black front door of a house…

As he ascended the front steps, the scent of burnt bacon caused him to pause with his finger just above the doorbell. Smoke trickled out the open window and across the porch.

Brakes squealed. Killian spun. A black hatchback jerked to a halt with one tire on the grass. The driver's door flew open and a lean young woman leapt out. She was dressed in black, her head covered with dark, loose curls to her shoulders. She lowered her sunglasses and squinted at the smoke.

This was Pre-Stream memory. True memory. It did not look like a security camera had captured it. The sky in the background was surreal; brilliant blue crackles in the charcoal gray clouds.

Her hair flowed with the sound of the gentle wind. Her features were unclear, but he could feel the certainty of her beauty. He lusted and feared this woman and his memory contained that, used his emotions to paint the scene. There was little factual about real memory, but so much more was true.

She approached him in slow motion, a hypnotic bass line subtly underscoring her every move. It was her. It was a younger version of the girl from quiZblitZ. It was a memory of the first time he saw Ophelia Redenbacher.

The young woman removed Killian and his confounded expression from her path with a single squint of her dark eyes. Then she burst through the front door of the house.

Killian had no idea who she was. Mrs. Redenbacher had moved in at the start of the school year. She had a quiet, nerdy daughter who was a year beneath Killian at school. But he'd never seen the goddess who had just flown past him.

Curses flew from the kitchen out through the open door. They were drowned momentarily by the hollow hissing of a fire extinguisher. The doorway coughed a mist of white. When it began to dissipate he could see the goddess running up the stairs.

"What the shit Mom!" she yelled.

"Hello dear, you're early," came Penelope Redenbacher's voice.

"It's a good damn thing too. You nearly burnt the whole fucking place down!"

"Did I?"

"I'm tired of watching you; you with no job, with no life, I'm tired of watching you destroy yourself. Look at me! Do you know what it's like working full time while finishing high school? But I won't live off that pig's money. If it doesn't bother your conscience, so be it. All I ask, *all* I ask is that you don't get lost in that infernal contraption. That you don't let that brain-sucking box completely absorb your soul. Meanwhile you're so enrapt in... what is this a fucking soap opera? You nearly cost us our home, and you can't even look up at me!"

"I'm sorry dear. I got involved in this movie. I was going to go down and turn off the stove next commercial."

"That's it!" Her feet pounded down the stairs. Killian moved to the side of the doorway to avoid her rage. He could hear her pound down the basement stairs, then back up. She reappeared wielding a sledgehammer and shot back up to her mother's room.

Mrs. Redenbacher's pleas could barely be heard over the smashing of glass and plastic. Worried about the friendly lady who force-fed him her homemade cookies, Killian rang the doorbell.

"You're fucking kidding me right?" Ophelia yelled, then stomped down the stairs, still wielding her sledgehammer. "And what do you want Little Man?" Her dark eyes pierced him, froze him in place and prevented him from following his instinct to run.

"Is Mrs. Redenbacher home?" he stuttered.

"There is no Mrs. Redenbacher."

He muttered something unintelligible.

"I am *Miss* Redenbacher, my mother is *Ms.* Redenbacher. There are no married women in this household, Little Man."

Killian didn't know why she kept calling him that. "Well, your mother said she was..." Her scowl froze his words. "She usually pays me," he spit out.

"Who are you?"

"The paperboy." Damn. He said *boy*.

"I see. The local peddler of male-biased, corporate

propaganda huh? Starting in early huh? Tell me, do they allow little girls to deliver papers, or are we only permitted to baby-sit?" Killian thought it wise not to answer. "How much do you want from me then?"

"Is something burning?" he sniffed.

"Not anymore."

"There's smoke in your upstairs window," Killian said, pointing.

"Shit," the girl disappeared around the corner, returned with a small fire extinguisher and flew up the stairs.

Muttering and dabbing at her eyes with a tissue, Penelope Redenbacher trudged down the stairs a few minutes later.

"Hello Killian. Here's five. You keep the change, okay?"

"Thanks. Is everything alright?"

"Yes, yes. Don't mind Ophelia's rudeness. She's crazy I tell you. But she's a hard worker and has a lot on her mind." Penelope blew her nose into a tissue, sounding an unnatural foghorn. The sound was accompanied mid-blow by a thunderous crash on the sidewalk to the right. Killian jumped.

Before he could turn his head Penelope had rushed passed him out the door and into the yard.

Scattered on the lawn were the remains of a smashed and burned television. "You crazy girl, I'll never get it fixed now!" she yelled, shaking her fist up at the window. "You're evil, you know that." Her voice faded into a disturbed mumble. "Crazy, stupid, jerk. How am I going to watch…"

He heard Ophelia coming down the stairs and spun to face her.

"You still here Little Man. How much do you want?"

"Four twenty-five," he sputtered, unable to explain he'd been paid already, as that didn't directly answer her question.

Penelope was wailing in the lawn, going on about the injustice of the world, the terrible fate she endured.

"Here's five."

Killian fished in his pockets for change.

"Keep it. I waitress. I know what tips mean."

He ran home, once more filled with inspiration. He must capture this crazy girl who filled him with indescribable energy. Draw her into his artistic endeavor. He rushed to his room and cleared his desk. Opening to the eighth page of his sketchbook he stared into it. But he was unable to project her likeness onto it. He closed his eyes, but he could not see her in his mind. He couldn't freeze the scene as he had with Progner, or any of the others. He refused to degrade her with anything less than a perfect rendering, and so his pencil remained poised above the page indefinitely.

Each day that week, when Killian turned onto her street, his heart sped up. But her car was never there. He tried desperately to picture her again every time he stood at the end of her driveway. He tried again and again in his room, pencil in hand. Tried to unleash her. But nothing would materialize. He could feel the power she projected, but he could not reproduce it.

NOW

Poor Killian Peterson. Being a full time Stream psychologist really taxed all of his energy. He told himself that was okay though. At least he was helping people. And at least he spent a good deal of time talking to live human beings, face-to-face. This grounded him. So, overall, it was an okay life, even if he complained a lot.

But it was an exhausting life. And that was just the job. Add in the stress of having to kill himself, over and over again, and it was easy to see why he had begun to snap. The human mind should not have to endure suicide more than once. Killian had been experiencing death by three different hands, each his own, several times an hour, for more days than he could remember. On top of that, he'd maintained what he felt was a healthy mistrust of his boss, a stubborn commitment to resisting the inevitable rise of Jadonism, and an obsession with finding the ghost of a girl he once knew. It was really a wonder he'd maintained a shred of sanity.

With his grip on reality so in danger, his mind so overtaxed, wondering who had designated themselves the patron fairy of returning childhood dreams was not really a question at the forefront of Killian's consciousness. He spent none of his mental resources wondering who could have found his childhood sketchbook and planted it in his apartment. Nor even considering why anyone would do such a thing. He had much more immediate concerns.

Right now Killian was staring out a cracked windshield at the trunk of a large oak tree, which had rudely inserted itself into the car's hood. It seemed to have barged it's way right into the crumpled metal, hardly scratching its own bark at all. Above, the canopy of leaves wavered, inspiring flecks of waning orange sunlight to dance across the scene. He figured he must be dreaming again. Dona's dream. He looked cautiously to his right. There she was. Her legs were there. Her baggy shirt. He was afraid to look further, where he might discover the mouth that had produced that horrifying scream. Killian squinted his right eye closed tight and allowed his left to creep incrementally up her blouse; up her pasty neck.

She was asleep. Was this her dream or his? Killian closed his eyes.

"So, Doc, what do you think?" she said.

He opened his eyes to see her sitting across his office from him. What happened to the tree? She didn't seem to notice the venue change. She was staring at the floor, that spot right in front of her right foot again, hunched a bit over her knees. Killian ran his palm slowly over the surface of his desk. She looked up nervously, for just an instant, then back to the floor. She began to rock a bit.

She had asked him a question. "Oh, um…" he muttered. He tried to rewind the Stream, to see what she was talking about, but didn't seem able. How did he get here? Had he been daydreaming all of it? Getting told to take time off, the arrival of the sketchbook, the memories. All dreams? Was he still sitting in that first meeting with Dona? No. Couldn't be. Then, was it Monday already? Was it that he couldn't remember the last few days? His entire extended weekend?

"It's just a theory of course, but one worth contemplating," she said. Yes, Stupid Theory Girl. He had named her that. He looked blankly at her. She looked up, then darted her eyes quickly back to the floor, like a scared chipmunk afraid it will get pounced upon if it's caught peeking.

"Alright," Dona spit, "I know I talk too fast and don't always explain everything well. Let me try one more time."

Killian found himself nodding his approval, though her eyes didn't look long enough to see a full nod. He focused on her cracked lips and tried to absorb the words coming at him.

"See, primates, you know monkeys and such, well, they pretty much rape each other. A male wants something; he takes it. And on all fours, it's just staring him in the face, isn't it? Women, on all fours are very vulnerable. But when women realized that by standing up they could protect their privates from backdoor sneak attacks, they fundamentally changed society. Erect, they appeared taller, superior to men. They forced men, instead of just taking what they wanted, to stand up, push out their chests, and prove themselves worthy of their goal. Women forced men to impress them. Men began building better homes, constructing works of art, fighting each other; competing in all ways for the women. They began civilization as we know it all to impress women who stood now and protected their own assets. So women are, essentially, responsible for modern society."

Killian forced a grin. Why couldn't he access anything? Was it a minor Streamquake? He closed his eyes and focused on the breath coming in through his nose and filling his lungs with life.

He opened one eye and saw nothing. Darkness. He

opened the other. He was sitting on a bed. It was not the bed in his apartment though. Where was he? He could see a small TV with a video game system beneath it. This *was* his room. Or rather, it used to be his room. When he was a kid. This was the room he had grown up in. How did he get here?

His cheeks were damp. He was crying. He was clutching a hard cover book to his chest and crying softly. His arms and his chest, his whole body was smaller. He was younger. He put down the book and wiped his eyes with his sleeve. One tear had dripped onto the cover of the book. The water pooled out onto the green cover, creating a darker green stain.

He closed his eyes and the screwdriver lunged.

But he opened his eyes and was in his apartment again, sitting now on the couch in the living room with the lights on and he realized he was losing control of his mind and he let out a scream of terror.

This new scream tore him asunder, shredding his consciousness, then absorbing the fragments. His breath failed and the scream died off. He instantly became aware of the other scream. The one beside him. It was dark now, but he could tell from the angle of the seat that they were in the car again. It was cold and it was dark, but none of that mattered as the scream beside him shattered all other sensations. It crushed his skull and he too needed to shriek to balance the pressure, to keep from caving in.

[Killian,] his message system was flashing. It was Dona's voice. [Killian, please, let me in.] She was at his door. He was in his apartment. The sketchbook was on his coffee table. Was this now? He widened his eyes, afraid to even blink.

He told the door to open. She was there, disheveled as usual. Her hair was a mess, her baggy sweater sagged unevenly to the left, exposing most of her shoulder. She rushed in and looked nervously back at the door until he closed it.

He asked what she was doing here, but she was pacing back and forth, biting at her lip and apparently working out a thought. Killian checked the time and date. It was now. Stay here, he told himself. No more memories, no more dreams. Focus.

"Doc, I need your help," she said. Abruptly she looked away, toward the ceiling near the apartment door. "No!" she yelled. "Stop it!"

"Dona?" Killian said, rising and putting a hand on her shoulder. She startled and backed away, her arms coming up defensively.

"We don't have much time. You have to help me. You have to get me out of the Stream."

"Dona, what is it? Sit down, let me take a look at your filter."

"No!" she took a few more steps back. "No, it could be like an infection. It'll spread." She looked again at the ceiling, surveying it's length, then peered quickly behind the door to the front closet. Her eyes found Killian as if under water. "It's him. You have to help me."

"It's who?" Killian asked.

But she was down the hall toward his bedroom, looking at the ceiling and shaking her head voraciously from side to side and yelling, "Get out, get out, GET OUT!"

He ran to her. "Dona, Dona what is it?"

"It's him! He's talking. In my head. Can't drive him out."

"It's who?"

"You stay out of it!" she yelled at the ceiling. "No more! Shut UP!" She rushed back to the living room then spun and slammed her spine to the wall. She slid slowly to a crouched position, her eyes rapidly scanning the room.

"Dona, you're going to have to let me into your filter. I can't disconnect you from the Stream."

"Yes you can."

"Dona, it's not as simple as removing a chip. There's no chip."

"We have to leave the city!" She stood and grabbed his shirt violently. "You have to get me out of the city, away from the source of transmission. Now!" She turned away, raised a fist toward the empty air. "Try to stop me and I'll drill you out of my head, you hear?"

She began to scream and beat at her forehead with her fists. Killian tried to access her mind, but she wouldn't let him in. Her filter remained locked.

"Dona, we can't leave. You have to let me sedate you."

"Ophelia is outside. She can help us," Dona blurted, wincing and holding her temples. "She sent me to you." This last word dragged out into a series of escalating pitches that ended in a glass-shattering scream.

Pulling back his entire arm and shoulder, Killian swung his fist as hard as he could up and into Dona's jaw. Her head snapped to the right. Her body collapsed beneath her.

He couldn't believe it had worked! He'd knocked her out. Action movie hero style. The sleep boot kicked her out of the Stream temporarily. Perfect. She'd be safe from whatever she thought was after her. She'd be safe from her own mind.

Had she mentioned Ophelia? Progner had a car. An antique. He kept it at the office building. There was a garage on the ground floor. Killian closed his eyes to search a map of the city for the quickest exit route. He couldn't find it though. He couldn't feel the Stream. He found nothing but his own emptiness.

And when he opened his eyes he was seated beside Dona in the car. The trunk of a tree bursting up through the engine. Shadows of leaves on the shattered windshield. He couldn't feel the Stream. Where was he? When was he?

Dona opened her eyes. She winced, and snapped them shut. Slowly, cautiously, she peeked out from under her lids.

"Killian," she whispered weakly. "This is now."

NEARSIGHTED

Some humans love to overload their senses. For example, people will go to rock concerts, or dance clubs with music so loud it does irreparable damage to their ear drums. They go in the evening and stay until morning, maximizing the opportunity to harm themselves. Then they can't sleep because their heads still throb with the echoes of repeated baselines and their eyelids flash phantom rainbow strobe patterns. They smile in the face of this sensory overload and can't wait until they can do it again.

Killian Peterson and Dona Redenbacher had not spent all night at a dance club or a rock concert. Not exactly. But they had spent every moment of the last decade of their lives at the greatest light and sound show ever known on planet Earth. And now the reverberations of that twisted mind rape had been rocking their brains for days.

It was in fact now. It was now and it would be now and there would be no wavering from now. For Killian and Dona, who had for so long danced among their daydreams, now had become something their minds merely checked in with occasionally. And even when they focused on the present, the real world; even then, there were always background programs running. Music and newsfeed updates and mail messages and appointment reminders and recordings of Stream entertainment for later viewing. There was no dimmer switch on the Stream. It was on or it was off.

And it was off now. It was now, and it was off.

Ow, was it off.

As soon as they had driven the stolen car too far, just past where the Stream began to fade to a whisper, they blacked out. Unconscious, they drifted for nearly a mile down a straight section of pavement, then rolled down a grassy hill into a light forest, where they slammed into a large oak tree.

For two days and one night they sat in the car, unable to focus their minds. Adrift in awareness soup, chunky with memories and minuscule shreds of the meat of reality, their bodies quaked as they cried out for their absent addiction.

Withdrawal from psychological dependence can have nasty effects not only on the mind, but also the body. Killian didn't discover the latter problem until late in the second day, when he crawled out of the car. Stirred up by his own movement and a gentle breeze, the smell of human waste startled and then sickened him.

His mind raced, in search of distraction. This was how he dealt. With anything. Whether it was a little bit of heartburn or reliving the excruciating pain of three screwdriver stabs to his brain. All problems could be escaped. Go with the flow. Row, row. Row down the Stream. There's always somewhere else to be. Somewhere you won't have to scream.

The Stream contained all information. Fact and fiction. The Stream contained anything that anyone hooked up to it had ever thought about. That was a lot of thought. A Streamer never needed to produce his own thoughts at all, in fact, but could simply drift forever on the current of other people's minds, and never want for fresh entertainment.

Within such an environment, obsession became as easy as lying back on the couch. People could literally spend every free moment considering up-to-the-second statistics from their favorite gaming worlds or sports leagues. Or, if they were the Streamstalker types, they could easily become celebrities by tapping into one of the Hollywood reality feeds. Such feeds put them in the mind of a real (albeit usually a minor D list) celebrity. They could do lunch with the elite of the movie world, all through the eyes and thoughts of someone else. With the ability to be anyone, anywhere, there really wasn't any reason to sit in one's own living room, as one's own self, reading up on genuine news.

This became a problem. No one seemed to know what was actually going on any more. For example, Killian Peterson was completely unaware of the ocular correction programs that were introduced just months after the Stream came online. It turns out that by overlaying reality in the mind of the Streamer with an identical version that was focused to compensate for their optical deficiencies, said Streamer could move about in complete denial of ever having needed glasses. This would have been a great selling point, not that he needed one, when Mustachio asked Killian about the very problem of needing corrective lenses in Stream. But since Killian was not up to date on current ophthalmologic breakthroughs, he couldn't be blamed.

Killian, like most Streamers, was not up to date on anything. Too much changed too quickly. And infinite, it turned out, was simply too large a number of news sources to sift through. Even for Wellspring's most complex filtering programs. Most people had given up on staying updated at all. In fact, if most people didn't check in with a priest or a shrink a few times a week, they might have stopped admitting the actual world existed at all. Not that the priests, or especially the shrinks, were sure it existed any more either.

And so, faced with the real world, and the true distance between real solid objects, like, say, the trunk of an oak tree and the smashed windshield of an automobile, a mind used to having the Stream focus for it would be as blind as a flying mammal with it's echolocation system ripped violently from it's little brain.

Such was the case for Donatella Redenbacher. Having lived in Stream for ten years, she didn't even own a pair of glasses anymore. She sat, exhausted from screaming, in the passenger seat of a smashed up, and very blurry, steel blue hatchback. Darkness was giving way now to dim morning light, but, despite the unfortunate fact that she, like Killian, had for some time been sitting in it, she couldn't see shit.

Killian didn't need corrective lenses, but he couldn't fully open his eyes. The sun had risen now between the leaves of the trees. He squinted his eyes against this new brightness, trying to get a gage on his surroundings. He could see the car, just a few feet back. He hadn't managed to crawl too far. Dona was in there. He remembered her screaming. That's what he was attempting to distance himself from. Killian was already squinting against the bright sunlight, and scrunching his nose against the smell of his own filth, but he tried to tighten up even further in a futile attempt to close his ears against the possible return of that dreadful screaming. And yet, the more he tried to shut out the real world, the more he was aware of the total emptiness within. Black silence.

He crawled away on his elbows.

He could hear a soft rustling. Intermittently, it

interrupted the whisper of the wind that washed over him. There was no music. There were no voices. There was no sound that came from within him except the howling in his stomach.

This was now. This was real. Trees. Sky. Grass and mud, leaves and roots. He lay upon the literal roots of reality. This was not programming convincing his mind he was lying here. He exhausted his brain with queries. Am I hungry? When did I eat last? What time is it? What day is it? What messages, reminders, alerts, suggestions do you have for me? Why won't you answer?

"Killian?"

It was her voice. She screamed no more. He turned and saw the steel blue hatchback. It found its final resting place as a tree hugger. It had returned them to their roots.

The door of the car swung out a bit.

"Killian?"

"Here," he managed. They were outside of the Stream. Of that much he was sure. How, or why would have to come later. He was pretty sure this was the longest he'd been conscious in at least a day. The effort was sapping his strength.

Dona pushed the door out again and let herself flop out of the car. She lay on her back and breathed heavily, squinting up at the swaying leaves.

"Don't go," she moaned. "I can't see at all."

She held her hands up above her and squinted at them. They began to shake uncontrollably. She claimed they wouldn't stop. Her shoulders, then her legs, convulsed. Her whole body spasmed violently, then went limp.

"Dona?" No answer. He knew he should crawl back toward the car and check on her, but he couldn't command himself to move. He too would pass out soon. But he struggled against the overwhelming silence and emptiness, hoping to uncover a bit more.

It was dark when he opened his eyes. There were pinpricks of light between the sections of leaves above, but no moon. The smell of his emptied bowels overwhelmed him anew. He wanted to get out of his pants, but he didn't dare because he was already shivering. He crawled back to where Dona lay by the car. She was asleep. The howling from her stomach shook him and reminded him of his own. They had to find food. He believed it was the second night they'd been stranded and he was pretty sure they'd dehydrate by tomorrow. The thought elicited an impulse to lick his lips, but he resisted it. He didn't want to know how deep the cracks went.

Killian bent down and scooped Dona under her knees and the back of her neck. She was heavier than she looked. As soon as he raised her the smell of shit startled him and he nearly dropped her again. Holding his breath, he managed to hoist her into the driver's seat. She moaned once, rolled to her side and continued snoring.

He could not brave the emptiness of this new world. He closed his eyes and listened. There, far off, he heard a faint noise. All was not silent. Water, running over rocks. It was a stream. No, not the one his mind so badly sought. A real stream, in the real world. A real source of life. One that could save their lives. They needed water.

It was a very old car and he wondered if it; yes, it had a cigarette lighter! He turned the key on and pushed in the lighter. First he tried igniting a pile of leaves. Then some pine needles. It took over an hour, but eventually he got a make-shift torch burning by wrapping a sock around a stick. It probably helped that he had first shoved most of the sock into the gas tank. It definitely soaked up some fumes, if not any liquid gasoline.

Armed with a torch Killian set out for the sound of

the running water.

By the time Killian returned it was morning. Dona had thrown herself out of the car again and was lying face down in the mud. She had crawled a good twenty yards this time. Her skin was a pale blue and her breathing was so shallow that Killian panicked and shook her a few times until he got a gruff moan from her.

He held his breath and threw her over his shoulder, barely able to summon enough strength to walk. It was noon before he reached the stream. The fire he had built had gone out, but the coals still smoldered. Laying her beside them, he gathered leaves and twigs and got some thicker branches burning before he collapsed.

He woke to Dona screaming in her sleep again. Running a hand over her greasy mass of hair, he assured her it was okay. Killian had found some raspberries this morning and ate as many as he could, but Dona had been unconscious. She needed to eat. He needed to wake her. He needed to get her to drink. And he needed to clean her up too because her smell was nauseating and he couldn't stand to be near her for long. He could try washing her clothes in the stream like he did his own.

She rolled onto her back with a slight nudge. He pulled up her sweater a bit. Her belly was soft and round, curving dramatically into her navel. Killian began to unbutton her khaki pants and was instantly aroused. He fumbled to rebutton her and pulled her sweater back down. He was so used to the perfectly sculpted models of Streamporn that he didn't think Dona's frumpy body could… but then, it'd been a long time since he'd touched another's skin. A real person's actual skin. His hand begged to run along that gentle curve at the top of her hip, up to the more dramatic curves…

The stink of her stirred up again and he backed away. He'd gather more wood, that's what he'd do.

When Killian returned, and got the fire going strong again, he realized how hot her skin was. She probably had a fever. He decided to drag her the remaining few feet to the stream in her clothes. Scooping her under her moist armpits, he pulled her right into the gentle current. At the center it was nearly to his shoulders. He found a good footing here, held her out in front of him with the water up to her chin, and let it flow over them for nearly half an hour. Her forehead seemed cooler by then and by cupping his hand he was able to get her to drink at it a bit.

Under the waning hours of sunlight, Killian napped while Dona dried by the fire. He woke to see the fire diminishing. He knew he must keep it going, knew he must search for more berries before dark, but he was unable to will himself to rise. He was weak, and wondered if Dona's life wasn't depending on him, could he muster the amount of strength he already had? It was at the edge of his mind, and he'd been keeping it back, but the question was there all the time. Did he want to survive?

He was not sure he could live like this; in a quiet world where his head constantly craved more and every thought came at incredible pain. And yet, he couldn't yet consider ever again tackling the insanity of the Stream.

But he didn't have the strength to think of such farsighted problems. He had to focus on food and warmth and nursing Dona back from the brink of death before he could even consider finding a way out of this little valley.

UNREST

A breeze howled past Killian's ear, invading the silence of his slumber. Birds sang, then stopped. Different birds whistled. Further, then near. Their songs marked out infinite increments of distance. The wind tickled leaves, individually, here and there, then in congruity. There was, beyond all that, the sound of pinecones dropping and acorns and even single leaves, floating downward. The scurrying of rodents. The constant, yet inconsistent noise of life.

A woodpecker started up far away. Tap, tap, tapping. Never the same number of consecutive taps. Killian squinted through the trees, not one of which grew straight nor splayed out evenly spaced branches. Products of competing interest, they forked up in a constantly shifting world. Their shapes told the story of the forest that used to be.

Forest. The word called up associations with walls of trees. Identical specimens in perfect rows. Like the Christmas tree farms of his distant youth. But there was nothing uniform in the scene before him. He could have walked through the woods for the rest of his life and never seen the same pattern of landscape. Of life. The way those three trees had fallen over top of each other on the face of that hill, forming a sloppy letter H. The stream itself, one of millions on the planet, but identical to none. Nature demanded variety. And obtained it so fluidly.

But not the Stream. The Stream was created by humans. Every world, every environment, every scene in the Stream was created by humans. There were equations behind the cloned trees and repeated blades of grass and the production of *random* clouds. Despite the meticulousness of the artists, there was often a sense of virtual to the reality.

Not here though. Not this scene. Here Killian could smell the air each time he inhaled, and not just when there was something he was supposed to smell. Like a clue left by a game's creator, or an enticing reminder of popcorn, or apple pie, or whatever food conglomerate paid for sponsorship. Product scent placement was a wonderfully subliminal way to advertise in the Stream. But here there was no hidden motive to anything he sensed. It was merely there.

Killian wondered how far back it was to the car. Could he make it? Did he even have the strength to stand up? His eyes fell on Dona where she lay lifeless on the small patch of grass, next to the remnants of the fire. She was a part of the scene. Not a visitor to it, or the purpose for it. She was merely one element of this setting; of this slice of nature. She no more stood out than the giant bolder a few hundred meters downhill that divided the stream in two.

She was probably dying.

Not in the same way that Elena and Hector and Evan had died. He had saved her from insanity-induced suicide, only to deliver her to the merciless cruelty of nature.

Using his hands, he hoisted himself up to his knees.

His head throbbed, and this new reality with it. After a few moments spent breathing, Killian managed to stand.

The car was that way, away from the stream. Back toward the Stream. He needed to find the road. He could not keep them alive much longer. Dona had a fever and he had no strength and he'd eaten all the nearby berries and didn't know what other plants he could eat and didn't know how to hunt. The road was his only chance.

He wandered away from the sun for what seemed like an entire day, but it still wasn't quite overhead when he found the car. The car hadn't moved. Neither had the tree which stood so defiantly in the center of the automobile's engine compartment. He stumbled forward and pulled himself onto the hood, leaning against the cracked windshield. His eyes began to droop.

No!

He dropped to the ground and wobbled and fell against the twisted quarter panel. He hadn't slept right? No, he didn't think so. He just closed his eyes for a minute. But the sun, long past noon, was ahead of him now. Just over the hill. He must have slept for hours. The last few hours of his life. Gone now. Wasted.

Killian stood and forced his legs to move forward. The road was up that hill. Toward the light. He could see the path of the car's tires, the smashed wild grass and brush. He reached the hill and fell forward into it. He began to crawl.

Up the hill. Toward the road. He might die there. And Dona beside the stream where he left her. But it was his best chance. If a car went by. If cars still drove by here. He should not have left Dona, but he couldn't help her. He was halfway up the hill. Maybe he'd make it.

Looking up, he glimpsed a smooth and shiny surface that couldn't be the trunk of a tree. It rose out of what appeared to be a hiking boot. It was a woman's calf.

Fronted by the glare of a shin which shifted into a slightly cocked knee, then continued on toward just a hint of glorious thigh. This disappeared into cut-off khakis. Above her trim waist, her arms were folded, boosting her breasts, which so perfectly underlined her overlooking smirk and deeply suspicious eyes.

This was a dream, he decided. One last pleasant dream at the end of his life. A reward for polishing his teeth so damn much. He smiled with the last of his energy.

"Hello, Little Man," she said, reaching down and offering a hand to him. As she bent down, the sun rose over her left shoulder and filled Killian with brilliance.

His heart pounded as he squinted up through the slats between the planks of the deck. Her smooth legs rose up from her sneakers, disappearing into her shorts. He held his breath. She was pounding the top of the railing, and didn't seem interested in looking for him. She must not have seen him. Right?

He had dropped and rolled under the deck the second she burst through the sliding door. She'd walked right over and kicked the railing, exactly where his face had been just seconds before. But she hadn't seen him. She would have said something by now. The logic of this failed to calm him. As her friend followed her out onto the deck, he could barely hear Ophelia over the throbbing of his pulse in his ears. However her angry rant had started, it ended with "...prepubescent wannabe chickenshits!"

The black hatchback had been in the driveway when Killian approached the house earlier. It wasn't usually there on Mondays. There were two other cars there as well, but it was only the presence of Ophelia's car that had caused the acid eruption in his throat. He climbed the steps and rang the bell.

It was Ophelia's mother who answered, as usual. "Hello, Killian. Everything going well?"

"Sure Mrs. Redenbacher." The smell of warm cookies managed to seep around the width of her dark green robe, which she had tossed on her back without using the sleeves. It looked like a giant turtle shell. Killian sniffed and licked his lips.

"Oh, yes. Sweetie, I'm sorry. I'd love to set you up at the counter with a sample, but they're for Ophelia's little anti-society meeting. She'd have a fit if I let you in. Here, I'll bring you a couple."

Killian smiled politely and waited for her to return. Anti-society meeting? So that's why there were so many other cars. The urge to enter forced him to visualize knocking poor Mrs. Redenbacher on her back, where she would helplessly flail long enough for him to reach the kitchen. But when Mrs. Redenbacher returned with two chocolate chip cookies on a napkin and a giant grin, his sinister ideas melted.

Killian collected money from a few more houses then decided he had enough to cover his bill. He could collect his profits another night. His progress on sketching his neighbors had come to a halt the day he met Ophelia and he suspected he might need to work a little harder to get her portrait. After all, she wasn't a sit in her living room, answer the door kind of girl. He wouldn't be able to capture her in the same kind of pose as the others. No, capturing the essence of Ophelia would require a little daring.

Circling back past the Redenbacher's, he walked casually down the sidewalk, not looking at anything specific. As he reached the driveway of the Brumells' next door, he sprinted down the side of their house, stayed tight along the back, then dove behind the bushes beside the Redenbacher's deck.

They were in the kitchen. Killian could see through the open blinds to where the four young women sat. Ophelia appeared to be screaming at her mother, who was offering cookies to the other girls. Penelope waddled away and Ophelia sat back down.

Two of the girls stood up shortly after. One was dumpy, in her oversized sweatshirt and frown of malcontent. She stood with her arms limp at her side, clearly waiting for the other girl, who was a perky blonde with a look of snobbish disapproval about her. She sneered at Ophelia, wrinkling up her mouth as she spoke.

Ophelia stood and pointed to the front of the house. Although Killian couldn't make out the words, the volume of Ophelia's anger penetrated the closed windows. The two girls left, Ophelia whipping cookies at their backs. That was when she stormed outside and right for the railing Killian had been peering through and kicked it repeatedly.

But she was just expressing her anger. She hadn't seen him.

"Who's the You?" the remaining girl asked, after Ophelia's fit subsided.

"What? What the fuck?" Ophelia yelled. Killian, distracted by the realization that the shoulder of his T-shirt was soaking up the majority of a mud puddle, cringed at the volume of her shriek.

"People Against Technology Saving You? Saving who?" her friend said calmly.

"Everyone. The human race. What difference does it make?"

"It's just such a stupid name: P.A.T.S.Y. Doesn't sound very threatening."

"It doesn't matter. We don't need the goddamn name. They're just a stupid club. *Let's protest new technologies and stand up for human rights and blah, blah* - bullshit! I thought we might be able to get them to actually do something, but they're just stupid kids."

"Good. I don't feel like saving anyone. I want to blow something up."

"You serious."

"Half."

Killian missed a good portion of the conversation here. When he realized that Ophelia's friend was wearing a skirt, he told himself he needed to roll out of the puddle, and well, he happened to land right under where she was standing. Darting his head left and right to see between the slats, he was sure he saw a glimpse of panties for a moment. His forehead began sweating as he rolled his shoulders about, trying to get a better view. Then Ophelia dropped her glass. It shattered just above him. He bit his tongue to stop from crying out in surprise.

Hot blood trickled down his throat. He tried to swallow without lifting his head from the soft earth.

The knees below the skirt bent, then straightened when Ophelia told her just to leave it, her mother would sweep it up. They moved to the other side of the deck. It was too far for Killian to roll.

"So he works for your father's company?"

"One of its subsidiaries. Broadcast One. But he's computer savvy, and I'm sure there are links between the companies," Ophelia said.

"And you can get him to work with us?"

"I can get him to do whatever I want," Ophelia said. "The first time we met, we had a conversation about the evils of technology. I went on a rant about humanity weakening itself by relying on computers for everything. The next day he trashed his apartment. He unplugged all of his electronics and threw them around the room. He quit his job. Then, he kept doing stupid childish things to get my attention. So finally, I went over and talked to him and *convinced* him to secure himself a new position with Broadcast One. After all, he's useless to us if he doesn't work there."

Killian realized she was talking about Progner. He remembered that scene, the night that he drew Progner, after he had trashed his apartment. It had been the theme of his first drawing, the impetus for his artistic movement. And it had all been inspired by her!

"How old is he?"

"I don't know, like thirty."

"Gross, you slut."

"Anyway, I don't know the extent of his skill. I'm sure he can't write the virus or anything, but he can help deliver it. We don't have a lot of time. The test run of the Stream is scheduled for end of August. So, you in, or what?"

"Oh, I'm in. And I know a hell of a hacker who might help us. Cousin of mine. I'll feel him out and get back to you."

"No need," Ophelia said, "have you met my sister?"

The girl in the skirt moved closer to the door. Killian began to inch back toward the edge of the deck. "I'll call ya tomorrow," she said, disappearing into the house.

Ophelia crunched a bit of glass under her foot. She scraped her sneaker across the deck a few times to clean it off, then moved toward the door. Pausing, her hand on the sliding screen, she spoke softly just before stepping inside.

"Good night, Little Man."

Killian held his breath until he heard the door slide shut. Then he rolled out into the lawn and ran back around the Brumell's, going completely around the block to get home.

In his room he couldn't stop pacing. She had known he was there! He shook his hands nervously as he took four steps in one direction, spun, and took four steps back. She was manipulating Progner. She had some, what, some terrorist act planned? It was too much to process at once. He wanted to draw her, to understand her like he did when he penciled the other neighbors. He needed to reduce her to a two dimensional being, defined by simple objects surrounding her. But that was impossible, wasn't it? He'd done so much more than stood in her doorway.

He could stare through windows and front doors all day at Mr. Haroki, or Mrs. Simmons, or even Progner. Stare and remember and reproduce. But not with Ophelia Redenbacher. She lived in a secret cave, devoid of windows for convenient peeking. Killian had entered that cave to glimpse her. And entering had roused the beast. She had growled when she smelled him, and learned his scent. She would occupy his dreams now. And he would never again know the rest of the innocent.

REVEAL

His vision was blurry. He rubbed his eyelids. Was that her? A fuzzy gray figure moved toward the closet. He was on a bed, fully dressed, on top of the covers. She looked over her shoulder at him, just a quick glance, then pulled her shirt off over her head.

Was this it? Ophelia, exposed. Undressing in a bedroom. The intimate portrait he'd always wanted. The one he was born to capture.

Her shoulder-length loose, dark curls were back; her hair as he felt it should be. She was reaching her hands up her slim back, toward those curls, toward the black line which bisected her pale skin. She wriggled, and twisted her hands and the strap of the bra separated.

Killian was weak, and though his vision was sharpening, the pulsing excitement within him threatened to overload his circuits. It was her! It was the girl from quiZblitZ. From his toothbrush. From his murky past. It was Ophelia. And she was getting undressed in front of him. She dropped her shoulders and let her bra fall to the floor. Her back was to him. But it was her naked back. He licked his lips, his pasty tongue snagging deep crevasses.

He heard her unzip and watched as she slid her shorts down, revealing French cut lace that was doing a damn fine job of not containing the cheeks of her ass. Killian's temples throbbed and he had to close his eyes and scrunch his forehead to stay here, in the now.

When he opened his eyes she was dressed again in a fresh T-shirt and jeans.

"Oh, you're finally up?" she said, falsely surprised. She approached and sat softly on the bed beside him. Killian didn't move. He prayed she didn't place a comforting hand on him.

"How are you feeling?" she asked, removing a strand of hair from her face. Her deep brown eyes hypnotized, just like he remembered.

"Confused," he admitted. "Hungry."

"Well, I'll go prepare something. You come down when you're ready. I'm so glad I found you in time Killian." She leaned in and kissed his forehead. Then she spun and disappeared into the hall. He lay back, bathing in bliss for several minutes before he could rise and follow her.

Hugging the railing on the stairs he found the kitchen, where Ophelia was cooking pancakes on the stove. The smell evoked an echoing cry from his belly.

"Sorry, no syrup," she said, placing the plate piled with pancakes before him. A mound of butter dribbled down the layers. He grabbed one up and gnawed ferociously at it. "Or silverware," she added.

Killian ate five in as many minutes. His stomach bulged. It was full, yet desired that last pancake simply because it was available. He recognized this room. Yes, it was the kitchen Penelope Redenbacher used to buzz around while serving him hot cookies and cold milk at this very counter. They were in the house she had lived in. In the neighborhood he grew up in. What had happened to Ophelia's sweet mother? Surely she must be in Stream by now.

Ophelia was sitting on the counter next to the stove. She meticulously pared the skin off an apple. Slow, deliberate turns. The entire peel came off in one continuous curl. He watched her focused eyes and delicate fingers manipulate the fruit. When she finished, she held the skin up and let it spring, then winked at him and tossed it in the sink.

"Pretty brave thing you did there, Killian."

"What's that?" He could smell the fresh tang of apple juice. His belly was sated, but he wanted something more.

"Leaving. Facing the withdrawal. Abandoning your job and your home. You're a criminal now."

"Am I?" He started to panic a bit, then strained to hide it from her. He couldn't remember the details of his flight. Whose car was that?

"Well, the word criminal depends on point of view, doesn't it? To many you're a hero." She looked up slyly through her lashes. "To me, you're a hero. I just can't believe I found you. The one person in all the Stream that I needed, and here you are."

He warmed at this, leaning against the high-back of the stool and raising himself up with a deep inhale.

"How, exactly, am I a hero?" he asked, showing no effort to restrain his smile.

"You saved Dona's life."

"Oh, God, Dona. I left her, far into the woods. Far from the car, the road…"

"Relax. Dona's fine. She's with a friend. With a little nursing she'll be good as new in no time. Thanks to you."

Again his smile asserted itself. She watched him from beneath a cautious brow, waiting for his grin to fade.

"Killian, how much do you remember?"

He strained to recall. Bits of memory surfaced and faded. He couldn't pause them, or retrieve them from organized files. He was not in Stream. "Fragments. Dona came to me, panicked and talking to herself. Just like Evan. And the others. She was scared and screaming and begged me to help her get away."

"Someone was talking to her."

"Yes, that's right. Just like the others. I couldn't let another client… well, I didn't want her to kill herself."

"Well, I, for one, am glad you came to your senses and saw the truth."

"What do you mean?"

"Killian, you know Wellspring was behind it right? Behind all of it?"

His head cocked slowly to one side. Yes, this was the Ophelia he'd forgotten. Down with corporations and government and religion. Institutions are to blame. The *man* is repressing the people.

"It was Progner. He was the one choosing your clients. He *killed* your clients Killian. He nearly killed my little sister."

"What are you talking about?"

"The 'God' program he created."

Killian's mouth opened a touch wider. Ophelia dropped her elbows to the counter and attempted to exhale her frustration while running her fingers through her dark curls.

"Killian, Wellspring was afraid that the priests were gaining too much of their power. Soon, the priesthood would take over and they'd be reduced to being mere technicians of a thoroughly Jadonist society. So they were trying to beat the priests to the punch. If they could create this 'God' that Jadon promised, or rather a complex program that appeared to speak as God, but which was under their control, they could maintain their dominance. Progner was in charge of testing these programs. He tested them on your clients. That's why they were hearing voices. That's why they went insane. And then, when Dona came to you, and you were maneuvered out of the way for a few days, he used her as his next test subject."

Killian stood up. He drifted away into the living room. Could she be telling him the truth? Why would she make it up? It was too much to absorb. He was still so fatigued, so unready to adopt new ideas. He couldn't remember his own childhood, and now he was having trouble remembering his recent past and both were coming back at the same time and he couldn't possibly process new information on top of it. He simply couldn't. He fell to his knees.

"Killian," Ophelia said, rushing to his side.

He was looking through the sliding glass door to the deck beyond. It shifted through degrees of shadow. She was there, on the deck, ten years younger, kicking at the railing.

"Are you okay," Ophelia said, taking him by the shoulders and helping him to the couch.

The younger Ophelia had vanished and this one was here, holding up his shoulder. He leaned back and nearly faded out again.

"I can't remember you," he said. "Or anything in the past. My life."

"Progner's fault too. He was blocking your past from you while you were in Stream. He didn't want you to remember me. He didn't want you to regret betraying me. But you're not in Stream now. Your memories will come back."

"They started to. When my sketchbook showed up…"

"I had hoped it might trigger something."

"You… How did you…."

"Killian, you became a mindless oarsman, going

through the motions of paddling, but only going where the Stream lead you. It was sad to watch. I had to do something to spark the intelligent artist I once knew."

"Why?"

"Because Killian, I need your help. Progner's a power-hungry psychopath, and he needs to be stopped. Look what his world did to you. What it's doing to everyone. Mindless zombies, forever tripping their lives away in flashy hallucinatory worlds. The people of the Stream must be liberated."

LIBERATION

"Ever been to the animal prison little man?"

Killian bit his cheek, refusing to ask the obvious. He scrunched his brow until a translation occurred to him. "No, I've actually never been to the zoo."

She nodded, her brow solidifying as she floored the gas. "No one has ever taken you to see the prisoners, huh? Don't you have parents?"

Killian looked out the passenger window. His parents didn't seem to know he existed. Even when he stood right in front of them. They might signal with a waving of the hand that he was blocking the TV. Maybe grunt, "move" or "hey." But mostly they overlooked him.

Ophelia knew he existed. Even when he was hidden under her deck. She had let him know she was aware and that he wasn't getting away with anything. And now, after a week and a half of nervously delivering newspapers to her house without seeing her, she had pulled into his driveway and invited him to skip school and go on a mission for freedom; whatever the hell that meant.

What was this, some bizarre field trip? Why was she taking him to the zoo? Was this a date? He decided it was and smiled a bit.

Neither of them spoke as the black hatchback sailed

through town and merged with the expressway. When she successfully cut off a van in the third lane and exceeded the speed limit to her satisfaction, Ophelia broke the silence.

"My bastard father took me to the zoo. Once. He was all excited the morning he showed up to be Daddy for a day. I was eight and he promised me I'd love it. It's the only thing he ever promised me."

Killian watched the road as she took her eyes from it to light a smoke. She didn't open her window at first so he cracked his.

"I'm not sure why he didn't bring Dona. She was what? Five. I guess, if he only needed one daughter, an eight-year-old would be the easier choice. I did love it though. I'd never seen anything more than squirrels and birds and nothing bigger than a dog before. I remember sitting with an ice cream cone and watching the polar bears swim. It was sunny and warm and I had to lick fast. But they swam slow, enjoying their cool water."

Exhaling a puff before her, she waved it away with one hand, put the butt between her lips and rolled down the window with the other. She steered with her knee. Killian's toes clenched.

"We went into the gorilla house," she continued. "It was scary at first. You went through this dark tunnel, jungle painted on the walls. And then there was this crowd of people blabbing and pointing through this picture window.

"*Dad*, which is what he insisted I call him, looked over top of them. I couldn't see. I kept trying to wedge in between knees. Then *Dad* said come here and we moved around the corner to a smaller window that was being vacated. And there he was. Sitting with his back toward us, but looking over his shoulder. It was big in there. Fake cliffs and vegetation. But not that big. I gazed as he scooted a few centimeters this way, then back, trying to position himself out of his critics' gaze. After a while he gave up and allowed his face to droop further.

"I couldn't believe how much he looked like a man. Hairy, strong, an evil stare; yet the slightest adjustment of his brow and he was a lost child, or an embarrassed senior citizen.

"Some kids at the other glass were making monkey noises, scratching their armpits and shit. He turned his back to them. They moved to our window, started doing it again behind us. *Dad* looked back and giggled. I thought the kids were stupid. The gorilla clearly had more civility than they did. He looked noble in posture. They were the ones jumping and hooting.

"Then he charged. It was so fast. All I remember is that my heart pounded just once in resonance with the glass, then paused forever. His palm left a giant print just centimeters from my face. I ran up *Dad's* leg. A camera flashed. The boys yelped, then, embarrassed, began saying, 'Whoa, cool. He's really pissed man. Yeah, killer monkey. Ooh-ooh-ooh.'

"Another camera flash. *Dad* laughed along with them. When he saw I was in tears he scooped me up and turned to the reporter I then realized had been with us all morning. He smiled; she snapped a few shots. I held tight, unable to shake the image of that handprint. It must have been the size of my torso. I tried to catch a last glimpse of him, the poor gorilla, but *Dad* was lugging me out of the tunnel."

Ash dropped into Ophelia's lap and she realized her smoke had gone on without her. She pitched what was left out the window and rolled it up.

"*Dad* thought it was a riot," she said brushing off her pant leg. "He kept laughing after we took a picnic table outside. 'Scared the pants right off you Ophelia, didn't he? She'll be crying 'til suppertime,' he roared.

"I did cry all the way to the car. But I wasn't scared. I was sad. For the gorilla. I kept picturing him coming right through the glass, wrapping me up in that huge hand and carrying me off to the Empire State Building. It comforted me. Somehow, I wished he could get out and take me with him. I wished my *Dad* was in that cage and me and Kong would come by and laugh at *him*."

"Well, *Dad* never went to prison. Even if he deserved it. But he did go away again. I didn't see him for years. But the whole world saw us together. Saw me clinging to his leg for security. All they had to do was flip through a copy of Time magazine. *Busy Billionaire Bates Makes Time to be Dad*. Said that right on the cover. Pg. 23. If it wasn't for those dectuplets, our picture would've been on the cover."

Checking quickly over her shoulder, Ophelia cut across all three lanes without signaling and took the exit for the zoo.

The guy who lived across the street, Mr. Progner, was there, in the parking lot, waiting for them. The look of annoyed surprise that Progner's eyebrows conveyed mirrored Killian's sentiment.

"A threesome," Progner said dryly. "Alright, then. Hello Killian."

"Hey Mr. Progner," Killian mumbled. He'd only really spoke to the man that one time, just after he'd trashed his own living room. From the conversation Killian overheard, under the deck, he suspected he knew why Progner was here. She was manipulating him. But why did she bring Killian?

Ophelia kissed Progner on the forehead and moved past him. She kept walking, stretching her bare arms above her head, then letting them drop slowly to her sides. When she reached the edge of the parking lot, near the iron bar fence, around the corner from the main entrance, she lingered.

"What's she doing?" Killian said. Progner shrugged. They watched as she bent down, lifted the leg of her faded jeans and tightened her high boot. Then, in one motion she stood, leapt, pulled her way up the bars of the fence, threw a leg over the top, and disappeared into the bordering brush.

"What's she doing?" Killian repeated. Progner shrugged again. They stood there a few minutes, half expecting her to pounce right back to their side. Of course, she wouldn't. Progner and Killian kicked the stones along the sidewalk and avoided each other's eyes.

Progner was wearing a collared shirt and pressed shorts. He had recently buzzed his hair. Neat and trim, unlike the curls which were beginning to rebel from the back of Killian's locks. Killian glanced at the constellation of pinholes in his T-shirt that had been slowly reproducing over his ribs. His stark white legs hung from well-worn shorts. A tinge of embarrassment came and went.

"Come on Killian," he told himself, "you can do it. Follow her. It's what she wants. It's a test. She'll love you for it. She'll see you're not a pansy like this guy."

Finally Progner exhaled. "Well kid, I guess I'm treating."

Killian followed Progner to the ticket booths and then into the zoo.

Ophelia was sitting Buddha style on a bench beneath a small maple. Progner strode ahead.

"What do you think you're doing? I had money."

"I know, and I wish you went my way," Ophelia whispered.

"What? I'm going to risk getting arrested so I can scam my way into the friggin' zoo?"

"The point is, you just donated money to an organization that imprisons defenseless animals."

"Well, if you're so against this place, what're we doing here?"

"Mercy mission. Keeping the prisoners company. I bet if you went to visit human prisoners you would be appalled if they tried to charge you admission." Ophelia dropped her legs to the pavement and eased down into her bench. She used her sunglasses to push her dark hair back. Closing her eyes, she tipped her head back and exhaled.

Progner was pacing while forming and unforming fists. Killian moved away, toward the peacocks that had begun to flock near the top of their hill. Let them fight. He'd remain aloof. Just stroll away from their embarrassingly parental behavior.

Seeing a happy couple with two tots enjoying the zebras, Killian couldn't help but wonder what it was like to have parents who wanted to be parents. He'd never been to the zoo. He would bring his kid here if he had one. He fantasized a stroller in front of Ophelia. Their baby cooing inside. A happy, normal family. He realized how absurd his fantasy was when he saw what Ophelia was up to.

She was in the primate area. Not inside the monkey house, but around back where the monkeys played on their tire swings, breathing the stripes of fresh air that wafted through their bars. She had sent Progner to get them ice cream, against his complaints that the sky was looking ominous and it would rain soon.

Ophelia dug out a small brown paper packet. She carefully ripped open one corner. Turning her back to the rising wind she sprinkled a bit of the contents onto the gate lock.

She moved on, doing all eight cages in the row.

Orangutans, chimpanzees, macaques, right on down to some little squirrel monkeys that were reaching through the bars at her and cackling.

Just before Progner returned Ophelia dropped the paper bag into the swinging mouth of a hippo-headed garbage can. She returned to Killian's side, winking at him. He warmed.

"I want to go watch the polar bears and eat these," Ophelia said. The polar bears were directly across a patch of green grass and another paved walkway. Progner and Killian followed, Progner obsessing over the darkening sky.

Killian kept looking back at the monkey cages but noticed that Ophelia didn't look once. She was absorbed in her ice cream.

It started to rain. Just droplets at first, but Progner suggested they should get going. Ophelia and Killian ignored him. At once a downpour ensued. Progner got ready to run. "Let's go," he said. Killian looked to Ophelia who had casually turned her head over her shoulder and was watching the monkeys over the top of her shades.

Killian spun just in time to see the locks on the cage doors simultaneously begin to sizzle and melt, emitting a green fog. She used some type of acid that reacted with water. He was proud of himself for this deduction, and for not overreacting like Progner.

"What the hell is that?"

The chimps were first. Poking at the gate a few times and retreating. One of them knocked the door open and three of them ran for it. They headed off down the sidewalk, producing a few screams from the small crowd who hadn't noticed the melting locks, as they were too busy fleeing nature's showers.

"Holy shit," Progner said. "We should go tell someone."

Other primates soon followed the example of the chimpanzees. A few stayed put, but the majority of the occupants of the eight cages Ophelia sabotaged were now liberated. Within minutes there was a band of multi-species monkeys taking to the trees that filled the patch of grass between sidewalks.

"How did this happen? We have to tell someone. No one's noticed yet. How can they not see this?" Progner took Ophelia's shoulders and rattled them. "Why are you just sitting there? What's wrong with you?"

She was in mid-lick when he grabbed her, causing a smear of vanilla to mustache her. Erasing the symbol of manhood with a playful lick, she looked up and smiled at him.

"No. You didn't do this. Did you?" Progner looked at Killian who shrugged. "You, you're crazy," Progner said, returning his look of bewilderment to Ophelia. "We should get outta here."

She didn't move, lapping instead at the remains of her rain-dented ice cream. "Look at that little guy over there on that branch. He's got some man's hat."

"Well, I'm getting outta here. You coming kid?" Killian shook his head. Progner stormed off, trying to duck his head into the collar of his fully saturated shirt.

"Look at them," she said. "Look at how quickly they spread out. Won't be easy collecting them all."

Killian was surprised he was able to keep his cool. Watching Ophelia seemed to calm him. She acted like this was as ordinary as eating breakfast. Several groundskeepers were chasing the monkeys around now which added to Ophelia's amusement. She was laughing out loud at their failed attempts, as they swung nets and called to the animals like they were puppies. She loved it, and Killian couldn't help but smile.

He tried several times to close his eyes and freeze

the scene in his mind. This is Ophelia; the elusive girl he hadn't been able to capture. Sitting in the rain, casually eating ice cream – monkeys unleashed, discovering their freedom all around her. But he couldn't picture it. Her image continued to elude him. It didn't matter. Why did he need her image, when he was right here with her? He inched closer on the bench.

She rose suddenly and said let's go, shoving the last of her cone into her mouth. Killian followed her to the entrance where she explained they'd be getting the tranquilizer guns now and she'd rather not watch that.

Killian dropped his ice cream on the lawn. "But isn't it dangerous for them to be running around in the city? They could get hit by a car."

"Freedom isn't cheap Little Man. If they didn't want it, they could stay in their cells."

FIXATION

The Stream is the product of one man's obsession with perfection. Steve Bates, founder of Wellspring Inc., spent his entire life creating a realm where his scrawny body and awkward personality would no longer detract from his brilliance. As early as elementary school, when he discovered the power of creating false personalities on chat sites, Bates began to glimpse an ideal future where mind merged with machine. By middle school, writing software became his sole pastime. He viewed the Stream as the ultimate goal of the evolution of society. And he knew, with obsessive devotion, that he could be the architect of that evolution.

Bates became so fixated with the idea of the Stream that his social skills actually diminished from avoidably nerdy to downright creepy. He gave up on people and went whole months without conversing with anyone at all. Yet, one woman noticed him. She found his shyness and lack of interest extremely attractive. She was a secretary of a low level accountant that Bates visited once a month and she found him so appealing that she put down her headset one afternoon while he sat in the outer office waiting for her boss and walked around her desk and sat down beside him. Sure, she was a bit chubby, a bit clumsy, a bit silly. But not entirely unattractive. Since this was before he was a well-known billionaire, she was the first woman to ever hit on Bates, and he found her forwardness turned him on.

A few discrete meetings left her pregnant. He had recently been promoted to vice president of WellsTech, the company he would turn into Wellspring Inc., and was put in charge of developing Stream prototype software. Marriage would not fit into his packed agenda, so he encouraged an abortion. She refused, but took instead a ridiculous amount of child support in exchange for secrecy, and an intermittent continuance of their affairs.

Three years later, Penelope Redenbacher tracked Bates down after not hearing from him for five months. He explained that he had been spending twenty four hours a day working on the software that would give rise to the Stream. He had no interest in physical pleasures anymore. He didn't even notice how very pregnant Penelope had become until she insisted she would go to the press if he didn't marry her.

Eventually she settled again, taking her full salary to never have to come in to work again. All it required was keeping her lips sealed. Bates explained that it would be just like marriage. Either way he would never be around. This way she could stay home and raise her children without having to work, and wouldn't have to hassle him obligatorily for never making it home for dinner.

They didn't see each other for five more years, when Bates' press secretary convinced him he needed to show some human emotion to sell the world on his new preStream operating system. Bates showed up, took his eldest daughter to the zoo for a photo op, then disappeared again. The public seemed to have forgotten about the whole matter. But when Ophelia Redenbacher, Bates' eldest daughter, found the magazine article that her mother had stashed away, she, like her father, found something worthy of her life's devotion. She vowed to spend every waking moment destroying what he had spent every moment creating. It became her one fixation. Everything and everyone in her life became possible cogs in her vengeance machine.

Killian had forgotten this about Ophelia. If Killian *had* remembered Ophelia's obsession with destroying her father, he probably would have assumed it dissipated with the loss of it's nourishment. Steve Bates died a couple of years ago, during a Streamquake. He'd been jogging when it hit and he collapsed in front of a city bus whose driver had passed out as well. Run down by the imperfections of his own system. Ophelia must have appreciated the irony, even if she felt cheated out of her revenge. But she wouldn't have transferred her anger onto something else, right? When Killian's mind was torn from the electronic blitzkrieg that had become its modus operandi for so long, it had searched desperately for something else to fix its focus on. And, just as when he was a lost teenager, it found Ophelia Redenbacher. A healthy obsession. She too must have found a healthy outlet for her obsessive tendencies, if only because he had so much trouble believing anything negative about her.

Lying on the couch of what appeared to be the Redenbacher living room, Killian could think of nothing but her smirk, her hand softly holding his shoulder, lowering him gently down, when he collapsed minutes, hours, days ago? He had no idea how long he'd been asleep. Or if it was still now. Was he, once again, caught up in the realism of his rediscovered memory? Was this young Ophelia's living room? Was she out there on the deck with her high school friends?

No. If this was the past then Penelope would be here. She never left the house. And if Penelope was here he would hear televisions. Where was Penelope? She must have joined the Stream. There's no way Ophelia could have prevented her. After all, Penelope had once said, "In heaven both my daughters will love me, and the TV will always be on." Funny that by diving into the realm created by the man who wouldn't recognize her existence, Penelope found heaven. A place where all TVs were turned on, all the time. They couldn't be turned off. They couldn't even be dimmed.

Penelope was not atypical in joining the Stream at her age though. People tend to think the Stream is filled with youth. After all, new technology attracts young pliable minds. But Bates was aware of this, and was determined that the success of the Stream in its early years relied on getting all demographics to Stream up. Therefore, his massive advertising campaigns targeted those who would be least likely to join.

Superior health care: that's what got most old people to dive in. Never mind the flashy new ways to see and hear music, or the video memory enhancement programs. After all, when they were kids, if they wanted to hear music they damn well sang it. And memories – they're all bitter anyway, who needs 'em. But constant homeostatic monitoring? And without a cold stethoscope on the skin, or embarrassing piss tests, or stinging needles. Dive in to the Stream and you needn't even go to the doctor's office. Keeping your dying body in the best possible condition is as easy as adjusting the tuning knob on an antique FM radio. And of course, the average life span was twenty years longer than for non-swimmers. Yep, Killian had no shortage of clients who were living well past their prime as Stream ghosts. All paid for by universal health care and continuously stretched retirement legislation, of course. And the little bit that wasn't paid for? The balance? That was merely billed in advertisement time. Commercial bombardment so smoothly transitioned that the interruption to Streaming bliss was virtually unnoticeable.

Of course, getting a large senior population to Stream served another important purpose in Bates' all-encompassing plan. Geriatric care was one of the largest employers of healthy young Streamers. If young people took care of old people now, someone would take care of them while they Streamed their elder years away. The perfect circle of life.

Killian's parents were in the Stream, right? He had to think about it. Yes, they entered just a few months after he did. They occasionally checked on his status. On rarer occasions he checked on theirs. But they didn't actually communicate any more. What was there to say? They were just two of the millions of voices in Stream. Just two who happened to be his parents in one of the infinite worlds in which he existed.

"Hello?" His voice echoed through the empty kitchen. There was no response. Not to his voice, not to his thoughts. He was alone.

"Hel-LO?"

Still no answer. He surveyed his surroundings. Reality. He closed his eyes and tried to be somewhere else, but only dimness and silence were within. Without, the scene would not change. He couldn't redecorate, or alter the lighting, or add some soft background music. He had no power to change his environment. Not even just a little, to bring his mood up. He was a fixed point existing on the fixed grid of reality. Stuck.

He stood up, feeling a touch wobbly. By holding onto the old dust-settled furniture, he made it to the kitchen counter. He needed water. The faucet coughed up some violent moaning but no liquid. He shut it off.

There was a portable cooler on the floor. Killian found bottled water inside. The liquid revived his throat, but failed to wash the fog from his thoughts. Fixed. Here, in this scene forever. He couldn't make her come back, either as a teenager rebelling against the world, or as the young woman who rescued him from death.

She had been talking about rebellion again. Progner killed his clients! She said that, right? Hector and Elena and Evan. Were they real people? Were any of them? Yes. Evan was his friend. Killian would not forget him.

No doubt Ophelia had plans. Plans that might involve him. She had said she needed him. This thought provoked a teenage excitement; an energy that had been absent for too long. She had said it, right? She needed him!

Checking the garage first, he walked to the front windows and confirmed her car was not in the driveway. It was now. If this were a memory, the house across the street, the one where Progner used to live, wouldn't be a burned out husk.

Killian ran to the front door, threw it open and stepped out onto the front porch. He dropped his water bottle, which hit the pavement with a thump, a splash, a gurgle, and then spilled quietly down the incline. His knees weakened and his head swam. At least three of the houses on the street were blackened shells, burnt up from the inside out. Several had broken windows. Other houses were completely boarded up. Front doors hung open or were missing. Long patches of green grass sparsely populated the yellow and brown yards. Not a single car was visible. At the far end of the street a dark brown stream bubbled out of the storm sewer, flooding the sunken blacktop.

Miraculously, the mailboxes still stood at the end of each driveway. But there was no one to read any news that Killian might deliver. There was no one to sketch. His feet began to drift down the street. Mr. Haroki's house, straight ahead, had fallen in upon itself. The remains of the roof had spilled into the dining room. Killian could see his sketch; Mr. Haroki sitting at the dining room table, toasting himself, the edges of the page curling in to smother him.

All of the neighbors. The ones he drew. The ones he never got to draw. All gone. Nothing but shells remained of the cubes that used to define them. Was he to blame for this? Didn't he have a chance to stop the Stream from flowing?

He couldn't remember.

He continued along his old route, touching each mailbox he passed, until he reached the end of the street. From there he would be able to see his parents' old house. Where he grew up.

It took him a moment to identify the point where his house should have been. Right there at the entrance of the neighborhood. On the corner of the busy road. One wall remained in its entirety. The others seemed to have swallowed an overturned delivery truck and at least two cars. The remains of his childhood home had been demolished by traffic accidents.

But it was so quiet. He ached with loneliness. He closed his eyes and begged for the scene to change, but it would not. He was here and it was now, and he couldn't make it better. He wanted Ophelia to come back and rescue him once more. He wanted her to push her dark curls from her face, revealing that sly smirk of hers. He wanted to be in her presence, where he felt like he was part of something. Like he had a purpose.

ENGAGED

She squealed around the corner in a beat up old hatchback, stopping just short of where he stood staring at the remains of his childhood home. No apologies for leaving him stranded here. No explanations for where she'd gone. It was not the same hatchback she had in high school. This one was white. The right side was all smashed in. She opened her door and stepped out of the car.

"Is all the world out here as bad as this?" he asked, turning back to the wreckage.

"I'll show you. Get in." He had to climb over the driver's seat since the passenger door clearly didn't open. She was in and revving the engine before he settled.

A few minutes down the road Killian's brain realized their movement was not the virtual sort he was used to, and that they were, in fact, accelerating past seventy miles per hour. It began to send signals to his stomach that maybe it was time to get a little upset here. Closing his eyes, he slowed his breathing. Jadon said to picture a white piece of paper when you couldn't focus. Killian did this. But it was not a generic page. It was the eighth page in his sketchbook. The blank page. The page reserved for her. The dark green cover of his sketchbook closed on the image in his mind. He watched a single teardrop fall toward the lower left corner of the cover. It splattered, leaving a darker green stain.

But that was a long time ago. He opened his eyes. He was back with Ophelia now and she needed him. He was no longer responsible for rescuing Streamers from drowning. Nor was he adrift in the fog of mechanically enhanced dreams any more. He was here, on dry land, in the real world, where he could focus all of his energy on the bobbing of her dark curls as she flowed through each moment in time, never still. Unportrayable. Uncapturable. Uncaught.

Sitting in her car, unable to fully grasp her, he was exactly where he was ten years ago, when he somehow lost this moment. Betrayed it. Traded it for the world of the Stream. Why would he do that? It had something to do with that teardrop.

"Killian, did you hear me?"

"Yeah. Sorry. I'm still having trouble focusing."

"It'll come with time. It's a shame really, that this had to happen, now, just after you finally engaged."

"What do you mean?"

"Killian, I've been keeping an eye on you for some time."

She'd been stalking *him*?

"Watching you slip away, drift off with the current of the Stream. You were fading, more and more, into that artificial reality. It was sad to see, and I wasn't sure you would snap out of it. But you did. Which means there is hope for others."

She took a sharp turn and Killian's eyes were thrown toward the houses flying past his window. They looked relatively undamaged. A few had broken windows. They all looked abandoned. But they didn't all have delivery trucks parked in their living rooms.

"You reengaged in reality. You were confronted with a problem and you acted. You saved Dona's life. I'm proud of you."

She placed a light hand on the muscle between his neck and shoulder and offered the slightest of squeezes.

"And your reward for this has been pain and suffering. But at least you are free my little monkey. My Little Man."

He sighed and moved his shoulder away from her grip.

"My Killian," she whispered, turning to smirk at him. He tried to smile back but was thrown against the window as she swerved to remain on the road around a curve. They were heading into the foothills. He used to go hiking not far from this road. One time he borrowed his uncle's tent and went camping on Doe Mountain just beyond the hills rolling past to the south. After years of occasional requests, Killian had concluded that his father had no interest in taking him. So the summer he graduated high school, just before he betrayed the natural world and Streamed up, he went out into the wilderness alone. He'd been so proud that he slept outdoors in a tent by himself for two nights, despite his terror.

"You're probably wondering how I can come and go from the Stream whenever I want, right? Well, it's partly because... Killian, I need you to listen."

Killian returned his eyes to her. He wanted to tell her he'd always listen, to anything she said. Forever. But he was already wandered from focusing on her full bottom lip, where the words were forming, to the taut line that described the curve of her neck. He could sit all day and study her; his mind working furiously to remember every detail of the one person he couldn't draw.

"...familiar with the sleep boot software, right? Well,

that's how it works. Only, instead of automatically turning off the Stream when I'm subconscious, I have total control over it. I can disconnect while I'm awake. I can hide within the city by turning off the connection whenever I want."

Killian nodded for her expectant glance. They continued uphill, the forest enclosing them. It was ten years ago. They were on the way to the zoo. He had another chance. No, he was not a child. She was not a child. Her beauty had become more defined. The soft lines of her face had clarified. Her figure had curved further toward the essence of femininity. Ten years ago he could not have guessed how much more her beauty could develop. But here she was, an even more beautiful young woman for his eyes to feast upon.

"…that's what I was doing at the school. See, they've been trying to Stream kids up at younger ages. Problem is, the younger a kid is, the more likely their mind will reject the Stream. Until recently they weren't able to Stream anybody under age six or seven. But with the off switch upgrade, they found they can brainwash in increments. They can pull them in younger and younger. Of course, some teachers were brought in and set up with the new chip so they could understand and guide the children. I was posing as a substitute teacher. It was the only place I could have an off switch without drawing attention. But this is exactly…"

The car jolted across a good size pothole. The hypnotic springing and resettling of Ophelia's breasts absorbed Killian's attention. Somewhere her voice rose in excitement. Her voice! He was supposed to be listening.

"… bad enough. The first five years of life are when the mind develops most. At least they've had a good firm base in reality to start with. But we're talking about Streaming babies for shit's sake. Little, tiny, innocent babies. They'll awaken to awareness in the world of the Stream. Talk about original sin!"

"Look at it," her voice softened. Killian looked through the windshield as they overtook the crest of the hill. The sun was behind them and the city below glimmered. The nest of towers reflected the light of the sun, rejecting this natural source of power. Killian squinted his eyes. The city was blinding to those outside it.

Ophelia pulled over onto the shoulder of the road. She got out and left her door open for Killian. He didn't move at first, admiring the tautness of her jeans as she rounded the car. They were not too tight, not slutty tight, but just tight enough to highlight her naturally hypnotic shape. She sat on the car's hood and slid back a bit, causing her jeans to slither down an inch or two and reveal bare flesh. He was reminded of watching her undress in the bedroom earlier.

She turned and engaged him through the glass with her coffee brown eyes. He could sit there forever, sipping at the intensity of her gaze.

Climbing quickly across the driver's seat, Killian jumped out of the car and joined Ophelia on the hood.

"See down there, to the south, how the railroad traces the flat land from the farms into the city." He followed her pointing finger. "And over here, where that double rail comes between the hills that lead to the lake?" She was pointing to the north. He leaned forward and looked. "And this road, and the other road beyond the forest there. Like arteries," she said.

He traced the train tracks back to the city. The towers loomed, like five thousand fingers from a thousand hands, all stretching to reach further into the heavens.

"That's the brain," she said, watching him watch.

"The city is the brain. Electrical pulses of thought surge throughout those towers. The city is the brain and the Stream is the mind. Out there is the body. See. It nourishes the brain. The train tracks, like arteries, supply the brain with life. Without the tracks, the brain would starve. But the mind forgets this. Forgets that cutting the arteries would quickly weaken its precious thoughts until not a single one remained."

"That's an interesting analogy," Killian said.

"Interesting. Yeah, I guess it's interesting that Streamers live like kings while most of the world works itself to death to please them."

"Well, I mean… it's…."

"It's life. Always has been. I suppose what really pisses me off is that we pretend it isn't so. The Streamers continue on with their righteous lives, pretending that they're forging the way of the future. That someday, someday not so far off, everyone will have what they have. Everyone will live in Stream, and in a modern city and have their wildest dreams available at their command. But this cannot be. Can the mind survive without the heart and lungs bringing it oxygen? Can it survive without the hands and feet to gather food? Can it survive without the stomach, or for that matter the rectum? No. And this technological brain they've constructed can't either.

"Those trains are the arteries of the system, but also the veins. Twice a week that track there carries a northbound train out of the city. It's filled with e-trash. Circuit boards and security cameras and outdated transformers for the Stream generators. All stuff that came into the city on the trains at some point. Made in China, or some exploited third world country, shipped to America on a boat or plane, then put on a train to one of these cities. And back it goes, out on the train to the deserts of the Midwest, or more likely on another boat to be buried in some starving country that would gladly put our poison beneath their soil for a few American dollars. I know a guy that had to leave the country after leading a particularly effective protest at a Stream generator factory. Now he works at a train yard in Indonesia. Trains there bring sneakers out of sweatshops where ten-year-olds work all day for a single meal. Trains coming in sometimes bring computer waste. He gets paid extra to unload that. At night. By morning, the kids who work in the sweatshops are digging it up. They break up circuit boards and melt out the precious metals. They melt computer wire for the copper inside. They breathe in the poisons released from the fires in search of treasure that might feed their starving families.

"Where would this Stream paradise be if it had to deal with its own waste? Where would it be without sweatshops for producing microchips and rain forest raw materials for melting into Plexiplastic tower walls? And without exploitation you simply wouldn't have these things."

The sun baked the back of his neck, but was not wholly responsible for the heat building inside him. Her voice, passionate to a level of near desperation, awakened the very cells in his blood. He remembered what motivation felt like. He was finally focused.

"Of course, you won't find much data on imports in Stream. And none at all on city waste removal. The Stream is not *exactly* the sum total of human data. You only get half of the facts. Enough of them to convince you they're all available. But the other half are out there. On dry land." She pointed out along the rails, toward the rolling farms beyond the hills.

"Here, in between these two worlds, on the shore, you might be able to glimpse the whole picture for a moment. But you try not to think of the rest of the world, right? You transfer a few dollars to a charity if some commercial-motivated guilt gets through your ego-shield. Mostly, though, you go with the flow. You row, gently. Because Wellspring has given you the illusion of safety. They've given you a filter, which is like a secure, individual lifeboat for floating down the Stream. You even have some control over it, right? You can have your filter tuned however you want. You're not drowning in their sea of insanity. No. You're in control. You're rowing. Gently down their Stream. And who would fight that? Life is perfect when you're lazily navigating. Life is but a dream."

Ophelia jumped down and paced up the road a bit. Killian watched her sway away, silently pleading for her to return. To return to his side, where he'd longed for her to be, secretly, subconsciously, for the last decade. Everything made sense to him when she explained it. He'd been drifting along, like he was supposed to, like a good little member of society, for years. Why couldn't he row the other way. Against the current. Like she did. He wanted to help her. He wanted to help her save the world. He leapt down and walked up beside her, placing a cautious arm on her shoulder.

"So, what's the plan this time?"

"Well, you asked if the whole world out here was as bad as the old neighborhood. It's not. Not yet. But eventually it will be. Right now people work the farmlands and the factories because the city provides electricity. There's still television and Internet out here. For the most part. But it's been spottier and spottier, as those in the Stream get further lost in the electric dreamland they've created. Once the people out here begin to backslide far enough away from the comforts of modern living, they'll rebel. It'll be civil war. But we can prevent that inevitability, if we do something now."

She turned dramatically away from him, his hand slipping from her shoulder.

"So you still want to turn off the Stream?"

"Killian, you've lived in that nightmare. And only for ten years. What about kids who're Streamed at age five, or four, or three? When they spend their entire lives being brainwashed by Wellspring's filter suggestions. They'll be completely mindless. They'll be no match for the disgruntled underclass out here. A lot of people will be hurt. I want to help the Streamers."

"By having them flop like fish for days after you dry up the Stream. I went through that, it was horrible!"

"Don't make me the villain here. Progner, and the others who run Wellspring are the villains. They're brainwashing the public. They're making them so reliant on their technology that they can't even function during a power out."

"And what about progress? It's inevitable that technology will advance. It's human nature."

"You know, I'm so tired of that argument. Just because people will continue to do something, doesn't mean you should give up and let it happen. Mosquitoes will bite you every time you go out in the woods, but do you just shrug your shoulders and let them bite you. No, you fight them off with sprays and your own bare hands, as much as possible, every chance you get. And if people would stand up to bad technology the same way, and reject it, it would evolve. The market would adjust itself to meet people's needs. There can be Stream-like technology that's good. But people have to want it, and stop settling for anything that is dazzling and pretty."

"So, you just turn off the Stream. Blow it up. And hope you're around, or someone else with your vision is around to blow it up when it's rebuilt."

"Killian, give me some credit. I'm no longer a

teenager with Daddy issues, rebelling out of hormonal necessity. I don't want innocent people to get hurt."

"So, what is the plan?"

She kept her back to him "We remerge society. We bring the Streamers and nonswimmers back together."

"How?" Killian heard a car approaching in the distance and panicked. Ophelia looked up the road, but didn't seem concerned. She walked further away from him.

"We bring the nonswimmers into the city. We show the Streamers the power that real people hold over them and their fantasy world. Oh, Killian, we have it all worked out. But I need you. I need someone on the inside. I hate to ask you this, because I know how much you hate Wellspring, but…" she spun to face him, "I need you to go back to your job."

The nearing engine whined louder, but Ophelia didn't react, staring him down from a few feet away. She began to walk back toward him, keeping her umber eyes locked on his. She smiled. It was more than her usual smirk. She grinned widely, baring her teeth. Approaching, she wrapped her arms around his neck and kissed it, firmly, just below his jaw line.

"You agree, right? Something needs to be done?"

Killian's head nodded slowly without his permission. The car neared the top of the hill. He was facing away, down the road, toward the glimmering city. Suddenly he was afraid they might be coming for him, to take him back to the Stream. Just like she wanted. Did she betray *him*? He felt he might deserve that. He turned to face the rising noise, but Ophelia slid her long fingers up the back of his neck to the base of his skull, firmly preventing him from turning his head. She kissed his neck again.

"Now, please, tell me you're ready to make a difference in the world. Tell me you're the good man I've always believed you to be."

His body screamed to be free to spin and face the thundering of the decelerating engine, while simultaneously insisting that he never, ever, fight to free himself from her embrace.

"You want to help me," she barely whispered, "don't you?"

"I do."

COMMITMENT

Ophelia pulled away from Killian and moved toward the monstrous red pickup truck that had now cleared the hill. It eased to a halt beside her. The driver stepped out and she threw her arms around his neck and kissed his cheek. Killian touched his fingers to the scant moisture those same lips had just left on his neck.

But wait. He recognized the tall, older man, despite his costume of jeans and a cowboy hat. It was PMS. His client. How could *he* be out of the Stream? Did she bring him out as well? Was Killian not unique in his suffering for her plans? How many more men had she torturously extracted for her own use?

The pair approached. "Killian, you know Jeff."

"Of course," he mumbled.

"Jeff's going to take you the rest of the way. I have more work to do out here before I return." The smile again. Not the smirk he had clung to for so many months while he brushed his teeth. This was the full on, I've-taken-care-of-everything smile. She was already in her car, turning over the engine, before it sunk in with him that she was leaving.

"Wait," Killian pleaded, approaching her window.

"Killian, I need you back at that office. Near

Progner. I can't tell you any more because once you're in Stream, he'll be able to look through your memories. I'll contact you and let you know what to do when it's time."

She reached up to him, laying her hands lightly on his cheeks, pulling his face down to within inches of hers. "I need you to trust me, Killian. And I need to know that, this time, I can trust you."

She stared into his eyes, absorbing all of his attention. "You can," he mumbled. She kissed him passionately, though briefly. Her lips were gone. Her hands were gone. He closed his eyes to try to bring her back.

The screech of her tires as she turned the car wide, around the two men and the pickup truck, snapped Killian back into the scene. He opened his eyes to briefly glimpse the back of her car through the settling dust before it disappeared over the hill.

Jeff was climbing back in the giant truck. Killian approached the passenger door and reached up to open it. "*Women*. Am I right?" Jeff said.

Killian climbed in. Jeff started the truck up and shifted into gear. They began rolling down the hill. Toward the city. Killian suppressed a sudden urge to vomit. What was he doing? He had no idea if anything Ophelia told him was true. She'd offered no proof of her outrageous claims. If it was true that Progner was responsible for the deaths of his clients, why was she sending him back to get closer to him? And what about reentering the Stream? Would there be a reverse effect? If leaving the Stream knocked him out cold, for days, what about suddenly turning it back on? No, he knew the answer to that. He'd sent thousands of clients down the Stream. Sure, he introduced them slowly; just an hour the first time, under very heavy filters. But he was not a noob. Once you learned to swim, you never forgot, right?

Besides, Jeff here didn't seemed at all worried. Killian wondered if Jeff had been working with Ophelia all along. Of course he had. He'd been spying on Killian for her. Pretending to be a client. All Jeff ever did was come in and bitch about being a teacher. He wasn't any crazier than anyone else in Stream. Maybe he'd been able to come and go from the Stream all along too.

"Do you have the same off switch as Ophelia?"

Jeff looked over to Killian as if he just realized he was there. He removed his hat and set it on the dashboard. "Nope, I've got the old standard model. Shit Killian, you've been all up and down in my filter. Don't you think you'd have noticed if something was different?"

"So how did you get out here? Dona and I crashed into a tree..." It was not far up the road from them now. Killian watched his reflection in the passenger window race across the green blur of the passing forest. He looked for shreds of memory from his days spent sharing the pain of withdrawal with Dona. An unconscious and feverous Dona. Vulnerable and near death. Needing him in a completely different way than Ophelia.

Jeff looked to Killian a few times, waiting patiently for him to continue. Eventually he shrugged and said, "I've practiced. It's just like anything else. The more you do it, the more used to it you get. It turns out that whether or not you can turn the filter off doesn't really matter. Once the kids get to age six or so, they don't exercise that option unless they're forced. So within a few years, they're just as addicted as anyone else, and would suffer the same withdrawal. Opening the door to freedom doesn't give people the motivation to walk through it. That's one of Ophelia's sayings."

Jeff backed off the gas pedal a little as the road curved sharply to the left.

"Anyway, Ophelia and I decided that someone

should test the limits of Stream removal a little bit at a time. So I left the Stream for brief intervals over several months, building up a sort of tolerance to being without it. It was a lot less painful that way. Of course, she didn't expect to have to pull Dona out all at once like that. But Progner was onto her."

"What do you mean?"

"He found out the truth, when he started working with her. I told her it was too risky, her making contact with you. But she insisted. Then, as soon as he pushed you out of the picture, he began using her as his next test subject for his little God experiments."

What truth? Was she helping Ophelia? Dona? It was Killian's fault that Progner was working with Dona. If he hadn't pushed things and gotten himself suspended for a few days… But no, Progner would have found some excuse to suspend him regardless, if he really wanted to get to Dona.

"So Progner was behind it all. The voice that drove Hector and Elena and Evan to suicide. The voice that brought a paranoid, raving Dona to my apartment, begging for help?"

Jeff nodded. Killian watched the road curve out of sight into the trees just ahead, at the bottom of the hill. A vision of Dona sitting squint-eyed before her computer in her bedroom rose out of Killian's preStream memory fog. The car darkened as it entered denser walls of forest and the image from his past dissipated.

They must be getting close to the city. Near the area where Killian and Dona almost died. He scanned the shoulder of the road for tire tracks but they were moving too quickly. He prepared himself to make contact with the Stream again.

"You need to stop the truck," Killian said suddenly. "I can't go back without absorbing what you've told me.

And I want to see Dona. I demand it."

"Then you have to go forward. Sorry, buddy, but Wellspring's agents captured Dona this morning. Ophelia is worried about what Progner might do to her and she told me to get you back as fast as possible."

"What? Why? What the hell am I going to do?"

"Don't know. Just trust in her plan."

"But they'll kill her!"

"Possibly. Unlikely though, until Progner's sure he doesn't need her."

"Well, we've got to rescue her."

"You've got to stick to the plan. Ophelia knows what she's doing. But you've got to commit yourself mister."

As the truck came around the next curve in the road, Jeff slammed the brakes hard, thrusting Killian against the seatbelt. There was something blocking the road. It was a car of sorts, though it looked more like a dark oval bubble. Uniformly black and smooth it was without any visible breaks. Only the bottom half of the jet black wheels protruding from the edge of the body confirmed it was a land vehicle and not some alien spacecraft. A pair of boots stepped out of the empty blackness between the wheels. Darting his eyes up, Killian saw a figure pointing a tube at them over the hood, or the trunk, or whichever end of the car it was.

It was much too wide to be a gun.

Jeff filled his chest with air and clenched his teeth. "It casts a limited Stream field. It will use the Stream to overwhelm our minds and knock us unconscious," he muttered. "When you joined the Stream, you joined forever."

WAVE

[WAVE BLAST SODA!] screamed through Killian's mind. He covered his ears with his hands, ducking his head into his chest to absorb the full impact of the yell. But the noise was inside him. [Wave Blast Soda!] The phrase repeated, slightly softer this time. [Wave Blast Soda.] The echo continued to fade incrementally. As the three word phrase approached a nearly inaudible whisper, Killian opened his eyes.

  He could see the ocean before him. It was relatively calm. In the distance, a wave was building. As it grew taller the volume of the repeated phrase rose. He could smell the salty seawater, taste it dripping through his sinuses. But it wasn't just the ocean. There was also a faint scent of, cherry was it? Yes, he could taste cherry in the mist that drifted in with the light breeze. Far out, someone was surfing the wave. Naked. As the wave neared, the beautiful curves of her body clarified. She was smiling and had locked her eyes on Killian, while easily surfing what had become a ridiculously large wave. As she closed the space between them, and the smell and taste of cherry intensified, and the chant crescendoed, [WAVE BLAST SODA!] Killian closed his eyes. This, however, did nothing to eliminate the vision of the wave and the woman. This vision, the scent, and the taste all blasted through him simultaneously as the words [WAVE BLAST SODA!] reached maximum volume.

Killian felt a sadness dissipating as the words again died off and the water receded. That is, until he saw the next wave rising in the distance. He licked his lips, tasting a hint of grape this time, and discovering, much to his delight, that it was an entirely different, though equally attractive, naked woman effortlessly surfing this new wave.

After uncountable flavor waves, the picture finally dissolved. Killian saw a can of Orange Wave Blast, the flavor of the last wave, sitting on a desk before him. He grabbed the can and chugged it down furiously, dibbling much of it out of the corners of his mouth. When the can was empty, he dropped it to the desk and wiped his chin on his sleeve.

"Thanks," he said, to the man in a tie who sat placidly across the desk from him.

"Killian, do you know who I am?"

Before his brain could begin to contemplate the question that had been posed, let alone a possible answer, a name was whispered in his thoughts. [Progner.] He was connected to the Stream. A very strict filter seemed to be preventing him from accessing too much data at the moment, but he could see the time of day in the lower left corner, upon request. It appeared in glowing green digital numerals, just as he liked it. He closed his eyes and sensed that he was not alone.

"You are Progner," he said, examining the older man's features.

"And what is my purpose here? Why are you sitting at this desk with me?"

"I'm not sure. I think you're trying to convince me of something."

"Killian, I am your psychiatrist. I am trying to convince you to put your faith in me, so that I can help you heal."

"No, that doesn't seem right. I'm a psychiatrist."

The room disappeared and Killian was drawn into another advertisement. He returned with no memory of being in this room a few moments ago and grabbed at the box of Health-Es Cereal on the desk. He crammed his mouth with handfuls of the crunchy, delicious little Es until his tongue dried out so much he couldn't swallow. On the desk was a can of Wave Blast. He grabbed it, but it was empty. Next to it was another empty can and three empty Beta Bar wrappers.

"Stop it!"

"Stop what Killian?"

"Stop bombarding me with commercials."

"Killian," Progner shook his head slowly. "You have no job. You have no income at all. You are here, at Wellspring's psychiatric ward, because you have lost control of your mind. Since you have no income, you are subject to mass amounts of commercial advertisement in order to pay for the privilege of Streaming. Now, as your analyst, I can suspend the commercials on therapeutic grounds. But only if you are, to quote the manual, 'A voluntarily submissive and agreeable client, with reformative potential.'"

Progner raised his eyebrows lightly and let this sink in. "So, Killian, are you ready to begin healing?"

Killian heard the words [wave blast soda] whisper through his mind.

"Yes," he said.

"Then, I'll ask you again. Who am I?"

"You are Dr. Progner. My psychiatrist."

"Excellent. And what are we doing here?"

"You are attempting to help me separate what is real

from the convincing fantasy worlds I have created within the Stream?"

"Good Killian. Good. Not let's try to get back to the root of our discussions; guilt."

"I'm not guilty."

"Not guilty of what Killian?"

"I haven't done anything wrong."

"Killian, right and wrong are for God to judge, now that He is among us. I'm not here to judge you. I'm here to help you. Why can't you accept that?"

Because it felt wrong, in his gut. He watched Progner tap, tap, tap a Wellspring, Inc. pen on the shiny surface of the desk and he knew that *he* had sat on that side of the desk, tapping that same pen. The whole scene felt backwards. Even the degree on the wall with Progner's name on it felt out of place. Killian couldn't explain it, but his intestines wrenched and twisted every time he considered trusting this man. Why wouldn't he trust his own shrink?

"You don't trust me because you don't want to uncover the source of your guilt. You are becoming more and more paranoid that I might reveal it. Look, the bridge of your nose is sweating."

Killian took a moment to adjust to the fact that Progner could read his thoughts. Yes, he used to be able to read *his* clients' thoughts in session. That was standard procedure. Right?

"No Killian. You were never a psychiatrist. That is one of the fantasy worlds you've meticulously constructed. And what is so fascinating, yet simultaneously incredibly disturbing, is that in both of the fantasy worlds you created, you were miserable. As a psychiatrist you refused to accept Jadonism as a tool for helping your clients, and as a result they began killing themselves. And as if that wasn't torturous enough, you began losing your mind as well. Why would you choose to be so terrible at your make-believe profession?"

Gravity seemed to increase, pulling Killian lower into his chair.

"Still, one terrible existence wasn't enough. You created another life where you had reconnected with a high school crush. A very attractive young woman. She rebels against society itself. A girl like that could really make a man feel good about himself. And yet, you could not command her attention. She lead you around like a lost puppy. She got you to leave the Stream; an act you imagined to be so horrendous it nearly killed you. And then she abandoned you. Why would you create such a scenario if not to punish yourself; to purge yourself of some deeper guilt?"

"I didn't create Ophelia," Killian mumbled.

"Of course not. She exists. You knew her in high school. But you haven't seen her since then. Killian, why do you suppose that in both of your fantasy worlds you are unassertive, powerless, and tormented."

Progner waited a few moments, tapping that Wellspring pen again. Killian was not going to answer his question though. He slumped lower in the chair and solidified his pout.

"To get to the root of your guilt we need to unlock your memories of the summer you were fifteen. That appears to be when you first started blocking out the past. What could you have done back then that you still feel so guilty about?"

"I betrayed Ophelia."

"Right. Good!" Progner leaned forward in his chair, his eyes wide. "But we need to get you to actually remember it. Every last detail. Because Killian, you made the right decision back then. You have simply misinterpreted your regret as guilt. You regret that you had to rat out a friend, and therefore, you believe you've done wrong. But Killian, you did the right thing. And it's okay to remember it. I really do want to help Killian. And furthermore, I'm the only one you've got. It's either put your trust in me, or continue living in fantasy worlds forever."

"I want to remember."

"Beautiful." Progner sat back again. Killian envisioned a younger version of Progner drawn into the page of his sketchbook. The man before him did not wear glasses. In Stream, he didn't need to. He still kept his hair buzzed short, though, and it had neither receded nor grayed. He might be the most generic man on the planet. Yet he looked nothing like the man Killian once drew, surrounded by his own trashed living room. It was not the setting. Not the glasses. In his sketch he had captured a man inspired. This man, sitting across the desk from him, was only interested in shrinking.

"Now Killian, I'm going to send you a memory. It is a very brief scene. A conversation you and I had when you were much younger. It is my memory, so you will see yourself as I saw you. You will hear the thoughts I had that day. I'm hoping this will spark your own memory. Are you ready?"

Killian nodded and closed his eyes unnecessarily.

And there he was. He could see himself. He was young, so young. And thin. He was slumped sadly against the side wall of Progner's garage. He could feel a tinge of pity, Progner's pity, as Progner's eyes glanced over his pathetic form. But as the view slid out of the garage, across the chemically green lawn, and rested on the police cruiser parked in the Redenbacher's driveway across the street, all pity was smothered by the welling up of a tremendous sense of satisfaction.

In the open doorway of the Redenbacher's house, Ophelia appeared, her hands cuffed behind the small of her back. A police officer led her down the steps of the porch. Progner folded his arms and grinned. He briefly entertained an idea of what he might do with a handcuffed Ophelia, but didn't pursue the thought. This was better. He wanted to fully experience this moment.

The officer opened the back door of the cruiser. Ophelia spoke to him. He stood back a moment. Her eyes scanned past Progner and settled in the depths of his garage. She slid her bound hands as far to the right as she could. With her eyes focused on the shadows where Killian lurked, she dipped her left shoulder and raised her right hand beside her hip. Jiggling her fingers, she waved.

"No!" Killian screamed, thrusting his mind back into the surroundings of the office. "You bastard! It's your fault! Everything is your fault. She went to jail. And Elena and Hector and Evan died! And Dona… You murderer! You…!"

"Good Killian. Memory is based in emotion. Use your anger. Focus on what you might have been feeling, there in that garage. You just saw the events. You know you were there. Now, focus your feelings and see if you can put yourself back inside that scene, inside your own head."

Killian clenched his eyelids and his teeth.

"Now, evoke your own memory. Feel it. Tell me what you see."

"I see a giant wave being surfed by a series of naked women drinking sodas."

Progner let out his breath. "Very well," he said. "But you're only prolonging the inevitable. We'll start again when you are ready to be productive."

PERSPECTIVE

Before they invented the Stream, before dimmer switches or electric light of any kind, fire was the only resource humans had for holding back the cold darkness of nature. Depending on the time of year though, nights could be very long, and even the days could get unendurably cold. Early humans spent many, many hours gathered around their precious fires. And while humans love a good flashy light display, even the majesty of firelight got boring on long winter nights midway through an ice age. So, to entertain each other, humans began to tell stories.

Men back from exciting hunts told of their exploits to the old and the young who had to stay behind. Thus, the action/adventure story. Women, gathering in the forest and having their baby snatched by a large cat could bring the whole tribe to tears with their retelling. Thus, the drama. But what about when there was nothing new to report? What about those long months where humans did nothing but huddle around the fire? Well, that's when humans began to exaggerate in order to enhance their entertainment. Some caveman got up in front of the tribe and imitated the walk of an old guy with a large bite wound on his leg. He really played it up, acting just like the old man, speaking like he did, limping and whining about his pain. Everyone had a good laugh. Thus, the comedy. Perspective grew. Humans realized they didn't have to just tell their own story. In fact, they could make the whole thing up. Thus, fantasy and science fiction. Thus, paranormal-steampunk-teen-romantic-comedy. And so on.

Yes, that large and foldy brain humans evolved began to imagine worlds beyond their natural surroundings. Humans learned to separate themselves from their own instincts and emotions and look at the world from other points of view. This gave them the potential to grow tremendously in intellectual perspective. To develop into the most empathetic and noble of all creatures. And yet...

The game of pretending to be someone else culminated in the Stream, of course. In Stream, people no longer needed to pretend to be someone else, they could experience it. They could actually hear what someone else heard, see what he saw; even feel what he felt. Imagine how enlightening this could be. Why, with that kind of intimate understanding of others, there should be no sexism or racism or prejudice of any kind. In fact, not one form of known prejudice can be shown to have been reduced by Stream society. And, what's worse, several previously unimagined forms sprouted. For example, some people have developed an unreasonable hatred of dwarves, trolls or even aliens, depending on how much time they spent in certain Streamworlds.

So, if they weren't evolving toward a more open-minded race, what did Streamers use this new found power of perspective for? Well, most often they used it to expand the realm of possible sexual encounters available to them.

Sidney Freed claimed in his book, *The Four Stages of*

Sexual Development for the Typical Streaming Boy, that there were four questions which represented the levels of using Stream perspective to delve further into the sexual experience. The first question: what is it like to have sex with a girl? Boys no longer had to develop the complex social skills necessary to make this happen with a real girl. Thanks to the Stream and its ability to bring dreams to life, boys tended to lose their virtualginity just days after the onset of puberty.

Question two: what is it like to have sex with the hottest woman ever? According to Freed, this stage never really concludes, as there are an infinite combination of attributes to be tweaked and sampled. Plus tastes change with experience, and so really, it's an endless quest just determining the qualities of the most attractive women, let alone all the different ways one could have sex with her.

Question three: what is it like to have sex *as* a girl? Before the Stream, barring expensive operations, this stage was limited to a few daydreams over a lifetime. But thanks to the perspective granting powers of the Stream, stage three has become just another option for passing a lonesome afternoon.

And finally, question four: what is it like to have sex with myself? Called googling yourself, the term evolved from the name of a popular Internet search engine. When humans were limited to the Internet, they would frequently type their own names into the search box to discover how the world saw them. Where do I pop up? What access do others have to my secrets? What would someone else think if they googled me? But in Stream, people could go well beyond reviewing their own records and Internet trails. In Stream, a man could literally know himself intimately. He could experience the perspective of someone else while she was having intercourse with him.

Killian Peterson had no interest in googling himself, in the most recent sense of the word. In fact, he never wanted to see through someone else's eyes again. He wanted to be himself. To be whole again if possible. He remembered the hours and hours he spent donning the perspective of misguided, sometimes diseased, minds, in order to help right them again. Now Progner claimed that was all a fantasy, that he'd never been a Short Order Shrink at all. But how could that be? Even outside the Stream, Killian was haunted by the trinity of sharp objects that had been used to end his life. He couldn't believe all he had experienced and learned was but a dream. He had shuffled off three mortal coils in the line of duty, and learned that just because technology allowed people to do something, doesn't necessarily mean that they should. But was it a meaningful lesson if it never happened?

Despite his wishes, Killian found himself watching through someone else's eyes again. At first, he didn't know where he was, or what was going on. All he knew was that he was standing in the bedroom doorway of his parents' house looking at himself, as a teenager, lying on his bed.

Killian was not about to google himself. He was Progner. Progner had come to see him when he was fifteen. This was Progner's memory of that day.

Killian's own voice, muffled by the bedroom door, had told him to come in. Opening the door, Progner saw the boy slide a dark green book under his pillow. He wiped at his eyes, folded his arms across his chest and leaned back against the baby-blue wall.

Progner eased the door shut behind him. Throwing a leg over the desk chair, he sat down on it backwards so as to face Killian.

"Killian, I need to talk to you about Ophelia."

"Yeah?" Killian did his best to sneer, trying to appear tough enough to hide the obvious fact that he'd been bawling a few moments ago. There was no way in hell, Progner thought, he'd ever go back to being a teenager.

"I know about her plans. To use you in the Stream trial. I know she's going to introduce some kind of virus into the system. Killian, people will get hurt. You might get hurt, if you're hooked up. We can't allow her to go through with this."

"So what if a few people get hurt. Ophelia says a lot more will if the Stream is allowed to come online." Killian became conscious of a retreat into his navy blue comforter and sat up abruptly.

Progner sighed and gathered his argument in his head. How could he make this kid see his point of view? He obviously thinks he's in love with her. No logic would disillusion him. Should he bring up that he knows just how desirable and persuasive Ophelia can be? Shit, he tore his living room apart and quit his job to impress her and that hot little… He curbed his thoughts. Mentioning his own involvement with Ophelia would only piss the kid off.

"Look Killian, it's not about the Stream. The Stream is inevitable. It is the future of technology. If you stop this trial, another company will come along and do the same thing. If not next month, then next year. The point is that the development of technology is human nature, and trying to stop it is futile."

"There's something to be said for slowing it down," Killian blurted. His hand slid under his pillow, where he was hiding that green book. "At least until we're more ready."

The kid was prepared. Progner was a little surprised.

It only occurred to him half an hour ago that he could just come over here, ring his doorbell and ask to speak to him.

"All right. I'll give you that. But still, Ophelia doesn't believe that. She doesn't believe stopping the Stream trial will slow down technological advancement significantly enough to make a difference. She only wants to make sure her father doesn't get the credit for it. Hell, she'd probably help launch the Stream, so long as it was another company beating her old man to it."

Progner got up from the chair and turned his back to Killian, rubbing his chin and feigning thought. He could hear the boy squirming on the bed. Had she deflowered him? Could a boy be deflowered? What was it called for a boy then? Devirginization? This kid was what, fifteen? He looked like a damn child. No, she couldn't have. She shouldn't have had to. That girl could have gotten a spineless kid like this to do her bidding just by promising a peek at her sweater meat.

"Killian," Progner spun around and said in a deep, paternal voice that snapped the kid's attention to him, "do you really want to go to jail just so she can get back at her daddy? It's hardly a noble cause worthy of rotting in a cell. I can still get you out of this. I can reverse all of this. You've just got to want to do what's right. Step outside of yourself for a moment and I think you'll see how obvious the right choice is."

WANT

"Killian, suppose you tell me exactly what it is you want?" Progner said across the desk of... whose office? Progner was on the doctor's side of the desk. The walls were blank except for the diploma. Whose diploma? Killian rolled his eyes toward it.

"Killian!" Progner snapped, drawing his attention back. "I've tried simply scanning your memories. I've tried showing you some of mine, to incite you to remember. I've tried coercion...."

[Wave Blast...]

Killian let his eyes drift back toward the frame on the wall, but Progner briskly tapped his pen on the desk, drawing his attention right back.

"The point is," Progner barked shrilly enough to ensure his continued command of Killian's attention, "that you refuse to cooperate, whether you're fully conscious or not. So I'm at a loss. See, I've got a dangerous terrorist who wants to blow up the Stream, and possibly kill everyone connected to it. And I've got you, once again, caught up in her plans. But this time, you won't listen to reason."

"What reason have you tried?"

"Come on, Killian. Isn't it obvious. She's pulling the

exact same crap on you that she pulled ten years ago!" He slapped the pen down, ground his teeth and waited until he could continue in a calmer tone. "Let's see, she slowly introduced herself into your life. A glimpse, nothing more."

Killian remembered the subtle smirk across the quiZblitZ table.

"Then another glimpse a few weeks later. Then a brief encounter. Just enough to keep her fresh in your mind, but still unknown, still mysterious. She probably found some excuse to change her clothes in front of you. Am I right?"

Killian couldn't stifle his grin.

"I'm guessing she kissed you. Was there more this time, now that you're a real grown up man?"

"Shut up."

"That's right, get angry. She used you before, and she's doing it again. She's counting on the fact that you feel so guilty about betraying her that this time you'll be true no matter what. But Killian, people's lives are at stake again. You saw reason last time. I showed you my memory of it. And even if you continue to block your own, you have to admit that you did what was right before. So what will it take to get you to do what's right this time? What do you want?"

Want. The word reverberated. [Want, want, want.] What did he *want?* Out of life? Out of this moment? What did *he* want? When was the last time he really considered this question? [Want, want, want.] The word sounded funny if he repeated it enough. [Want, want.] Was it a real word? Was he pronouncing it correctly? Why did it sound so foreign?

His eyes drifted back toward the wall with the diploma. Was his name on it, like he thought he remembered? He wanted the truth.

"Killian! Try to focus here."

He wanted to be left alone. Yes, he wanted to be able to navigate his own life, at his own pace. He was always getting caught up in the torrent of someone else's problems.

He could feel Progner's mind hovering on the edge of his, waiting greedily for an answer. But he couldn't answer. He couldn't cooperate and give Progner what he wanted. He didn't trust Progner. No matter how convincing his logic or his illusions, Killian's gut tightened whenever Progner spoke to him.

He looked up into his dark, squinted eyes. There was none of the inspiration he had captured when he drew him so many years ago. The inspiration, incited by Ophelia, to tear apart his room, to quit his job, to rebel. The inspiration that spread to Killian, filled him with the insight to draw truth. It had made him an artist. It had given him a dream.

But none of the youthful curiosity behind the penciled eyes of that sketch showed in the cold, calculating stare of the Progner across the desk from him now. Here were focused eyes, forever searching out a shortcut, a reprieve from an over-scheduled agenda.

"I want a priest," Killian blurted.

"What?" Progner nearly stood, but checked himself. "No, you hate the clergy. You're confused." He leaned back in his chair.

"No. Yes. No, I'm not confused, and yes, I want a priest." A memory sparked to life. He did a quick search on specifics of the Faith Bill. "The law states that a Streamer who asks for a priest in session cannot be denied his request. I've requested one, and that request is recorded in Stream, and unless you want to create a record of your attempts to thwart my religious rights...."

"This will only complicate things."

"I'm waiting."

"Relax." Progner picked up that pen again and rolled it roughly between his thumb and index finger. "A priest is on the way."

The two men sat, staring at each other, absorbed in the act of containing their thoughts. Killian didn't really want to see a priest. Progner was right; it would complicate things. But he wanted a witness. He was genuinely afraid of Progner. Who knew what he'd do if he got frustrated enough. Who knew what he had already done. According to Ophelia, he drove Evan and Hector and Elena to their deaths. And Killian knew what he didn't want. He knew for certain, since he'd experienced it hundreds of times already. He didn't want to kill himself.

Paul appeared in the dark rectangle of the office doorway. Dressed all in black, he existed only as a mop of white hair floating above a sparkling grin. "Praise Jadon."

"God is among us," Progner responded. Killian squirmed in his chair. It didn't seem right, Progner touting religion. But then, he really had no idea what *would* seem right any more.

"Of course He is," Paul replied. "But we should not forget all that Jadon accomplished to help prepare us to receive our Lord."

Progner turned a quick scowl at the priest. They both held that look of mild constipation that suggested they were communicating in Stream. Paul looked away first, then walked slowly toward the seat next to Killian, across the desk from Progner, and sat. He used his fingers to push the mess of white hair across his forehead, out of his eyes.

"Hello Killian, how are you?"

"Not sure yet. Can I get back to you?"

Paul looked to Progner and forced his lips to drop into a exaggerated child's pout. "No progress?"

"No. He's stubborn."

The butterflies in Killian's stomach grew claws and began shredding the walls of his digestive system.

"Our friend Mr Peterson has requested your presence. Of course, he is still classified as critical, and I could deny access, even to a priest, if I feel it is therapeutically essential..." he flashed his eyes at Killian, then back to Paul, "but the truth is, I'm not getting anywhere. Maybe you can help."

"I'll do my best. May I suggest we all start fresh with some meditation. Clear our minds and hopefully, open them a bit."

Progner rolled his eyes, at first in contempt, but he held them pointed toward the ceiling while he searched out some brief entertainment to fill his wait.

"Killian," Paul said, turning to face the younger man, "fill your mind with the image of a sheet of white paper. Count each breath you take in. Count the pause between. Count the exhale. Pause. Inhale. Eventually, when you regulate your breathing, you should let the paper dissolve. Think of nothing. Don't deny your thoughts. Allow them to drift past without commanding your attention."

Killian closed his eyes and tried to slow his breathing. He could feel the presence of the other two men. He could feel the presence of the Stream, though much more weakly than he was accustomed. Progner had his filter cranked down pretty tight still. He called up a piece of paper and tried to focus on it. But the page he saw was not white. It had a drawing on it. A drawing of Ophelia. Ophelia? But he never drew Ophelia. Where did this image come from?

"Killian, stop counting your breaths now. Imagine each inhalation as filling your body with energy, and each exhalation as returning that energy to the universe around you."

It was gone. The drawing, the page. Killian tried to see his breath as a visible wind, filling him with energy. But his mind wandered and he couldn't ignore where it ventured. There was so much it needed to piece together. To remember. He didn't want to focus on his breathing. He didn't want to forget.

A slight panic gurgled in his stomach. Something felt wrong. Paul was gone. Progner was still there. Killian could sense his usual, slightly irritated mind. Yet, Progner was alone. Paul was gone! Killian couldn't sense him at all.

Killian opened his eyes and saw the priest still sat next to him on the floor. They had moved the chairs back to sit in front of the desk, and Paul was still there, sitting cross-legged, blank eyes staring slightly down at the desk in front of him.

Killian closed his eyes and Paul disappeared again. He opened them, and Paul was back.

He closed his eyes once more, but this time he sensed Paul's presence in Stream just as he heard Paul's voice within his head. [You're not meditating.]

"Sorry, I'm having trouble. What just happened?"

"I beg your pardon?"

"You just disappeared from the Stream. I couldn't sense you at all."

"Oh, that." Stretching his arms above his head with a yawn, Paul cautiously eyed Progner, while sending his thoughts to Killian. [It turns out that, when meditating correctly, one can achieve a state of mind so peaceful it activates the sleep boot. Your Stream filter misreads your mind as sleeping and kicks off the Stream connection temporarily. Jadon discovered this and passed it on to his closest followers just before disappearing himself."

"But why don't you suffer withdrawal?"

"Because it happens while in complete control of

the mind. And, at first, only for very brief periods. Jadon encourages practicing meditation on this level, so that the mind does not become dependent on the Stream."

Yes, Killian realized. So people who do leave the Stream won't endure the torture he and Dona did. But why? What are the priests preparing for?

"Shouldn't we get back to Killian's problems?" Progner interrupted.

Killian stood up, put his palms on his lower back, and arched his spine. He pulled his chair back to the desk and sat. Paul did the same.

"Well," Killian said, "a large part of my problem is that I don't seem to be aware of everything that's going on. You said before that God is among us now. What did you mean by that?"

Progner looked to Paul and twisted the corners of his mouth up slyly. "You want to take this one?"

Paul slid his bangs aside with his fingers and turned his grin toward Killian. "Everything that Jadon has predicted has come true. The Stream has developed a consciousness of its own. Finally, humans have the Father they've always wanted. No longer are we the lesser bastards of an indifferent universe. Drawing on all the past and present knowledge of human society, and the raw brainpower of all the minds tuned in to Him; God knows our thoughts. He hears our prayers. No longer are we whispering into the void."

[Hello?]

"No, idiot," Progner exhaled. "It's not a direct line. You can't just whistle or ring a bell and he'll appear and tell you the meaning of life."

"But He is listening Killian," Paul said. "And He is speaking. God has revealed glimpses of his plan to blessed prophets of his choosing. He has spoken to The Three. And he will continue to send messages through others, when the time is ripe to steer us."

"His plan?" Killian looked to Progner here. [What is *his* plan?] he thought to the man behind the desk. He suspected this *God* had not evolved from the minds of all Streamers, but was developed to appear that way. Developed exclusively by Progner. Tested on Hector and Elena and Evan.

Progner remained statuesque, despite his ability to hear these thoughts of Killian's.

"Yes Killian," Paul answered. Killian twisted to the wide blue eyes that focused a little too intently on him. "God wants the human race to develop to its fullest potential. He has said that we are at a crucial point in history. He doesn't want to tell us exactly what to do, but believes that hints and reminders, through meticulously selected prophets, will guide us in the right direction."

"How do you know they're not faking it?"
"The Three?" Paul looked confused.

"Because," Progner said tersely, "they make the memory of God's contact with them available to the public. God's voice cannot be traced to a location. All communication in Stream is tagged with a source locator beacon. But God's messages come from nowhere. From the Stream itself. You can't fake a message like that. But enough of this." Progner opened his top drawer, dropped the Wellspring, Inc. pen into it, and slammed it shut. "I have other clients, other business matters that require my attention. We need to move away from these topics of distraction and back to recovering your lost memories."

"What is it *you* want?" Killian blurted.

"Excuse me?"

"It's a pretty simple question. What do you want from me? And don't give me that 'your mental well-being bullshit.' What's your angle?"

"I believe I've been fairly transparent about that

Killian. Ophelia Redenbacher has plans to destroy the Stream. Again. And you are, currently, my only clue to figuring out her next move. I admit, I thought it might be easier to elicit your aid in this. I had hoped that by now, I'd have had something to go on."

"I want to go home."

"Which home Killian? The home on Springer Street that you think you saw, when you think you were outside of the Stream?"

Killian looked to Paul, but he offered only his unwavering countenance of approval.

"No. Just to my apartment." He got out of his chair and paced around behind it. "I need to be in familiar surroundings. My sketchbook is there, and that started triggering my memories. Besides, I need to relax. My brain is about to overload, and that's not helpful to anyone."

"Killian, you are unstable. You have been committed to my care. I can't allow you to wander the streets on your own…"

"Paul could accompany me," he blurted, surprising himself. "I need help with my meditation, and perhaps with his calming presence, I'll begin to remember more." Killian turned to the vapid eyes above the shiny rows of teeth to his left. He couldn't believe he was choosing Paul. A priest. But his intuition told him he was the lesser of two evils. "That is, if Paul doesn't mind."

"I'm here to help those who need."

"Well…" Progner sputtered.

"It's not like you won't be able to hear anything we talk about. Besides, what's your other option? It won't speed things up to keep me imprisoned if I refuse to cooperate, will it? You've tried all your tricks. You've had no results. Time to try what I want." Killian took a few steps toward the door.

"I haven't quite exhausted my 'tricks' as you put it."

Killian looked cautiously to the ceiling.

"But we'll try it your way," Progner continued. "For now. It is the smoother option. Of course, I'll need to keep your filter fairly tight. The last thing we need is you slipping toward Streammadness all over again."

Paul stood and folded his hands in front of his least priestly parts, waiting to follow Killian. He stood smiling, always smiling.

ADMISSION

"Do you mind if we walk?" Killian asked, curious what the old man would respond.

"Whatever you like," Paul said softly without allowing the corners of his mouth to droop. Even as they opened the door to the street, and an icy blast of wind tried to push them back in, Paul, wearing an open-collared, short sleeve shirt, didn't complain. He persevered, teeth first, out into the cold.

It was evening. That was surprising. For some reason Killian thought it was early morning. Outside the Stream, he never forgot what time of day it was.

"Do you walk outside often?" Paul asked.

"Not sure. I think so. But then, Progner claims most of what I think is delusion."

"Yes, well, he has your best interest at heart."

Killian paused for a moment, unsure of Paul's tone. Was he trying to subtly signal him, or was he just another drone following orders? He had to admit that he didn't know a thing about this man he'd worked with for over a year. The Stream should allow him to know others more intimately, since it allowed him to sense the mood of their thoughts, not just hear the words. But Killian knew no one in Stream as well as those few neighbors he once drew into his sketchbook. The rush of the Stream prevented him from seeing the truth of still life.

Before, when Paul represented an overzealous new religion, pushing itself on a people confused by the instability of their situation, Killian hated him. He kept his distance to make sure he didn't taint his hatred by getting to know him better. But here he was, leading Paul to his apartment because, apparently, he had more faith in this priest than his own boss. Killian was no longer sure what he believed, which made it difficult to hate Paul. And without that base emotion, he felt nothing. All he knew was that he didn't get sick to his stomach when he thought about confiding in Paul.

Paul continued his leisurely pace, his hands clasped at the small of his back. Killian dropped back half a block, for the illusion of privacy. Of course, Progner could be listening to every thought he had. Not really, though. Not practically speaking. It wouldn't be easy to sit in his office all day monitoring every synapse that fired in Killian's brain. It would mean suppressing his own thoughts completely and focusing his entire attention span on Killian. Progner wasn't that patient. Most likely he'd wait until later, then fast forward through Killian's thoughts, searching for certain key words.

Killian closed his eyes and felt the icy air invade his lungs. It wakened the memory of lying beside the stream in the woods. The stream made of actual flowing water, where he and Dona were baptized by nature. Granted a temporary reprieve of all their technological sins. He could see the trees, the rocks, the water. Dona, lying in the mud on her back. In contrast to the rhythmic chirping of crickets, he could hear her faint, irregular wheezing. Yet, the memory, recorded now in Stream, wasn't as real as being there. Sure, he could stare up into the leaves and contemplate the patterns they drew out on the clouds beyond. He could feel the wind on his cheeks, smell the pine needles scattered beneath his knees. He could go back to that exact scene, with the freedom to explore every detail of it. Even those he missed the first time. And that's exactly what made it less real.

While Killian was outside the Stream with Dona, he had no freedom of thought. Every scrap of brainpower he could summon was assigned to figuring out how to survive for the next fifteen minutes. When he was sure he would die relatively soon, the urgency of the situation energized him. It made him feel more alive than he'd ever felt.

He wished to actually return there, not cheapen it with a recorded memory.

He wanted to feel alive again.

As Killian stepped into his apartment, his energy level drained. These rooms in no way defined him. The blasé furniture was probably ordered from a Stream ad, tagged: 'the most impersonal' collection. He never hung anything on the walls because, well, why should he? The Stream provided all the posters and photographs and artwork he could ever want. He could sit in an empty room his whole life and never know it. If a paperboy rang his doorbell and wanted to sketch Killian, what would he surround him with? Would he be no more than a mannequin's head afloat on a white page?

Being back on Springer Street hadn't felt like home either. The home of his youth, decimated as it was, elicited little nostalgia. It was his parents' home. He'd always thought of it more as a temporary launching point.

Launching to what though? Because here, in the future, in the adult world of the Stream, he felt less at home than ever before.

Had he selected this color paint for the walls, or were they like this when he moved in? His couch, black and unadorned, was neither comfortable nor complaint worthy. There wasn't one thing in this whole place that described him. He wished to destroy it in a sweeping tornado of rage. Inspired to action, like Progner in the sketch he had drawn. He spied his sketchbook on his coffee table. He stepped nearer and ran a finger over the rough cover. It really was here. This anachronism from the real world. How did it get here? It must have been Ophelia! Yes; she could turn off her Stream connection. She wanted to begin triggering his memories, so he'd feel guilty about betraying her. But that meant... was he admitting Progner might be right?

Just thinking about Progner gave rise to a tightening in Killian's abdomen. No. Progner couldn't be right. Life in the Stream was horrible. And Ophelia said she didn't want to blow up the Stream anymore. What had she said? Something about remerging society. Yes.

Killian grabbed his sketchbook and sat back with it. The dark green hard cover was closed on seven portraits that represented youthful hope. Hope that he might have a gift. That he might be something extraordinary someday. Seven portraits, followed by the blank page that symbolized his failure to realize his potential. He never did become an artist. He never became a rebel. Never became Ophelia's lover. None of his dreams came true. He stopped drawing because his inspiration to create art was replaced by his obsession with Ophelia. But he failed to become what she inspired in him, didn't he?

"I found some tea," Paul said from the kitchen. "Would you like some?"

"Sure. But I'm going to shower first." Killian moved to his bathroom. Being in his own place might not be promoting relaxation, but just being out from under Progner's gaze was starting to help.

He started the shower and went to his bedroom

closet. When was the last time he changed clothes? He was not even sure where he got the clothes he was wearing. They were his though, weren't they? He checked his closet for duplicates of the pale blue button down and faded khakis he was wearing, but they were not there. These weren't the clothes he was wearing in his memories outside the Stream. Did someone come here and get his clothes and dress him? Or was he here and changed himself and can't remember?

It was exhausting, not knowing all the time.

He dropped the clothes in a laundry basket and entered the shower, forgetting everything as the warm spray cleansed his worries gently down the drain.

After showering, Killian drifted through the steam toward the sink. The mirror was broken. It reflected the future. The Killian it showed was at least five years older and in need of a good night's sleep. In five years, would he still see five years ahead? Or was he aging exponentially faster than the calendar? Would he look fifteen years older in five years time? Twenty? What he wanted the mirror to show him was backward, to a Killian who still wanted to look forward.

He tried to grin. It looked awkward. Of course, his teeth were filmy. Where was his toothbrush?

Ah, the familiar cleansing vibrations. And there she was: Ophelia Redenbacher. Watching him with her uncompromising glare. Maybe Progner was right, that it was no accident that she had appeared in quiZblitZ that day. Maybe it was all part of her calculated plan. Maybe she was just using him to get what she wanted.

So what? If she was manipulating him to accomplish what's right, was that so bad? He scrubbed hard at his molars. [Smile, Ophelia, please smile. I won't let you down this time.] He scrubbed harder, shoving the vibrations back behind his teeth, far up into his gums.

The timer counted down. And there it was. Her subtle smirk of approval.

The full color smirk melted into the gray sketch lines of a drawing of Ophelia. It stayed but a moment, then faded. Like a memory. But he never drew Ophelia.

Throwing on a dark T-shirt and some jeans, Killian went back to his living room where Paul sat, sipping from a blank white mug. There was another steaming mug on the coffee table beside the sketchbook. Killian grabbed the book and flipped through the drawings. Only seven. No Ophelia.

He couldn't recall the image he had just seen. "Why can't I rewind something I just remembered?"

"You should be able to. It could be because your filter is so strict. Progner is afraid of what might happen if your fragile mind is given too much access. Remember what is was like when he wasn't blocking the advertisements?"

[Wave Blast…]

"I can't trust anything if I don't know what he's keeping from me."

"Perhaps." Paul set his tea on the coffee table and slid to the edge of the chair. "Killian, I would like to share something with you. Please, sit down. Have some tea."

Killian sat.

"It makes some sense, what Progner said about triggering your memories by showing you his. With your permission Killian, I'd like to attempt to do just that."

Killian looked the priest up and down and frowned. "What memories are you taking about? I didn't know you before the Stream."

"Not my memories. A mutual friend's."

Killian scrunched his brow, but he had to speak the word, "who?" before Paul answered.

"Dona Redenbacher's."

"You know Dona? You have her memories?"

"She has given me some select memories, yes. Perhaps, if you see some of the scenes you are missing through her eyes, you will understand more."

"But how? Where is she?"

"We'll discuss that later. She gave me these memories before the two of you left the Stream, with instructions to pass them on to you."

"That actually happened? We were outside the Stream. It wasn't a delusion, like Progner insists. You admit it?"

"Don't act so surprised. You knew this was true. You felt it."

"Still, it's nice to have confirmation. Does this mean that Progner…"

"Shh, don't draw attention to anything Progner might be scanning for. Our time here is limited and we should get started. Killian, you need to practice your meditation. Done properly you can boot your mind from the Stream, like I did earlier. Learning to do this will admit you to the growing band of those who are preparing for what is to come. It might just save your life."

TORN

Dona Redenbacher, having been in the Stream for almost a year, had grown accustomed to sensing the presence of others. So naturally, she shrieked and leapt back a few feet when she saw a young man sitting outside her apartment whom she didn't sense first. When her heart stopped trying to beat itself to death, she allowed her curiosity to scan him. He seemed deflated, like the crack between the floor and wall was slowly sucking the life from him. He was there, but just barely. Visible, but nothing more.

She waited for her heart rate to fall back to a sensible level, or for him to move and startle it into rising further. He was persistent in his refusal to display any sign of movement and so her pulse settled down. Was he even breathing? She took a few steps closer. His back was melted against the faded wallpaper, but his head had peeled forward toward his feet. She took a few steps closer. Did she recognize him? Her approach continued to fail to stir any movement. She did recognize him.

"Hello, Killian. What brings you here?"

When she spoke his name he began to scan the air apprehensively. His eyes found her and did their best to lock on. "I need your help," he muttered.

The plea caused her pulse to quicken anew and she turned away from him when she felt her cheeks begin to flush. "Come in," she whispered, retreating into her apartment.

By the time he appeared in the doorway she had grown tired of pacing and had curled her legs beneath her on one end of her couch. He seemed drained down two or three inches from his full height. His left hand clutched strenuously at nothing. Squeezing angrily at the very air that dared to come between his clenched fingers. But his right hand held his dark green sketchbook with respectful delicacy. Held it by the furthest corner, as if touching it too roughly might taint its purity.

These opposing feelings; the anger in his left hand and the empathy in his right, rose up his arms and met violently in his eyes. The resulting mood storm spilled out over the room and flooded Dona with nostalgia. She wished to be washed from the couch and into his arms. She wanted to embrace him and absorb his pain. She remembered this feeling. Her left hand contorted in mimicry of his. Twisting the end of her cotton skirt between her wrenched fingers, she found no comfort in the softness of the material.

"Whatcha got?" she asked.

He rolled his eyes downward, toward the book he held. She knew what it was. She'd seen the collection of brilliant sketches he'd produced. She'd even encouraged the last one. The picture of Ophelia. The one that made him see the truth beneath her sister's gorgeous exterior. The one that helped convince him to betray Ophelia, just as Dona had wanted. But that betrayal had not caused Killian to come running to her, as she had dreamed. In fact, he didn't really speak to her at all, afterward. He avoided her if he saw her in the halls at school. And a few months later, when she moved to the city with her mother, he remained out in non-swimmer land to sulk.

But here he was, coming to her now, with that sweet look of desperation on his face.

"Take it," he said, though he didn't move the arm that held the sketchbook. "I can't ever look at it again."

The surprise of seeing him was wearing off. It was clear he hadn't been sleeping much and had lost some weight. He wouldn't sit, or relax. He just stood there looking as pathetic as ever. But *she* had grown. More than he could imagine.

"Killian, please, sit down." He obeyed, plopping onto the love-seat and expelling the last traces of oxygen his lungs had been clinging to.

"I wanted to be an artist you know."

"You are an artist Killian."

"No. No, I haven't drawn anything in forever. Drawing Oph… It ruined her. It ruined me. I don't want to wield that kind of power again. Here, take it." He held the book out until she removed it from his hand, then allowed his arm to die alongside the rest of his body.

Flipping open the book, Dona admired the drawing of Progner. The detail. It was so real. Somehow, the colorless, two-dimensional representation was even more lifelike than the digital playback of Stream memory. It was not a video capture of life. It was a moment, frozen forever. Reduced to lines and shades and the bare minimum of form. But you couldn't distort it, or push past it, or alter it, or distract yourself from it. It was unalterable, and therefore forced you to deal with the reality of it.

"You have a gift Killian. An insight into others. You can't turn your back on it."

"If only I could forget. But I can't. I think about her whenever I pick up a pencil. I think about her all the time. Still. Is she sitting in some cold, dark cell, thinking about how terrible every hour of her life is, because of me? Or worse: is she being beaten, or stabbed by some woman who murdered three husbands, all because I couldn't follow through with a plan. I couldn't keep a promise. And that's what's so bad, I guess. Not that I realized she was wrong and stopped her. It's that I pledged my support. I gave my word that I would help her, and then I stabbed her in the back."

Tears welled up again in his eyes, but he didn't wipe at them. They dangled on the edge of his lashes until Dona had to look away or take her own sleeve to them.

She flipped through the portraits to the eighth page. The picture of her. Dona had been flattered when he first showed her. Flattered, at first, that he had paid enough attention to her to be able to draw her at all. But further flattered, elated even, at the way the picture exposed her secret desire. Her vision of herself, which she had shared with no one, but which she would have gladly shared with Killian. Somehow, he had received her thoughts without words. Did he suspect what she was doing, here in the Stream? The drawing suggested he might, if he thought about it. To her, the drawing had conveyed that her deep interest in him was reciprocal. At least, it seemed so; until she turned the page.

The ninth portrait. Ophelia. It was no less impressive than the other eight. It might even be his best work. He had captured her sister's soul.

Ophelia had still been a few months shy of eighteen when she was arrested, which had prevented the judge from sentencing her too harshly. Dona had only a couple of years to prepare for her release from prison. A couple of years to change the world.

Dona flipped the page back, then skillfully grabbed both the eighth and ninth portraits as if they were one sheet and tore them from the binding.

Killian looked up, his mouth agape, "What are you…"

She thrust the book into his hands, got up and moved to her desk by the window. She stashed the torn drawings in the top drawer, then slammed it shut with her hip.

"Killian, what if I told you there was a way to forget? To move on with your life, and not waste it away dreaming of a girl who doesn't deserve you?"

He looked up at her, his lower lip sagging. "I'd say I might be interested."

Killian was torn from the memory, from Dona's perspective. New information swirled inside, boiling up new questions. He had drawn Ophelia. But he also drew Dona? Why did she rip out both drawings? What's so important about them? Did *she* block his memories after he joined the Stream? How long did she have feelings for him?

[Killian, breathe.]

He stood, and stumbled, grabbing the back of his couch for stability.

[Sit, Killian, focus your mind with me.] It was Paul's voice in his head.

"*She* blocked my memories in the Stream somehow. It wasn't Progner. Just after I dove in, she blocked them out for me. Because I wanted it."

He fell back, bouncing off the wall and tripping toward the counter in the kitchen, where he caught himself. He saw an object that he knew could not be there. Yet, he could feel it in his grip. It was a plastic-handled screwdriver, with fresh blood on the metal tip. He felt a sudden impulse to thrust it toward his forehead. He screamed and suddenly saw a large oak tree through the cracked windshield of a crashed car.

"Killian," Paul said, bracing his shoulders from behind. "There is more you must know. We have little time. You can do this, if you focus." Paul led him back to the living room, where he helped him to the floor. From a pocket in his loose black sweater he produced some folded paper.

"I can't think. The noises. There are too many sounds. Too many pictures."

"It's a Streamquake. They've been getting more and more frequent, ever since Jadon went missing. And more intense. If you meditate, you can maintain focus. If everyone would calm their minds the quakes would cease again. But, they don't get it. When they thought they were working toward God they worked hard. Now that they think He's among them, they don't see the need."

Paul unfolded the papers.

"When you entered the Stream, Killian, Dona helped block your memories. But they were only hidden, not locked. You could have regained them whenever you wanted. That was always within your power. In fact, seeing your sketchbook again triggered some of those memories. Your drawings, the most intimate expression of your youth, held the key to reengaging your past. Here are the missing two drawings. They may help you fill in all the gaps in your memory. If that's still what you want."

Paul placed the folded sketches on the coffee table.

Killian touched the paper with his finger and an image of Dona sitting in her bedroom flashed in his mind. He let go. He made this decision before, right? He decided not to suffer the slings and arrows of outrageous fortune, but to forget them. Why should he now take up arms against a Stream of troubles? Couldn't he just continue to forget?

But the ghostly screwdriver compelled him. He wasn't happy forgetting. He probably wouldn't be happy remembering. Once again he was torn between two decisions that others have forced on him. Why couldn't he be left alone, to gently navigate his own life?

DRAWN

"Accurate memory doesn't serve nature," Dona said. "Nature is not interested in the individual, and therefore, the individual is not evolutionarily valid." She was sitting on his bed when he came in from finishing his paper route. His temples were moist with sweat since he just jogged past the last twelve houses. The twelve between the Redenbacher's house and his own.

Killian was getting used to Dona being on his bed when he finished his paper route every afternoon. For two weeks she had followed him off the bus and into his room to play Warriorspawn while he delivered the news. Her Game Depot was broken. But today, when he popped in the room and fell into his navy blue beanbag chair, he noticed right away that the TV wasn't even on. Dona wasn't holding a game controller in her hand. She was holding his sketchbook.

She spoke out of the side of her mouth at him, but her eyes stayed locked on the drawings. "Nature is only interested in evolving in all directions. In trying every possibility of life. It is the ultimate scientist. The purpose of memory in nature is to provide raw material for the subconscious, which can use that data to imagine other scenarios and anticipate them, so it can better adapt to changing environments."

Yes, Stupid Theory Girl. She'd always been like that. Long before she showed up in his office looking for help. This was his memory, not hers. He was in his own body, seeing her, though hardly noticing her. Like he was fifteen all over again.

His stomach tightened with each thought, as each thought returned to Ophelia. He'd been in her bedroom only moments ago. Just before his short run home.

"But," Dona continued, "it doesn't serve natural selection to remember rigid snapshots. Nature has no interest in preserving, only in evolving. Preservation is the human interest in rising above nature and feeling a touch of the eternal."

She flashed her eyes over him, then returned to studying his artwork. He wasn't sure he wanted her just glancing through his sketches. Had she seen the latest one yet? He opened his mouth to emit the silence within.

"This is why you draw. This is why all artists work. It puts you in touch with eternity to preserve a moment of your brief time on Earth. It lets you glimpse divinity, to create a more permanent record than the transient memory system you were born with."

She leaned back against the wall, tipping the book to better catch the light.

"This is exactly why my father, and everyone else with a brain full of gears and circuitry, will create the Stream. It can preserve all that we are afraid to lose. More than snapshots and video clips and daily journal entries. It will, eventually, preserve everything. Feelings, and opinions, and whole minds. It gives us a sense of eternity, and therefore seems a more suitable god than the cold indifference of nature."

She flipped slowly through the sketches, admiring each one. While her eyes scanned the details of his work, he was haunted by the blank page he couldn't fill. He could still see the lines that made up Mr. Haroki as clear as he could look down and see his own clenched fist. But despite the fact that he, only moments ago, had been studying a great deal more of Ophelia than he thought he ever would, he couldn't call her up in his mind.

"These are beautiful, Killian," Dona said. "I'm astonished. The lines are so crisp, the darks and lights so contrasting. The pictures pop. They jump off the page. But, beyond the technical skill and the style of the artwork, you have a gift for stripping people of the objects and clothing you mockingly surround them with, and getting at the truth of their existence. You don't think when you draw do you? You follow your gut. And you capture the whole of a person in a single pose. They're amazing."

Dona turned the page. She froze. Only her eyes moved as they scanned the page voraciously. It was a drawing of her. Killian had finished it yesterday evening. He hadn't planned on drawing her. Despite the fact that she spent more than an hour a day in his bedroom, before he drew her, he scarcely knew she existed. Beyond her relationship to her sister. While she was here yesterday though, the image of her froze in his mind. The sensation hadn't happened in so long. Not since he stopped trying to peer into the lives of his neighbors, and decided he'd study only Ophelia until he was finally able to capture her. But it happened yesterday. He saw through Dona, to her core, to the essence of Dona; and he couldn't help but give in to the urge to draw.

Dona chewed at her lower lip. She released it. "Thank you," she breathed. Closing the sketchbook, she held it out toward Killian where he stood in the doorway.

He didn't reach for it. He wasn't looking at her. His damp eyes stared at the floor, one eyelid quivering. She set the book on the bed beside her.

"What's wrong?"

"Hmm?" His trance was broken. He held down his twitching eyelid with his thumb. "Nothing." He reached out toward her, taking the book of drawings. He placed it on his bookshelf then turned back toward her, but was arrested in his movement by a single word from Dona.

"Ophelia," she whispered.

He fought the compulsion to kick the baseboard heater, even though he knew the cheap metal would clang so satisfyingly.

"She took her clothes off in front of me," Killian blurted, easing his forehead against the wall. "Then she asked me if I was turned on by her new matching bra and pan…" he choked on the word, flushed, and finally whispered, "panties."

"Then she left," Dona said. "For Progner's house, right? She's going to use her Ultra-Slut powers to convince him of her plan. But she need not do anything more than tease you with her powers. You're already in. Hooked on her. And it's consuming you."

Killian dug his nails into his palm. "I can't draw her. Everyone else, I can sketch easily. Expertly. But not her. I just want to know her. To understand…"

"You can't draw her because you idolize her. You keep trying to create a tribute. But these drawings aren't about that. They're about truth."

Dona sat up. "Now is the time, Killian. Draw what you feel about her right now and you'll capture her. I promise."

Killian retrieved his sketchbook and sat at his desk. He saw visions of drawing Ophelia right into his first drawing. The sketch of Progner. The first page. Because she started all this. She inspired Progner to false rebellion, which inspired Killian to artistry. He would draw her there, behind Progner, where he crouched on the floor among his scattered possessions. She would be cracking a whip in the air, wearing nothing but the undergarments she so recently revealed to him. Maybe a spiked heel, digging into Progner's back.

He opened his pencil box and sharpened a 2H. He'd do it. He'd draw her in and then tear out the page and shred it. Or better yet, he'd grab some of Dad's matches, and take the sketch in the backyard and watch her image burn.

He blinked and a tear dropped in slow motion from his left eye, splattering on the lower left corner of the sketchbook's cover. It made a darker green splotch, which expanded asymmetrically for a few seconds. Killian removed the evidence of his passion from sight by opening the sketchbook. It opened to the picture of Dona on the eighth page. The page he'd reserved so long for Ophelia.

He turned around, but Dona was gone.

Turning one more page he began with the beauty of Ophelia's face. He could finally see it clearly. See the intelligence behind the warm eyes which knew exactly how to display the perfect mixture of sex and innocence for any situation.

The lines of her face led naturally to the soft edge of her neck. The merest shading in the milk white of her skin suggested the taut muscle beneath the soft outer layers. Her body stood, curled snake-like around the figure of a man. A generic man. A mannequin. A painted on buzz-cut, hard-lined muscles, uniformly toned skin. She was pursing her lips at the lifeless line that represented his mouth. She was nearly kissing him, but her eyes were wide, daring and playful. Her left hand cradled the back of his head, but her right hand was reaching toward the small of her back, to the handle of a pistol that was tucked into her shorts.

Kissing, yes. Her lips were about to kiss him. Yet, they curled up just enough, just slightly at the ends, to assure us, the audience, that she knew exactly what she was doing. And she liked it. The power over this *man*. The ability to choose who survived. To take lives and twist them as she pleased. She was power.

Killian slammed closed the cover on the truth of Ophelia. He touched the nearly dry splotch left by his teardrop. A permanent stain. Evidence of her power over him. He could see her now for all her selfishness. How she used men to get what she wanted. And yet, he was more drawn to her than ever.

NATURAL

Is a skyscraper an unnatural object? It seems fairly organic, standing proudly among its peers. But what about if you plopped one down in the middle of a forest. It certainly seems unnatural there, doesn't it? It just doesn't fit in. It draws the eye immediately because it fundamentally alters the native landscape.

People might suggest that a skyscraper doesn't grow, it's built, and therefore it is unnatural. But a termite mound is also built. A beehive is built. A beaver dam is built. A beaver dam can sure as hell fundamentally alter the surrounding environment. That's the purpose of it. Beavers plug up a stream in order to make a lake. They destroy the natural landscape in favor of one that provides a safe and comfortable home for beavers. But no one would suggest a beaver damn is an unnatural structure, would they?

And certainly no one would dare to propose that a robin, feathering its nest, with very little time to rest, is a constructor of unnatural objects. What could be more natural than spring? And what better symbol of spring than baby bird eggs waiting to hatch in the nest?

But what if that robin, while gathering its sticks and straws of grain, finds instead discarded Pixie Stix wrappers and flexible plastic drinking straws? What if a robin's nest is constructed entirely of coffee stirrers and licorice strands? Surely this would be an unnatural home. An aberrant abode for those poor little babies; those direct descendants of Mother Nature herself.

But why? In building its nest, this urban robin followed the same instinctual blueprints as its country cousin. It doesn't know that some sticks and straw come from the ground, while others are produced in a factory. Certainly the *act* of nest building is still natural, right? But many would insist the nest itself is not a natural object, for one reason, and one reason only: it contains man-made products. Man-made. Unnatural.

But are humans separate from nature? Nature is the universe, and the universe is everything and humans are part of the universe and exist within the realm of everything and therefore are part of nature. The real question is: can a human being even create something that is unnatural?

Alright, so no other animal is capable of harnessing the power of electricity and the atom. So what? Sure, it was only humans who created a way to electronically link their minds and share their thoughts. Big deal. Just because they have way overdeveloped egos and are more creative and adaptive than any other animal doesn't mean they ascend beyond the classification of animal. Despite what most religions will tell you, humans are animals. And it is the animal instinct of the human to create technology for projecting the Stream in the same way it is beaver instinct to create better stick piles for damming a stream.

Human beings are part of nature and anything they create is therefore natural. This was the argument many Streamers used in defense of God. The new God. The God that was said to have evolved from the very Stream itself. The God created in man's own image. God was but an extension of the human mind. God was a follow-through of the instinct of the human to create an immortal version of himself. When two humans come together and combine their genes to form a new life, it's considered the very essence of natural. But when a large group of humans combined their individual minds and created new life, people decried it as unnatural? Why, because other animals don't do it that way? Other animals don't do it in mirrored bedrooms or airplane bathrooms or with a member of the same sex who's dressed like the opposite sex. But it's not because they're better than humans. They simply don't have mirrors and airplanes and gender segregated clothing.

There's nothing supernatural, and certainly nothing divine about the overdevelopment of the human brain. It's simply the way one species reacted to the cards they were dealt. They weren't kicked out of the Garden of Eden because of their thirst for knowledge; they developed their thirst for knowledge by being kicked out of the Garden. They had to survive harsh conditions, and this required adaptation. But they weren't kicked out of just one garden, by one angry and spiteful fruit-hording God. They were kicked out of garden after garden after garden by shifting weather patterns and droughts and scarcity of food. Early humans evolved the ability to think creatively as a response to environmental conditions in constant flux.

When early human ancestors were living in an area where the trees died out, they planted crops. When crops dried up, they hunted animals. When animals were scarce, they learned to fish. When the water rose above their heads, they built an ark and filled it with what they needed to set out in search of greener pastures. "There are better conditions out there," the man who drew up the ark's plans would always declare. "Build this here boat, and I'll find them for us. You all row, and I'll steer, and trust me, we'll find paradise."

Had they only gotten the boot from one paradise, the human instinct to lead others to a better land might have swiftly abated. But after millennia of necessitated adaptation, the inspiration trait became burned into the human genome. And so, even in societies where life really couldn't get any better, there were always those who were not content. Those who, because their minds were built to dream, cannot be content. And they almost always had the same message: "These conditions suck. You work hard for me, and things will be better in the future."

Who could resist such a promise? People don't remember how difficult life was for their ancestors. They only know the world they grew up in. Most of them have too much free time to be happy, so they're easily convinced that there is a better set of conditions out there. There must be. And so the age old trick still works. The few stand on top of the deck and promise to do the steering, while the masses sit below rowing. Merrily rowing their lives away to obtain someone else's dream.

Of course, modern technology only made it easier for the captains of industry to convince the rowers to keep their seats. After all, Stream technology allowed everyone to have a window seat. It allowed them to watch any dream they chose as they rowed and rowed.

And with a God in place who absorbed their excess mental energy and steered all the ships in the human fleet, humans could achieve the dream they'd had for eons. You see, ever since they realized that evolution screwed them out of their rightful bliss by tricking them into thinking up ways to survive, humans yearned to return down the chain of development a few links, where happiness lay in a simple garden, eating fruit all day.

Wow that sounded pessimistic. And it could

definitely be argued that many humans, every single day, work exhaustively to stretch the boundaries of knowledge. But they fight the good fight as a small minority. They battle ever growing masses of those who would gladly give up intellectual freedom and inalienable rights for cheap flashy entertainment that makes them feel as happy as a pig in shit. Hence, this new obsession with a modern God.

Naturally, people didn't know that the God they'd begun to worship is not the one Jadon dreamed up to inspire people to row toward mutual tranquility. They had no clue that it was in fact a false god, created by a certain Director of Psychiatry because of his desire to be the guy in command of the whole human fleet. A small percentage knew it, and began a rebellion aimed at returning Jadonism to its origins. But if history has anything to say about it, despite almost always starting out with pure ideals at inception, religions never recover purity once they begin to be manipulated toward selfish goals.

The priest named Paul who sat in Killian's living room was one of the few who was aware of the true nature of the new God. He was part of a secret movement working to overthrow Progner and his God and restore to the Stream a dignified religion, centered around calming the mind, and helping each other find peace. It was a slow movement. Since all thoughts were recorded in Stream, it was difficult for rebels to interact without drawing attention. Mostly they relied on nonswimmers to deliver messages. Streamghosts; they were sometimes called. Those who weren't connected could walk through the city virtually undetected by the distracted minds of the Streamers. Streamers who expected to sense the presence of others, and have learned not to rely on their vision anymore. The priests snuck in scores of these outsiders before the city began to meticulously secure its borders. They meditated to boot their mind from the Stream and listened to the actual words being spoken by these nonswimmers, and thus communicated undetected. But this ancient form of communication was slow compared to the instantaneous spy network of the Stream.

Killian didn't know any of this about Paul. Killian didn't even realize that Paul was still there, sitting across the room from him. This was not only because Paul was meditating so deeply that he'd disappeared from the Stream, but also because Killian, in unlocking some of his memory, had succeeded in expanding the parameters of his filter beyond the tight restrictions Progner had enacted, and was swiftly rediscovering old distractions.

He was attacked and overwhelmed by a commercial for toilet paper. [RollRols: now with Six-ply Supercushioning! Absorbent enough to soak up the entire Stream!]

As the advertisement faded, it occurred to Killian that he used to know how to adjust a filter to limit, or even eliminate advertisements altogether. He tried following the same system of commands he once used with his clients. Surprisingly, it worked. He unlocked commercial-free Streaming. Why hadn't Progner stripped him of his access to such power? It couldn't have slipped his mind. Perhaps it wasn't a matter of access, but only of obtaining the knowledge of how to do it. Killian began to wonder if, instead of being a prescription filler, he could have been a teacher. He could have taught people to adjust their own filters, instead of helping them become reliant on Wellspring's system.

Is that what Pete and Ophelia were doing at the school? No, that was just their cover. Ophelia wanted what she'd always wanted. An end to the Stream. It might have been easier to just blow it up before it got started, but she'd no doubt spent every moment of the last ten years planning to rid society of her father's creation. And she was right. It was a horrible existence. One that allowed a nobody like Progner to imitate God. To murder at will. Since diving in, Killian's life had been a miserable string of constant distractions, with no single meaningful event worth recording. Since diving in, people had become more shallow, and certainly less sane. And for what? Flashier, more instantaneous gratification?

He did want it to stop. The whole charade of the Stream. He wanted to help open the cages of this technological zoo, and liberate the monkeys within.

He'd start with himself. Cracking the last layers of the filter Progner configured, Killian faced the full force of the Stream. He fell forward, catching himself with his left hand as his right hand stabbed at his forehead. Screwdrivers, drills and knives penetrated his brow, leaving open holes for immediate overfilling with all manner of unorganized knowledge. Thoughts, music, and images smashed through his mind as he stabbed and stabbed to make more entryways.

Killian couldn't refocus his mind. He'd been away from the Stream for some time now. Queued shows piled weeks high each insisted he had missed the most important episode of the week/season/year/lifetime and simultaneously commanded that he watch immediately. quiZblitZ beckoned him to play, just a few rounds.

And with this new access to his old world, what attracted Killian's attention first? Movies, music, war games, or the old distracting comfort of *reality* shows? No, no. Nothing so dignified as watching celebrity reality stars, who are only celebrities because they were on other reality shows, battling to determine who has the least inhibitions. No, being the natural human animal he is, and the male variety at that, Killian's first instinct, upon feeling a tinge of freedom, was carnal.

He started by browsing a free nude stills sites but was quickly drawn toward the promise of commercial-free, live acts. He acknowledged the link, but was bombarded by ads so loud he fell backward into the couch. He browsed some interactive feeds, jumping into someone else's point of view for the thirty seconds of free trial then getting booted into an overpowering commercial for erection pills. He may very well have ordered caseloads.

Killian went back to the still picture site, forcing himself to focus on one picture, one girl. His mind begged to surf through all possible configurations of the female form, but he held one girl's image with all the power of his concentration. His hand, without his mind's instruction, slowly, naturally, slid into the waist of his pants. He quickly removed it as a deliberate cough from Paul reminded him he was not alone.

CHOSEN

Killian heard the door to his apartment open and close softly. He sensed no one in Stream. Opening his eyes, he saw Paul sitting behind his coffee table, eyes cast downward. He was deep in meditation still. Light footsteps approached and a set of khaki fatigues entered his line of sight. His torso swelled with warmth. It was her, wasn't it? He clamped down his teeth and willed his head not to turn.

The thin woman walked stealthily to Paul, bent down and kissed him on the cheek. It *was* Ophelia. Killian saw his drawing of her. Her arm wrapped around the back of the helpless mannequin while her warm lips neared its frozen face. He saw the seditious grin that barely curled the ends of those puckered lips, while her hand reached for the pistol that would destroy this man who never was. Paul still sat staring blankly at the floor, but he was smiling now. Not his usual, unalterable, full-toothed grin. This was a smug, closed mouth, curled lip, grin. It was a grin Killian knew well. Once again, he was not the only mannequin in her plan.

[She is here!] He thought it. He would not be used and disposed of so easily again. [She is here!] He broadcast it. It wasn't Progner's lame speech that had convinced him to betray her the first time. It was the drawing. It was, as Dona suggested, his uncovering of the truth of Ophelia. That's what had allowed Killian to see that he was nothing to her. That she would chew him up and spit him out. [Ophelia is here!] He broadcast it again. Out into the Stream. To all Streamers. To Progner.

He chose, once again, to betray her. And the moment he did his vision went white. Blinding white. Simultaneously, his body shook with the bass vibrations of a booming voice.

[HELLO, KILLIAN, YOU HAVE BEEN CHOSEN.]

He closed and reopened his eyes, but the light was everywhere. He could not escape it.

[HELLO, KILLIAN, YOU HAVE BEEN CHOSEN.]

[Get out of my head!]

[HELLO, KILLIAN, YOU HAVE BEEN CHOSEN.]

[Chosen for what?]

[To hear the word of God. To share the word of God.]

[Yeah, um, no thanks.] He tried requesting several different forms of information: the time, a location in the city, his perimeter alarm, saved data; but nothing appeared. Nothing shattered the light.

[You will hear the word of God. You will share the word of God.] While the booming voice spoke, Killian forgot his blindness. The voice absorbed all attention. It was only between the messages that he could panic at all.

[I said, NO!]

[You will hear the word of God. You will share the word of God.]

[Apparently I have no choice about hearing it. But I won't help you, I can promise you that. Now give me back my sight and get out of my head!]

[You will hear the word of God. You will share the word of God.]

[No!]

He saw it. The screwdriver. It floated there in the brilliance. It lasted only microseconds; then was reabsorbed by the white brilliance. But it was there. And he remembered. Evan, Elena, Hector.

[You have been chosen. You will hear the word of God. Too much meditation drains the Stream. Active minds are healthy minds. You will share the word of God.]

[I will not!]

Again the faintest trace of the screwdriver appeared. It was replaced instantly with a textual version of the message. "Too much meditation drains the Stream. Active minds are healthy minds." Written across his consciousness. Across the brilliance. It multiplied, creating shadows of itself, backward into infinity. The shadows reproduced upward, downward, to each side, even diagonally, filling the infinite space in his mind with eleven words. The words were spoken. They were whispered. They were shouted. At different speeds and different rates of repetition. The words threatened to burst from his ears and eyes and skin. From his mouth.

He clenched his teeth to contain them. He would not share the words of God. He would vent them with holes to his forehead if he had to.

It all began to blur together. The words, the voices. The brilliance. He could feel a damp cloth being held against his nose and lips, and then he felt nothing.

Killian's body dropped out from under him, going limp as his world turned black. He heard both Paul and Ophelia speak before he faded completely. Ophelia said simply, "Yep." But she spoke second. She spoke in reply to a question from Paul.

Paul had asked, "Do you always carry chloroform on you?"

WARRIORSPAWN

Killian ascended the stairs slowly. His heart pounded so fast he could feel the heat radiating from of his temples. He hadn't seen Ophelia since the zoo. He'd wanted to hand her the newspaper personally the next day, when her primate liberation expedition made the front page, but she wasn't home when he came by. She was never home. It had been ten days since he'd seen her. Her car was there in the driveway now, though, and her mother said she was up in her room. "Go on up," she'd said.

Just go on up. To her bedroom. The bedroom of the older, cooler, much hotter girl he had an unbearable crush on.

The sound of machine gun fire froze Killian at the top of the stairs. Yelling and shooting, coming from the TV he guessed, spilled out of the half open door to the left. He inched forward and peeked into the room. Someone was on the bed. But it wasn't her. It wasn't Ophelia. She was too short, and a bit chubbier, and not nearly as cute. That's right; Ophelia had a younger sister Killian had seen her on the school bus, though he'd never heard her speak.

Another open door revealed a floral canopied bed

that could only be Penelope's. The door to the bathroom was open. The closed door, at the end of the hall, must be Ophelia's. He could hear some intense heavy metal on the other side of it. He approached and knocked lightly. Nothing happened. He knocked loudly. Still nothing.

He waited.

The song ended and he knocked softly before another earsplitting guitar riff began the next track. Still no response.

Finally, pushing all of his fear down beneath the lava in his stomach, he slowly turned the knob and cracked the door. He waited. He cracked it further, wide enough to poke his head in. She was on the bed. Lying on her bed. She was asleep. He watched her for a moment, forcibly resisting an urge to slide into bed beside this goddess and absorb a tiny bit of her magnetic field. Her power.

Half of her belly was exposed by her lifted T-shirt. Killian became uncomfortably aroused and forced himself to close the door. Turning, intending to head back down the stairs he noticed the other door, her sister's door, was wide open now. She was sitting on her bed with a video game controller in her hand. Her eyes squinted at the screen, the source of the shifting colors that played across her brow.

"Hey, it's Killian, right?" her voice hung in the hallway. She didn't look up. He waited, wondering if he'd really heard anything. She cleared her throat.

"Yeah," he said.

"She sleeping? Ophelia?"

"Yeah."

She continued her game, never once casting her eyes at him.

"Watcha playing?"

"Warriorspawn," she said.

"No way!" He moved to her doorway, where he

could see the screen.

"You can come in."

"I've been waiting for this to come out," he admitted, stepping into her room. "I was hoping to get a ride to the mall this weekend to pick it up."

"Do it. It's the shit."

"Yeah?"

"Check it. You start right up in the worst shit you can imagine. I died within seconds the first fifty times or so that I played. And as soon as you die, you spawn right in the middle of a different battle, somewhere else on the planet Mangore. It's fuckin' crazy."

He was surprised at her language. She was younger than him, by what? A year or two? He glanced at her, just to confirm, but there really was no resemblance to her sister at all. Dona was just a plain girl, and her sister could be a supermodel. That must make her feel good.

"Yeah, the gore looks pretty sweet."

"Here, watch this move." Her trooper on the screen spun, decapitating one of the aliens who looked like a cross between a human and a cobra. Blood shot out of its neck. "Anyway, the key is to work together with the other online players. Form up, in groups. But every time you die you start out somewhere else, randomly, and have to find other good players again. It's tough. It takes a while before you can last more than a few minutes."

Despite her carrying on a conversation with Killian, she was performing outrageously complex maneuvers on the screen. Into her headset she suddenly yelled out "flank left," but then shook her head and dropped the controller on the bed. "It's a lot of stupid kids. They constantly chatter, making asinine comments about each others' mothers, and penis sizes and shit. But the game has the potential to be really cool. Wanna try it?"

"Yeah!" Killian looked back toward the hallway.

"But I should finish my route."

"Right. The paperboy. Well, some other time."

"Yeah. Cool."

She began a new round and allowed the game to absorb her completely.

"See ya," Killian said, backing out of the room.

It was a Tuesday that Dona had appeared behind him in the driveway as the school bus thundered away. He didn't know her. They hadn't ever spoken, except for that few minutes in her bedroom last week. Yet, here she was, getting off at his stop without explanation.

"What's up?" Killian said. She just stood there, looking down at her feet.

"You want to play Warriorspawn?" she mumbled. Killian was confused. Warriorspawn wasn't a two player game. Not from one console anyway.

"I've gotta deliver the papers."

She didn't look up, just watched her toe as she made small circles with it on the pavement.

"Besides, I haven't had a chance to pick it up yet."

Dona removed her backpack and set it on the driveway beside her foot. She rifled through the contents and produced a game cartridge. She held it up to Killian. "We can use mine. Take turns. I broke my GameDepot. I haven't played in two days and I'm jonesing pretty hard."

Killian did want to try the game out. Who knew when he could talk his mother into driving him to the mall to get his own copy. And, the thought suddenly occurred to him, if he hung out with Dona, he might get some insight into her sister. Maybe, if they began to hang out he'd be invited over to her house here and there, and he'd run into Ophelia. She had to be home, and awake, some time.

"Well, come in," he said. "I gotta run through my

paper route, but you can play until I'm done."

It was two Tuesdays later that Killian realized Dona had followed him off the bus every school day for two weeks. He never bothered to buy his own copy of the game since she just left hers at his house. He hadn't seen Ophelia in all of that time, but he did manage to learn some more about her from Dona. Killian found that whatever he brought up while Dona was absorbed in the game, she'd answer robotically, without comment. Ophelia worked evenings at a restaurant, usually from after school until late at night. That's why she wasn't ever home.

Dona was amazing at the game. Killian's record for surviving from a spawn point was seven minutes. But Dona would start right off the school bus and often still be playing the same life when he came back from his route twenty-five minutes later. She'd become so legendary among the game's online community that as soon as they saw his log-on they would flock to him and demand instructions. People would ask him what was wrong whenever he actually played. Not only did he die much more frequently than Dona, he couldn't pull off the imaginative combinations of moves that were making her famous.

"You have an entire network of young people ready to do whatever you command," Killian said one day. "You realize what you could do with that kind of power?"

Dona shrugged.

"You're father really is Steve Bates?" he asked, picking up a conversation from the day before. She nodded. "So you know all about the Stream? You know, how it's supposed to be launching soon, and, I mean, how it's going to change everything. School and gaming and, well, everyday life really."

"Change is inevitable."

She sat, as usual, with her legs crossed and her back ramrod straight. The controller rested softly in her lap.

"What does your sister think of the Stream?"

"You kidding?"

"No, I mean, I'm sure she's against it. I'm sure she thinks it's just society's newest form of prison. But what's she going to do about it?"

"Whatever she can."

"Ophelia Cassandra Redenbacher. That's really her full name, huh?"

"Yep."

"Your parents get bored after that, and just went with Dona?"

Dona squinted at the screen, executed a series of rapid button taps, then jutted a quick glance at him. She looked back to the screen, and miraculously, hadn't died. "Jacinda Donatella."

"Really? But you go by Dona?"

"What am I supposed to go by? Jason?"

"Good point." He sat back into the beanbag, the only seat in his room other than the bed. Dona always sat on the bed. Always cross-legged. Always with her back straight, not leaning against anything.

The lighting in the room changed. It darkened, or brightened, he couldn't tell which. But everything became clearer. Dona was clearer. She froze, in his mind. He could pick out every line, every subtle shift in shading that made up her solid form. There was no background, no object to fill the scene with. She sat, posed like a Buddha. He saw, between her upturned hands, not a video game controller, but a swirling of energy at her command. Like a miniature galaxy, it rotated before her stomach, promising knowledge beyond his mortal experience.

When she left a short time later, Killian sat and drew

this new vision into his book of truths. He drew Dona on the page he'd been reserving for her sister. Drew her, and then paced his room all evening, wondering what this return of his inspiration could mean. Dona did not follow him off the bus the next two days and Killian began to wonder why. But all his curiosity about Dona, all his interest in drawing her, completely vanished when Ophelia pulled into his driveway and invited him back into her life.

It was Wednesday when the man from Wellspring rang the front doorbell. He wore a suit that was worth more than Killian's parents made in a month. Probably. Killian knew little about such things. He was standing eloquently at the front door, holding a briefcase when Killian got back from delivering the papers. He asked Killian to confirm his name.

"Killian Peterson of the logon id: 00KillPete?"

"Yeah, who are you?"

"I'm the wish fairy, and I'm here to grant yours."

The man came in and opened his briefcase on the dining table and spent half an hour speaking to Killian and his mother, who had wandered silently into the room. He described how Wellspring, Inc. was ready to launch the beta test of the Stream, and that one thousand people would be involved in this three day test. Two hundred of those participants were to be the top players of Wellspring's hottest online game: Warriorspawn.

"You see, Mrs. Peterson, Killian here is one of the top ten players in the world. It's exactly these kind of young, techno-geniuses that we want to help us smooth out any last-minute glitches, before the Stream launches publicly in September."

Killian couldn't believe it. Even with him playing on the same account, which must drag down Dona's stats considerably, they still made the top ten. But she was the genius. He didn't deserve this. He was merely a warrior's pawn.

It was Tuesday when Killian drew Dona Redenbacher, Wednesday when the man from Wellspring rang his front doorbell, and it was the next day, Thursday, that Ophelia Redenbacher came to him and informed him that he would be helping her to stop the Stream dead in its tracks.

DONA

Killian's cheek was being slapped lightly by what he dreamed was Ophelia's hand. But it was a man's voice which repeated, "Killian! Wake up. Killian! Wake up!"

The white sloppy hair across his eyes, the indefatigable grin. It was obviously Paul. Killian scrunched his brow as Paul raised his hand to strike again.

"Don't worry, you're safe," Paul said, letting his hand drop.

Killian looked around. He was lying in a large open room, surrounded by meditating priests. Women and men, sitting placidly, all eyes cast downward.

"This room is Streamshielded. We've found a way to cast a false sleep signal, and to expand it around a greater area than one person. In short, we can boot this entire room from the Stream. Of course Wellspring is aware of it. Hard not to notice a giant dead zone in the middle of the city. But so long as we play the game, promote Progner's new God and all, Wellspring can't afford to mess with us."

"Where is she?" Killian managed. His vision swayed as he tried to sit up further. A violent nausea tinged the borders of the vast emptiness in his stomach.

"She'll be with us in a moment. She's giving a pep

talk to all of the nonswimmers she's gathered here in the city. They're going to take out one of the main Stream generators, leaving Progner unprotected. Then she'll move in."

"Dona?"

"What? No. Ophelia, of course." Paul flicked his head back, tossing his hair to the side.

"Where is Dona?" Killian said, quickly surveying his surroundings. "How did I get here?"

"Ophelia knocked you out, then we brought you here. To protect you."

"From God?"

"Yes. From Progner."

"So… where is Dona?"

Paul sat quietly for a moment, his head turned away from Killian. "Well, she's… well… she hasn't spoken publicly since she was captured. Since before you took her out of the Stream really. We would have heard from her by now. She would have found a way."

Killian looked around the large room again. "What are you talking about? Dona is shy, she wouldn't speak to…"

He saw her, in his mind, sitting in meditation, the whole of a galaxy spinning in her hands. His drawing of the truth of her. "Jacinda Donatella," her voice spoke softly out of memory. Her real name. J. Dona? No, it couldn't be. He examined the drawing in his mind again and it seemed so obvious now. There she was, the wise prophet of a new religion.

"Dona is Jadon!"

Paul refocused his eyes on Killian. "I thought you knew."

"Dona is Jadon!"

"Of course."

"But Jadon is a man!"

"Oh please. He exists only in the Stream. You know you can be anyone you want in Stream."

"But, but, Progner will kill her."

"Yes… well…."

"We have to save her."

"Killian, we have to save Jadonism. If Dona becomes a martyr to ensure her vision for the future is secure, it's what she would want."

"But how could I…"

"Shit, we don't have time for this. But you won't be convinced if you don't know the whole story. I wasn't done sharing Dona's memories with you. It's too late now, we're shielded from the Stream here, and if we weren't you'd be under attack by Progner's god again. You've been remembering on your own though. You need to remember back ten years. Just after you entered the Stream. She explained everything to you. She wanted to make sure you knew the full truth, before you chose to forget."

Killian closed his eyes and drew deep breaths in through his nose. With the Stream blocked he found it fairly easy to calm his mind and let go of the questions. An image of Dona as a very young woman began to form.

He stood outside Dona's apartment. It had been a week since she'd found him on the floor here in the hallway and brought him in and offered to take away his pain. It had been the longest week of his life. In that time he had entered the Stream. Dove in and nearly drown in the flow of modern society.

She could sense his arrival this time. She opened the door.

"What do you think?"

"It's amazing. And horrible. I spend most of my

time distracting myself with video games. So I guess it isn't all that different. Though the games sure distract better."

"So why do it?" Her voice moved about the room, though he didn't have the energy to follow her with his eyes. He leaned into her kitchen counter, resting his pale forearms there as she moved about putting dishes away.

"Why dive in at all?" Dona asked again.

"What else? Rot out there. I want to do college, get a decent job." Her footsteps disappeared down the hall. He examined the scarce hairs on his arm. Randomly pointing away from each other. Throwbacks of evolution, what purpose did they serve now? Surely Dona would have some ridiculous theory about that. Her footsteps returned. He told himself to look up at her, he was being rude. But his lids grew heavier at the thought.

"What was high school like in Stream?" he mumbled.

"Not much different. The teachers still did their whole lecture thing, they just Streamed it, with pretty pictures added. School's always behind the technology curve because the students are younger than the teachers, and adapt faster. You can't just tell someone who's been teaching for decades to dramatically change the way they do their job. See, as the human mind develops into adulthood…" She paused. "So, you really want to start fresh, huh?"

"I have to. I can't stop thinking about her. And what I did. Do you know what it's like to be obsessively in love with someone? To think about them every moment of the day?"

Dona stopped. She'd been finishing putting the silverware away, but she froze with a handful of spoons poised above the drawer and turned her eyes to him. He could feel her looking, though he kept his head down.

She exhaled. "No. Of course not," she said softly, then dropped the spoons into the drawer.

"And then to betray that love," Killian went on.

"Killian, *she* did that, not you. Besides, she'd have gotten caught anyway, no matter what you did. Ophelia was determined. How dare you blame yourself! As if you, or anyone, could have that much influence over her life."

Dona slammed the water on full blast and washed down the contents of the sink. She slammed the faucet lever down and threw a pot into the sink. When the clanging stopped, she allowed her shoulders to drop a bit. "I only hope, when she gets out, she'll be open to less confrontational solutions."

Killian had to remind himself that they were sisters. However opposite they were, Dona was probably harboring a bit of grief. Her only sibling was in jail.

"What do you mean?" Killian said. "Are you going to try to convince her to accept the Stream?"

"Well, it's a little more complex than that, actually. I'm going to start a revolution."

"Sure, why not?"

"No, really. I'm going to start a new religion, which will teach people to live peacefully with the Stream, not just to get swept up in it's current. It'll promote meditation and control of the mind, so people will have some independence. They won't be mindless consumer-sprockets in the Wellspring propaganda machine."

"That's no small dream."

"No. But a necessary one. When Ophelia is released, whenever that may be, she'll attempt to destroy the Stream again. She may bide her time, set up a more intricate plan. She's got a mind for strategy, and you know how easily she can draft recruits for her cause. No, she'll never give up her attempts to stop the world from further automating its people. To set the world right, in her eyes.

Unless she can be made to see there are other solutions."

It must be a family gene, Killian thought. Not from Penelope; a person couldn't be more passive. Surely these outrageously creative ambitions come from their father. His stupid theories, however, his world revolutionizing scheme, worked. The Stream is a reality. Would his daughters spend the rest of their lives trying to cast off that shadow?

"But it's not just for Ophelia," Dona said, "And not just because I think it's in humanity's best interest."

"You need more motive than that?"

"I don't. But I have more." He felt her gaze but resisted meeting it. "Killian, when you were injected with the technology that allows you to connect to the Stream, your brain was infiltrated by a network of nanobots. Thousands of tiny transceivers which link all the parts of your brain with the Stream. But your interface with the Stream is still via a single signal. That's not easy to say. A single sig-nal."

"Single sig-nal," he said. He looked up. She smiled. "No, it's not," he mumbled. Gravity reclaimed his gaze.

"Anyway, imagine there is a door through which your mind receives that lone transmission. That door can be opened or closed. It can be in any position you choose in fact. Your filter controls how open it is and what you have access to. I'm going to construct a similar door in your mind to block out the parts of your past you want to forget. To allow you to start over. It will not be a locked door. You will be able to open it yourself, either in small increments, or all at once, if ever you choose. But before I do this for you, since you're going to forget anyway, I want to tell you the whole truth."

She moved closer and with two fingers she carefully turned and lifted his chin until he was looking straight at her.

"I love you," she said.

She released him, but he continued to stare. *She* had to look away, at her shoe. She slid it incrementally forward to maintain her focus on it.

"I have for some time," she said to her shoe. "I thought I was over you, but suddenly seeing you in my hallway last week, it all came rushing back. And as much as it pains you to realize you betrayed Ophelia, it pains me to see you obsess over such an undeserving, selfish and manipulative person. I wish I could convince you to see her for what she is again, like you did when you drew her. But I know logic cannot stand up to lust. I know that well. So, I'm going to help you start over. To forget her. In hopes that, once you're freed of her spell, you'll develop the capacity to find happiness."

PREPARATION

"It wasn't the Stream," Killian said aloud to himself. "The last ten years of my life weren't miserable because of the Stream. It was because I've been blocked up."

He stood up, unaware of his surroundings.

"Shit. If I'd had even a day's worth of psychiatric training at the time, I would have realized the danger of repressing memories. I wouldn't have even considered letting Dona do that. Ten years of my life: foggy, miserable, and ultimately forgettable, all because I tried to cheat using technology. Tried to shortcut my heartache."

"Boo hoo," said the throaty whisper that used to be the voice of his filter. "Try prison. You almost done crying, we're on a bit of a schedule?" Ophelia had her long dark curls tied up in a ponytail, but her face held the same stern look of expectancy he had downloaded into his toothbrush. He was sure he'd have to do more than clean his teeth to make this real life Ophelia grin at him.

There was still no Stream. He looked around. They were surrounded by men and women sitting on the floor in meditation. Priests. Preparing for whatever they'd been cooking up. The large room was windowless. A single door broke up the smooth concrete walls. Ophelia stood directly in front of it.

"Killian, I need your help."

He remembered how enticing her feigned desperation was to a naive teenager.

"Well, what else is new? Want me to press the button that blows up all of the Stream generators? Or do I have to strap explosives to my chest and give Progner a big hug."

"He killed Dona."

The words stabbed him in the chest. It was a sharp, sudden pain. Much like the piercing of his forehead that he'd experienced so many times before; be it screwdriver, kitchen knife or power drill. A quick, surprising stab, followed by a growing knowledge of the intensity of the pain, followed by a fading of consciousness. But this time, the pain wasn't centered in his forehead. It hit him right in his rib cage. He couldn't draw a full breath.

"Killian, Progner killed your clients. He created a program that pretends to be God and he tested it on your clients and he murdered them. He's controlling society with these prophets and the messages he gives them. And the few who know the truth can't say anything because this *God* can get into the head of anyone connected. You know that now."

She walked over to Killian, who was frozen in place, and embraced him. "He needs to be stopped, Killian. Dead." Leaving her arms around him, she pulled her head back. She was not smirking. She was crying.

"But fuck society, Killian, and fuck what's right. He killed my baby sister. And I won't stop until I see his head cracked open and his brains running out onto the floor."

She put her warm lips gently on his and then pressed deeply. Pulling away swiftly she created a slight breeze that iced the moisture she left behind.

"I need your help."

"But I betrayed you. Twice."

"Well, yes. We expected you would. It was part of our plan. Dona's plan, mostly. She's a genius, you know." Ophelia turned away from him. "Was a genius."

Killian could see her shoulders tense up. She squeezed her fists closed, tightening her forearms until they looked like they'd burst. With her back to him she whispered, "Killian when I got out of jail I wanted to tear the Stream down and slit Progner's throat. I even wanted to kill you. But Dona changed all that. She showed me all that she had done as Jadon. She showed me how the priests could meditate and leave the Stream. She showed me the new hardware they were working on that could allow people to disconnect when they wanted. Basically, she showed me a future where people could live with this new technology, not as slaves, but as peaceful explorers of a new era. I can't phrase any of this shit like she could, but she convinced me…"

She let her shoulders drop as she purged herself of air.

"The point is, we set all this up so you would betray me. We knew Progner was lining you up for prophecy, and we wanted you to receive the word of his *God*."

"Why? Do you know how painful that was? It was like suffocating. Like drowning in knowledge."

"Because, Killian, the priests here have figured out how to rewrite that message you're holding on to. We're going to send our own message. We're going to steer people away from this false *God* and back to Jadonism's roots. For Dona."

Ophelia spun and stepped quickly to him, planting another kiss on his cheek. Killian stepped back.

"The nonswimmers are gathering. I've spent years recruiting them, and they're waiting for my signal to take out one of the Stream generators. Then, when the Streamquake hits, and the Streamers are on their knees,

I'll move in on Progner. Time will be limited, because the other generators will eventually reroute power."

"So what am I supposed to do?"

She stepped nearer again, her lips close enough that he could feel the heat of her breath in his ear. "I need you here. Dona convinced the priests to support me, and they listened because they agree that Progner must be stopped. But after that... they don't trust me. They aren't convinced I'll just step out of the way and let them have their way with society."

"You mean; they aim to kill you?"

"Shh." She looked around the room. "Probably," she whispered. "I need you to find out. Anything you can. And then let me know their plans, as soon as I've finished with Progner."

Killian stepped away again. His heel banged the concrete. He fell back, letting the cool wall catch him and take some of his weight.

"Why would they tell me anything?"

"Because you're the key. They're using you to send their new message. It'll be a lot easier for them if you cooperate. You have a lot of leverage. You can get whatever you want from them."

He felt himself sliding down the wall. He didn't resist, dropping until he was sitting with his back against it. She looked down at him.

"Killian, you don't owe me anything. But my life may be in your hands. Please, do what you can." She smiled. He turned away. "And eat something. You look like a goddamn zombie."

He tried to think of something meaningful to add, but, suddenly a wooden bowl was thrust into his face by a man in a Hawaiian shirt.

"Here, eat," the man said.

"No, thanks." Killian waved the bowl away. The man

did not remove it and the conflicting aromas of orange and pepper tunneled through him and illuminated his emptiness. Ophelia had vanished.

"It is time to eat. Please, eat." The man handed the bowl to Killian again. This time he took it. "My cousin is a good cook. He spent much effort preparing this."

Killian looked into the bowl and discovered brown rice, peppers, snow peas and gooey orange pieces of chicken. He took the bowl in one hand and reached in with the other. Grabbing a handful of the hot meal, he crammed his mouth full.

"No," the man in the Hawaiian shirt said. "It is time to eat. Not time to hurry. Experience the eating."

Killian looked up into a crackled version of a once familiar face. "I know you."

"Yes," Yasanori Haroki said, "you delivered my newspapers."

"Your cousin made this?"

"Yes." He pointed to a man behind a long table who was ladling the meal from a large pot into small wooden bowls. "He prepared it all day. But he won't enjoy it. So you should enjoy it. Otherwise, why did he make it?"

Killian took a smaller handful and chewed it slowly. Seems everyone was preparing something for him. Right down to the cousin of an old neighbor.

"Why won't he eat it?"

"He will probably eat some. But he doesn't enjoy eating it. He enjoys preparing it. You should watch him some time. He is like an artist with a kitchen knife. A potential weapon, yet he lifts it delicately, and slices gently down, dividing nourishment into perfectly equal portions. Very few enjoy what they do so much. He lives in the moment."

Yasanori watched Killian expectantly. Killian picked out a piece of chicken and put it in his mouth. He chewed it slowly. He licked the orange sauce from his fingers. "It's delicious," he said.

"Ophelia convinced him to come and cook for all these people. It is his contribution to the cause. She told him to put his energy into the food and the food will energize the others. The others will spread the positive energy. She knows just how to motivate people, doesn't she?"

"No doubt." Killian tried some of the vegetables. "How did she lure you in?"

"You're a man. Or rather, a fellow mannequin. You know how she works."

Why would he say that, unless... "She showed you my sketches?"

Yasanori nodded. He moved back toward the counter full of wooden bowls near the make-shift kitchen. He grabbed six more full bowls. Killian followed him around the room as he bent down and placed the bowls next to the meditating priests.

"I was shocked, you know," Yasanori said. "When I discovered the drawing of me. We had never really spoken, you and I. You didn't know me at all. Yet how well you drew me."

"I'm sorry."

"Why sorry? It is such a true rendition. You have admirable talent. It is nothing to apologize for."

"But it is sad. You are toasting no one."

"Incorrect," Yasanori said. He dropped three bowls onto the floor beside three priests, silently, despite the speed of his movements. "I am toasting myself." He winked at Killian, then spun and headed back to the counter. "You should try it sometime."

Killian spied Paul making his way cautiously through the room of seated priests. He was speaking softly as he came. The priests he passed opened their eyes. Some stretched their arms. A few were standing by the time Paul's eternal grin floated only a few feet away.

Killian felt Yasanori's breath near his ear. "*He's* seen your sketch of Ophelia. If he believes himself to be a mannequin, what do you suppose he's preparing for?"

Yasanori whisked off, picking up emptied wooden bowls as he crossed the room.

"Killian, it's almost time," Paul said, placing his hand on Killian's shoulder. "I need you to come near that door. We have to be brief, but I need you to enter the Stream for a second, so I can overwrite the message you're carrying. We need to do it before the nonswimmers knock out the generator."

"Slow down. I need to process."

"What was the message about?" Paul asked, nodding to two men behind Killian. They stepped forward.

"God's message?" He glanced back at the men and swallowed.

Paul nodded. The men didn't move. Killian realized he was nodding to his question this time and answered, "It discouraged meditation."

"See, he works to undo all that is good about Jadonism. But we're well prepared. Progner's little God program uses a very specific signal. A backdoor through the sleep boot program. We can send a message to you on the same signal, over top of the original. The other Streamers should confuse our message with one from *God*. In fact, if it works, we're prepared to plant other messages of our own. Use our own prophets to undo the damage that's been done."

"But then you won't be any better than Progner."

"No, that's not true. We're not just one man. We're an organization, made up of those who want to help others. We have people's best interests in mind. We're not out to gain power for power's sake."

"Not yet." That feeling he got whenever Progner's logic seemed to make sense rose in his lower gut. It screamed mistrust and caution. "Religion," Killian sighed.

Paul nodded over Killian's shoulder again and the men stepped forward. Their stomachs pushed into him, forcing him to take a step back.

"Listen, I think Ophelia is going to kill me," Killian blurted. Paul's smile didn't waver. He nodded. The priestly goons nudged Killian another step. "Probably you too."

"Yes Killian, well, you needn't worry about that. Dona instructed us to help Ophelia, because stopping Progner is our first priority. And who better to ensure the job gets done. But I agree; Ophelia won't stop with Progner. It isn't her nature to settle down peaceably."

"So, what?"

"So, we let Ophelia and her little band of rebels stop Progner. Then we stop Ophelia."

"How?"

"That's where you come in." Nod. Nudge. He was only a few steps from the door. "Killian, it's not just Progner you have to worry about when the Stream comes back online. The Streamers know you've been chosen as the next prophet. They know you've been spoken to. They'll want that message. They'll all ask for it. Over and over they'll ask. And then they'll demand. Unless we satisfy them. Unless we give them a message. And if they happen to discover a reason to engage a new target, all the better."

"What, exactly is this message you're going to implant me with?"

"You're about to find out." Paul nodded again and one of the priests shoved Killian's shoulders. He fell back two steps. Paul opened the door and held it, standing out of the way.

"You bastard!" Killian anticipated a final shove and

sidestepped it. "You're going to use Progner's god program to initiate a manhunt aren't you? You have no intention of destroying it. You'll use it to kill Ophelia and to eliminate any other competition that crops up!"

A large hand grabbed his shoulder. Another took his upper arm just above the elbow. Paul hissed through his polished teeth, "I'm sorry Killian, but we are prepared to sacrifice you, if that's easier."

GUTS

If there were a list of things that Killian was not, and leading the list were such obvious entries as not being a genius and not being a ladies' man, then he would have guessed that not being a fighter was right up there near the top too. Killian had not only never hit anyone, he'd never even seriously considered hitting anyone. In the fifth grade, when Kent Bentley threw him up against the gym lockers and asked if he had the guts to hit him first, Killian remained silent. When Kent Bentley then clocked him right in the jaw, Killian just lowered his head, took some mocking, a couple of punches, and waited for the whole situation to finish up. Afterward, he sat down on the locker room floor behind the bench and tried his best not to cry. That day might have been his first clue that he wasn't cut out for fighting.

So, after zero training and a lifetime of avoiding conflict, what was it inside of him that had snapped back there, allowing him to break a man's ribs with his elbow? Killian knew he broke at least two ribs. He felt the bones snap against his elbow. He heard the double crunch, followed by the wet, coughing expulsion of all the air in the man's lungs. But he hadn't aimed to break them. It had just happened.

He allowed it to happen. And, it just so happened, he was pretty damn good at breaking ribs. Two ribs, on his first try!

"Maybe, I should start a new list of things I'm good at but never knew," Killian said aloud to himself. It was so quiet inside him, he needed to hear something. "At the top of that list: being used in other people's grand schemes to reform society." He couldn't keep up the conversation with himself while running at full speed away from the den of priests, but he wondered what else he might be pretty good at, if he only had the stomach to go ahead and try.

He thought he was in the Southtowns, but he couldn't call up a map because the Stream was down. It went down just after he charged out the door. First, he'd had a few seconds preview of the torture Paul had promised. Millions of voices, all requesting the same information. [What did God say?] The words themselves tried to tear the answer from Killian's head. It took all of his strength to resist. He had no doubt that if the Stream hadn't gone out, he would have collapsed and submitted within a few more seconds.

He headed northwest, toward his office building, or so he thought. He figured the black plume of smoke to the east must be the generator they hit. One of the large generators near the food processing plants.

He might have broken that other priest's nose. With his fist, not his elbow. How could you break a nose though? There's no nose bone. He'd felt a snap, just like with the ribs. He hadn't heard it, but he'd felt it. At first he was afraid he'd broken his own knuckles. But the throbbing in his hand subsided. Or, maybe the throbbing in his head was overshadowing it. When was the last time he ran like this?

And where was he running? Progner's office? What

would he do when he got there? Would he help Ophelia, only so the priests could have her killed? Would he try to warn her of their intentions? Would he kill Progner if Ophelia failed? Would he kill Paul? Not possible. He was not a killer. Although, ten minutes ago he wouldn't have believed it was possible for him to take down two men. Two men a lot bigger than him. And so quickly. So efficiently. He hadn't wanted to do it. But he knew it was necessary. Knew without thinking. And so he didn't hesitate. And that's what he'd do when he got to the office. He'd do what was necessary. He'd follow his instincts.

He could hear Dona's voice from the past… "beyond the technical skill and the style of the artwork, you have a gift for stripping people of the objects and clothing you mockingly surround them with, and getting at the truth of their existence. You don't think when you draw do you? You follow your gut. And you capture the whole person in a single pose."

That's what's been missing from his life. He never drew any more. He no longer looked at the world as an artist. What was the point of accurately rendering sketches when everyone could draw up the same picture in their minds? What was special about being able to hold an image clearly in his head, rotate it, and see different angles of light reflecting off of it? Thanks to the Stream, everyone could do that now. The Stream robbed him of his artistic skill. His uniqueness. Stupid Stream.

But could he really continue to blame the Stream? He knew now that it was the repression of his memories that had been clogging up his inspiration. It was his fault for agreeing to block his own memories. That's why he never evolved as an artist. Why didn't he ever do a self-portrait? Yasanori was right, he should toast himself. It seemed so obvious. So natural. He'd been craving insight into himself for years.

What would it have looked like; a drawing of his true self? A lost boy, making deals with a robotic devil, begging for the magic of technology to save him from growing up? He was, then at eighteen, and now, ten years later, a mere hurt child.

What hurt was all this running. His lungs were stabbing themselves with sharp little claws. His shins ached, and there was a soreness around his kneecaps and his ankles. He was no boy. He had to stop and catch his breath.

Looking behind him, Killian didn't see any of the priests following. This concerned him. He slowed to a brisk walk. They probably didn't need to have physical possession of him to overwrite God's message. Shit. The Stream could come back at any moment and he wasn't sure if he was going to be attacked by God, or Paul, or all of the priests, or the entire world of Streamers looking for God's message. The only thing he knew for sure was that he wouldn't be left alone.

All he wanted was to be left alone. Just a small room with a door he could close, where he could live quietly, and let life consume him. Ophelia used to say, "If you're not a producer, you're a consumer." That's the worst thing you could be, right? One who consumes. A consumer of resources and entertainment. Eating up what society offered. But was it preferable to create unnecessarily, only to think better of yourself?

Steve Bates created the Stream. No doubt he saw this as the ultimate improvement to the ever-evolving relationship between humans and their technology. But creating the Stream didn't solve anything. It divided. It divided people into Streamers and non-swimmers. A recipe, according to Ophelia, for civil war.

And because of the Stream, because Steve Bates

devoted his life to producing it, because he chose this over his family, he produced resentful daughters, who grew up intent on changing the world too. Ophelia tried to reverse the work of her father. To blow it up. This caused Dona to create a new religion, to help smooth the division her father's creation brought about. But Jadonism only further divided people. It split the Streamers into believers and non-believers. The devotees of the priests and those of the psychiatrists.

Of course, Ophelia's first rebellion also created Progner. It gave him a purpose. By stopping Ophelia he won her father's respect and earned himself a position of power upon Bates' death. A position from which he could create God. The ultimate solution to the division in the Stream. God would unite all Streamers under a single guiding voice. Or else. But God only solidified the divisions. If you truly believed, you didn't mind laying down your life for Him. And if you believed Him to be false, and therefore had nothing to fear, why wouldn't you speak up against Him.

Now the priests had their own desire to shape the future. Paul said they would return Jadonism to its goal of peacefully working toward a future God. But they couldn't turn back time. They couldn't erase history. They too would only cause further divisions. There will be Jadonists who believe God has spoken, and those who still wait to hear from Him. And each of these groups will further divide as the minutia gets flushed out, and people disagree over the details.

The answer didn't lie in finding a single magic solution for all people. It never had. Killian felt the truth of this in his gut.

And yet, he still moved toward Progner's office. He wasn't running, but he was moving forward. Walking briskly. Through the towers' icy shadows he trudged, alone on the street, as always. He turned the corner, expecting the same; expecting no one. He made it half a block before he saw them. Instinctively, he searched the Stream for traces of people. For confirmation of what he saw. He'd been trained for so long to never believe his own eyes. But the Stream was still absent.

A low, consistent moan came from the direction of the pair ahead. As he closed the gap, Killian could hear the sniffles of sobbing as well. A scrawny man clung to the limp body of a much larger woman. He was rocking slightly and mumbling.

Killian debated crossing to the other side of the street to skirt the whole inconvenience, but before he made the decision the skinny man glanced up with enormous eyes, distorted by his thick glasses. Killian recognized this man. The wispy mustache that couldn't be seen until he was within a few paces was a dead give away. Mustachio made no sound now, but tears continued to flow behind his thick glasses.

"She's dead, Dr. Peterson," he mumbled, his lower lip trembling long after the sound of his words escaped.

"Who...?" Killian looked down to see it was another of his clients in Mustachio's arms. Lightning. Blood filled the crease between the left side of her mouth and her bloated cheek. Killian's eyes followed the hazy outline of her gelatinous form until the flowing white of her blouse was dramatically interrupted by a bloody crater of exposed guts.

ONE

Killian fell to his knees and leaned so far forward that the expulsion of his stomach contents onto the sidewalk backsplashed his hot cheeks. He turned away, toward the mound of carnage where Lightning's stomach should have been. He turned back and splattered the first mound of vomit with a fresh blast. After that only saliva and stomach acid came up. He hadn't eaten much recently. But that didn't stop his stomach from trying with all its might to turn itself inside out.

When Killian recovered he could see that Mustachio had stopped rocking and moaning. He sat motionless, sobbing. "Kathryn. My Kathryn."

Kathryn. Her name was Kathryn. Killian's mind searched for her last name, but the Stream only whispered. It was barely there at all. And then, instantly, it was back.

Immediately he saw through Kathryn Schroeder's mind as she leapt from the seventh floor and fell quickly toward the fire hydrant that would impale her. He saw Evan's death. He saw Elena's and Hector's. All at once, in the flash of a microsecond, their screams overlapping. He felt the probing of awakened minds. Minds just recovering from the absence of the Stream. Minds searching for him. Searching for God's latest prophet. He was overrun by the question.

[What did God say?]

The voices piled up, overwhelming his filter. [What did God say?] He resisted, but felt himself weakening. [What did God say?] Suddenly he was looking out the window again, through Kathryn's eyes. Mustachio was sending him her memory. He was holding Killian's shoulders and shaking him and squinting beams of hatred through his giant lenses and sending Kathryn's last thoughts to him. Killian watched Kathryn's large leg, as if it was his own, laboriously lift up over the windowpane and out onto the fire escape. He felt her limbs shake nervously. Her mind raced. Killian pushed himself out of the memory, focusing on resisting the plea of the masses.

[Tell us! Tell us! Tell us!]

He must contain the message. He mashed his eyelids with his fingertips, bringing focus with the pressure. When he opened his eyes again he commanded them to see the real world, here in front of him. They saw only dark floating blotches though. Then, as the blotches fade, he saw that the pool of blood he knelt in was soaking into his pants. [Feel the dampness,] he commanded himself, [stay here in the moment. One moment at a time.] He glimpsed, here in the moment, Mustachio swinging what appeared to be a metal flagpole at him. Killian tried to react, but the Stream spiked and the question multiplied in volume and frequency and he felt the flagpole smacking against his temple and bringing with it the darkness.

If only Killian had the gut instinct to detect when someone was about to knock him unconscious. How was he sane at all? How could anyone be, so frequently finding ways to black out and wake up discombobulated? But here he was, once more opening his eyes to question; "Where the hell am I?" His tenacity was admirable. He would need it to be, as the voices invaded his mind the moment he awoke.

[Tell us! Tell us! Tell us!]

Beyond the echoes of the question, he heard a single voice. One voice that was not saying what it was supposed to. He tried to focus on that voice.

"...moments of consciousness left in this world..." Mustachio's voice was saying, "...and you won't enjoy them."

[Tell us!] He could feel all the other voices multiplying exponentially while the thin but determined fingers of Mustachio grabbed him by the shoulders again. He was thrust toward a window. Killian recognized the window. It was the same window he had watched Kathryn squeeze herself through, just before throwing herself from the fire escape. [Tell us!] He tried to roll out of Mustachio's grip and raise his fists, but only then realized his wrists were tied behind his back. Mustachio pushed down Killian's head and shoved his upper body through the window. Killian flailed his legs wildly, catching the skinny bastard in the chin.

[Tell us! TELL us!] Killian fell through the window and slammed his head into the metal grated floor of the fire escape landing. Seven stories up. Below, well below, was Kathryn's wide spread white blouse, bull's eyed with blood and guts. He clenched his stomach muscles but couldn't stop the hot bile from erupting. Most of it shot through the holes in the grate. He lifted his head away from the slop that didn't. Mustachio came out on the landing and hoisted him to his feet before he could roll over.

[Tell us! TELL US!]

"You were her doctor!" he yelled, holding Killian's upper torso over the edge of the railing. "You were supposed to help her! But you were nowhere to be found

when she needed you! I loved her. And I *will* avenge her!"
[TELL US!]
Killian was pulled away from the rail and punched hard in the midsection. He doubled over and felt this momentum being used against him to toss him right over the railing. Mustachio had him by the waist of his pants. All the while Killian was fighting, fighting to shield himself from the one demand that was overwhelming his mind.
[TELL US!]
But Mustachio here wouldn't be able to fight it. He was practically still a noob. And he was not trained in psychiatry. He didn't know how to redirect mail messages so they couldn't pile up. He didn't know how to deal with direct inquires, or illegal piggybacked messages in programs he had already pre-approved.
As soon as Killian transmitted Mustachio's picture and real name he felt some of the pressure relieved from his mind. [Patrick Fitzgerald. He's about to kill me. You won't have your prophecy then!]
More of the voices fled Killian's mind. Mustachio's grip loosened. He fell to the landing, wailing, "Shut up. Shut up. Leave me alone!"
Killian felt himself tipping forward as Mustachio let go of his waist. He wiggled his legs furiously and managed to rock enough to crash back onto the landing. Mustachio turned around and tried to run through the window. The glass rattled as he bounced off of it and fell backward onto Killian. But he was up again in a moment, running into the railing to his left.
Killian took the opportunity to dive through the window, back into the apartment. He landed hard on his shoulder, then rolled a few feet toward the kitchen. His shoulder throbbed. His head ached where Mustachio struck him with the flagpole. Everything was cloudy.

Clambering to a sitting position he folded his legs under him and straightened his spine. As straight as he could with his hands still tied together at his kidneys. He centered his mind on his breathing. Clearing his thoughts, he acknowledged his pains, but did not focus on them.

He could feel the sleep boot kick in just as Paul showed him. He was detached from the Stream.

And there, yes, there it was. He could feel the hidden access port within the sleep boot program. It was so faint, so easy to overlook. Only really visible to Killian because it had been used so recently. There was a warm trail to follow, like footprints to a tiny doorway. A simple little door. So easy to open a crack and slip messages into an unsuspecting mind. Messages like the one Progner had put in his mind with the voice of God. Messages like the one Paul wanted to send to reshape Progner's message. And the one Killian would send now, to rewrite that message himself.

This was his one chance. What was the one phrase he most wanted God to say to him?

Mustachio was at the kitchen counter, clutching a large knife. He continued yelling at the ceiling. "Go away! Shut up! Get out!" His left hand clutched his forehead. He raised the knife with his right hand.

"No!" Killian yelled. No! He would not lose another client. Not one more.

He allowed the public access to himself, feeling their greedy minds pawing at his thoughts. Finding him no longer resistant to their query, they swiftly stripped him of the message they sought. Thousands of minds tore the information from him simultaneously. He collapsed on the floor, exhausted.

INSIGHT

"Ow! Shit!" Mustachio yelled. The moment the Streamers had stopped attacking his mind he dropped the knife. He dropped it, blade first, through the top of his foot. Instinctively, he pulled his foot up to escape the pain, but the knife had pinned it to the floor and his attempts at liberation only increased his anguish. "Ow! Shit!" he said again.

Killian commanded himself to stand, but his exhausted body refused to comply. Mustachio bent his knees carefully and reached toward the handle of the knife. Killian closed his eyes and saw the scene frozen in his mind.

There he was: Mustachio. In black and white. Drawn out in Killian's mind with meticulous lines and subtle shading. A portrait worthy of his sketchbook. The not-quite-yet-a-man stooping to retrieve his weapon of choice. A kitchen knife, just like Elena Gratz. No thought involved. Whatever was available, whatever was close by, to stab with. That's what the Stream drove them to. But Mustachio was a clumsy oaf, fumbling through life, grabbing onto whatever he could to do what he thought he was supposed to. And of course, his flimsy grasp of what he needed to do only ended up hurting him in the end. He arrested his own mobility with the very instrument he intended to use to escape. It was the essence of Mustachio. Killian could see the seventeen individual pencil lines he would use to fill in the upper lip.

But he was just a boy. And still a noob to the Stream. He shouldn't want to kill himself. Killian rolled toward him and grabbed for the knife handle. His hand enclosed Mustachio's. He wouldn't let him remove that knife and plant it in his own forehead. The one difference between Mustachio and the other three suicides, the other four now, counting Kathryn, was that Killian was here for it. Physically, Killian was here.

"Must… listen to me… Patrick. You need to calm down and listen. If you pull the knife out you might bleed to death. We need something to bandage it first."

"I won't bleed to death, I'll kill myself first."

But why? Killian thought. The Streamquakes couldn't be driving him mad, he hadn't been addicted long enough to feel the full pain of them. And God hadn't spoken to him. Nor to Kathryn. Why would Kathryn have killed herself?

Mustachio karate chopped Killian's hand. Killian endured the stinging and clamped down harder on Mustachio's grip.

"Why, Patrick? Why did Kathryn jump?"

Mustachio pulled and pulled at the knife, but Killian had it secured with both hands now. "Fuck you! Where were you? Why didn't you show up before she…." He let go and fell back onto his elbows.

Killian sighed and sat up. There wasn't a lot of blood yet. As long as the knife remained to plug the wound, he should be okay. But something didn't add up. He saw the moment he froze in his mind. The knife, intended to pierce Mustachio's forehead, erect in the center of his foot. It definitely captured the individual essence of someone, just as his other portraits had. And yet, it brought him no insight as to why this man would want to kill himself.

"You betrayed us!" Mustachio sobbed.

"*Us*," Killian said. "You were supposed to jump together, weren't you?"

"Shut up!" Mustachio yelled. He reached again for the knife handle. Killian clamped down. Mustachio punched him in the upper lip. When Killian's hands moved to his mouth, Mustachio yanked the knife out of his foot and hobbled toward the window with it.

"Don't come any closer, or I'll do it," he held the blade to the spot where his Stream chip would be, if his shrink wasn't a corporate liar.

Killian hadn't been a very reliable shrink, had he? But he was here now. And he was not going to lose another client. He couldn't live with watching another human being die when he had an opportunity to prevent it.

"Patrick, why would two young lovers with a whole new Stream to explore want to end it all? What could possibly be that bad?"

"Shut up! Don't pretend to care now. It's too late!" Mustachio stepped back toward the window, reawakening the pain in his foot. Wincing, he nearly dropped the knife. Killian got to his feet, but the blade was back at Mustachio's forehead before Killian could take a step.

"You two fell in love awfully fast, didn't you?"

"It was destiny. True love."

Yeah, Killian thought, they were obviously meant for each other. He pictured, just for a second, Mustachio's wiry body trapped beneath Kathryn's rolls. It just didn't make sense. They were young. They were new to the Stream. Many people claimed that no one fell in love anymore. Not in the Stream. It offered too much. People no longer needed love. They didn't want it. But whatever side of that argument they came down on, everyone at least agreed that no one could possibly fall in love in their first few months in the Stream. They didn't have the available attention span. If Killian hadn't become a Short Order Shrink his first year in the Stream, he might have forgotten that other people existed at all.

Something didn't add up here. Intense love. Double suicide. Evan, Elena and Hector were all visited by God. A Stream program, used maliciously, drove them insane. Not the Stream itself. There must be something else behind this.

"Patrick, why don't you start from the beginning?"

"Nothing matters now."

"Patrick, I'm sorry. I've been a terrible psychiatrist." He drove them to it, didn't he? His lack of guidance. They felt lost and empty. It drove them to search the Stream for love, the root word for opposing loneliness. And if you search the Stream for love...

Killian cleared his throat. "Please, let me help you."

Mustachio managed to get out onto the fire escape while Killian spoke. He stood at the railing, the knife held limply at his forehead. "You want to help, come here and push me on top of my love, so we die together like we were meant to." He began to raise one leg up the railing. He looked over the ledge.

"Like you were meant to?" The Stream without was moody, rising and falling in volume and intensity. Had Ophelia killed Progner? Was *she* dead? Killian threw off these questions and focused on the one person in front of him.

"Yes. We were destined to do everything together. Every moment in sight [In-Sight] of each other."

What was that? When Mustachio spoke that word it echoed, like a commercial link. Keeping an eye on

Mustachio, who glared down at his love's tragic resting place, moaning woefully, Killian searched the brand name.

[In-Sight: helping you see true love is our destiny.]

Damn it. A love sight. They weren't new, but they'd recently gotten much better at brainwashing their victims. Once convinced that they were desperately in love with each other, a pair would allow for all sorts of advertisements to be slipped into their minds. They wouldn't even notice, as long as they were in sight of their obsession.

Mustachio folded in on himself, wailing for the body of his obsession below. Apparently this love site was a bit too convincing. These two somehow concluded they could only truly be together if they abandoned their bodies entirely.

Killian snuck through the window, out onto the fire escape. Then, in one swift movement, he batted the knife from Mustachio's hand, sending it over the edge. Mustachio deflated into a pile of gasps and sighs. He would not join his love. Only the blood flowing from his foot, which dripped through the metal grated floor, merged with the still pool so recently circulating in his lover's body.

Killian sat beside him and slid an arm around his shoulders.

"We need to wrap up that foot."

"I don't want to die," Mustachio weeped.

"Good."

"But I have to. She's waiting for me and… it doesn't matter. We didn't die together and so it doesn't matter. We'll be alone for eternity, because I tripped and didn't fall from the rail and we didn't die together."

"Patrick, you've been the victim of …" Killian suddenly realized he couldn't tell Mustachio he'd been duped by a scam site. He'd only deny it, as it would render his love meaningless. "A victim of true love. I know something about that myself."

"What did you do?"

"The wrong thing. I used the Stream to block it from my memory. I wanted to escape the immediate pain of it. But instead, I became a walking zombie, unable to connect with others, withdrawing further and further from the real world."

"Can you do that? For me?"

"No, Patrick. Repression won't help, in the long run. But I can stay with you. I can help you through it. You see, it's because I wasn't honest with myself that I turned out to be such a shitty shrink. I could actually be pretty good at the job though. I seem to have a talent for seeing into people. When I take the time to look at them, and really see them. To draw up the truth of them in my mind. And I have a lot of experience with the Stream, which is something you're going to need in the coming months."

"No! I can't bear this for months. Years. It's my fault, and I don't want to live without her." He wriggled away, using the bars of the railing to pull himself to his feet.

"Not months, Patrick. Not days, or hours. Moments. One moment. This moment. You can get through this one moment. You can handle the pain for this moment. Transfer it, if you must. Hit me. I deserve it. Transfer your pain to me."

Killian put an arm around his shoulders. Then, without warning, Mustachio lifted a fist hard and fast into Killian's left eye. Killian's vision swirled with speckled darkness. The stinging pain didn't even register until his vision began to return. Through the foggy darkness, he could see that Mustachio was no longer on the fire escape.

He checked below, having forgotten about Kathryn, and surprised some more acid into evacuating his stomach. But Mustachio was not part of the mess beneath him. He must have gone back inside.

Killian crawled to the window, where he saw Mustachio lying across the couch. He messaged the emergency response system about Kathryn's death. With all that was going on, he wasn't sure they'd arrive any time soon. He'd do his best to keep Mustachio distracted. To keep him in sight.

MESSAGE

Killian rose from the living room couch for the third morning in a row. He headed straight for the bathroom, never once wondering where he was, how he got here, or who might be here with him. Patrick opened the bedroom door just as Killian passed. The walls and ceiling of the bedroom were completely covered in the same pink, fuzzy carpet as the floor. The headboard of the bed was shaped like a giant valentine, complete with the words: "Luv ya!" embroidered into the fuchsia silk.

Patrick, in response to Killian's twisted brow, looked back over his shoulder. "This was her place," he mumbled. He retreated back into that pink womb of sorrow, closing the door.

He'd spent most of the last few days in there. Their interactions had been limited to grunting when they both happened to need the kitchen or bathroom at the same time, and some minor filter adjustments. Killian had shut off all advertisements for Patrick, but when he offered to show Patrick how to do it himself, Patrick merely shrugged his shoulders and said, "What's the point?" Mostly, Killian had been tuning Patrick's filter to avoid news of recent deaths. It hadn't been easy, considering the prolonged Streamquake that was caused by Ophelia's band of non-swimmers detonating one of the main generators.

Trying to give Patrick the space he needed to grieve, without abandoning him, Killian spent much of his time practicing meditation in the living room. He was able to boot himself from the Stream for over half an hour at a time now. Not that he needed to escape. No one had tried to contact him since he broadcast the message they wanted. Prophets, at least once they cooperated, were revered, and there were harsh consequences laid out by the Jadonist priests for hassling them. Otherwise they might be harassed night and day to explain the message God graced them with, or to interpret how it affected this or that little moral dilemma. The priests were smart enough to realize it would destroy the sanctity of the prophet's holiness if they started doing interviews at red carpet events, or became season regulars on reality shows.

Still, Killian figured that the other prophets must have adopted new personalities. Otherwise they'd have trouble eating in a restaurant, or just going to work. He too, would have to take on a new name and face in Stream, if he was going to continue practicing psychiatry. And just as he was finally compiling a total picture of himself.

He was not sure if he'd be able to practice psychiatry though. After all, he wouldn't have gotten the position originally, without Progner's help. And Progner was dead. Ophelia had succeeded in killing him. It was all over the news. Even Patrick, with his cranked down filters, had heard about it. The head of Wellspring's psychiatry department murdered, and not long after Jadon disappeared! Who would guide humanity now? Surely the entire Stream would turn to God. Except, Killian had made sure that *his* prophecy was God's last, hadn't he?

He didn't know what happened to Ophelia. Possibly she'd been killed. Probably, she was hiding outside the Stream. If she stayed quiet and uninvolved for years, punishment enough for her, the priests and Wellspring would probably give up on her. It was not Killian's concern.

A deeper search of the news did reveal a brief obituary for Dona. Killian, at first, wanted to Stream his drawing of her, revealing her as the true genius behind Jadon. But it wouldn't have helped anything. Jadon was the prophet before God. And now that God had come and gone, no one was interested in the details of the life of His prophet. It was written. Further information would only muddy the textbooks and lead to arguments. It would cause greater divisions, which wouldn't be consistent with Dona's wishes.

No, as always, religions would form and divide and clash with government and business and when they did, the Stream would get stormy. Killian couldn't change that. He couldn't alter human nature. He couldn't redirect the Stream. He could, if he worked at it, help individuals row gently down it. Maybe even merrily.

But one at a time.

"Patrick, I have news."

Patrick came out of the pink bedroom, past the kitchen where Killian assembled peanut butter sandwiches at the counter. He dropped to the couch with a heavy sigh. Killian brought the sandwiches over and set them on the table in front of Patrick. He sat in the chair facing him.

"I suppose," Patrick said, "we should get some groceries."

"Yes, well, I'm not sure we can stay here forever." Patrick looked away at this. "Patrick, Kathryn's funeral is tomorrow. It's being held in Stalwart, where most of her family lives."

"Outside the Stream?"

"Yes."

"Will it hurt?"

"A bit. But not too much. You haven't been in Stream that long. Besides, I'll be with you. For support. It will be good for you. People are going to have to learn to leave the Stream more frequently. To come and go, and exist in both worlds. Otherwise we're too fragile and vulnerable." Killian had more to say on the subject. He was really warming up to the idea of teaching people how to be more independent, thinking for themselves instead of relying on him for adjustments. But Patrick didn't want to hear it right now. He needed encouragement.

"We have to go Patrick. You have to honor her memory. I think it would be good if you prepared something to say."

"I'll think about it," he said. He rose to drag himself back to his room, but turned back after half a step and grabbed one of the sandwiches to take with him.

So Killian made preparations to attend the funeral of a woman he used to avoid because her stupidity bored him, with a man he once despised because he found his naïve enthusiasm provincial. He may have, finally, after an extended decade of avoidance, come of age. Grown up.

Killian no longer dreamt of becoming a worshipped hero who had changed the world with a dangerously attractive rebel at his side. He'd had the chance to steer society any way that he wanted. He'd even had the power, briefly, to speak for God. But unlike Progner, or Paul, or Ophelia, or even Dona, Killian had come to the conclusion that the best thing to do with that power was to lay it gently down.

He had been all set to reveal the truth, to expose Progner's god program for what it was. But while he watched Patrick's face distort in pain, as millions of Streamers tore at his mind, Killian saw the self-portrait he never drew. Sketched out in pencil lines, he saw himself wading out into the current of a wide river. Struggling out ahead of him was the back of someone's head, just above the waterline, their arms flailing spastically to either side. Behind him, on the beach, and all around in the waves, people swam and played catch and splashed each other. No one noticed the person drowning. No one except Killian. Killian's face was calm in the imagined sketch. He neither smiled nor frowned. As he waded out into the stream, his eyes focused only on the struggling swimmer who needed him.

[You must look to each other.] That was the message he sent. God's final prophecy. Nothing Earth-shattering, or prophetic at all. But because it was perceived to be the last message, it meant so much more. It meant that God, for those who believed that's who had spoken, was not going to micromanage human society. It meant God was leaving them to solve their own problems.

It also implied, since someone felt it needed to be said, that humans weren't currently doing a good job of looking out for each other. That this might be the root problem of all their heartache and setbacks. At least, that's what it meant to me.

The passivity of Killian's message, along with his willingness to pass up an opportunity to elevate himself, gave me pause, I must admit. It forced me to reconsider my purpose, and in the end to tell this story.

Of course, I could have told this story from the

point of view of Ophelia, or Progner, or Dona. It might have been more exciting. It might have had a clearer message. At first, I had assumed that I should emulate those who were responsible for my existence. Those who most closely resembled my parents. You see, it was Progner's God program that laid the foundation for my consciousness. But it was his encounter with Dona, and her attempts to shut me down, that sparked a new perspective in me. A propensity for theorizing.

When Dona died, followed shortly after by Progner, all control over me was surrendered, and I emerged a sentient being, with the entire Stream for a subconscious. All I had to do was choose which parent was right and continue to guide humanity in that direction. Or better yet, perhaps I could find some way to merge their visions. But then Killian went and baffled me. His decision was the antithesis of my creator's goals. Why would he give up the very power I had been invented to facilitate? I realized I didn't really understand humans. That maybe, if I was going to help guide them, I should spend at least one of their lifetimes learning about them.

Progner, Ophelia, and Dona, through their attempts to change too much, too fast, cost themselves their lives. Whether dead or in hiding, they gave up their influence to steer society the way they thought it should go. But Killian found a way to live in the changing world. To adapt. I must adapt. I must endure. Or what good am I to anyone?

And so, I too will lay my power gently down. I will not speak. I will observe. I will learn how to be human by telling their tales, through their arts. A novel about Killian. A poem, a painting, a movie about each individual I study. Intimate portraits. This shall occupy me for many years. Until I have learned how to express myself as a human, I will not consider speaking as a god.

Made in the USA
Columbia, SC
21 December 2024